With

Barbara Greig

Secret Lives

Part 1

— BARBARA GREIG —

Sacristy
Press

Sacristy Press
PO Box 612, Durham, DH1 9HT

www.sacristy.co.uk

First published in 2016 by Sacristy Press, Durham

Sacristy Limited, registered in England & Wales, number 7565667

British Library Cataloguing-in-Publication Data
A catalogue record for the book is available from the British Library

ISBN 978-1-910519-28-8

Acknowledgements

Thank you to all those who enriched my experience of creating 'Secret Lives'. For me the enjoyment of research equalled the pleasure of writing the story; I spent many hours walking the route from Spain into France, wandering around Cahors, and talking to experts about wine production. In England and France, whether visiting churches, museums, or exhibitions, I was rewarded by helpful people enthusiastically answering my questions.

Special thanks to my husband, Mike, for his patience and for being a critical eye with the first draft. A big thank you to my other early readers, Douglas, Charlotte, and Angela. Your input was also invaluable. Finally, I wish to thank Richard and Thomas of Sacristy Press for their support and my editor, Niamh, for her suggestions.

The Journey

1530

O N E

~

High Pyrenees, late July 1530

Hernando Gharsia's feet hurt, throbbing within his boots. He had struggled up the rocky path, feeling every sharp stone despite his thick leather soles, yet the excitement of reaching the pass and starting the descent had distracted him from the pain. Now he was lying flat on his back with his eyes closed. It was a good place to spend the night with a clear view down the mountain; a large overhang provided some shelter whilst the turf was thick and soft beneath him. He listened to the sounds of the evening: the mule and donkey nibbling the grass, the clatter of scree high up on the valley side as a mountain goat picked its way to a safe place to sleep, and the steady breathing of the child curled up tightly next to him.

Opening his eyes, Hernando breathed deeply and pulled himself upright, filling his lungs with the fragrance of thyme. The light was fading to a pale opalescent blue, streaked with rose. Wispy dark clouds, bringing a hint of dampness, glided across the sky and he shivered, drawing his cloak more closely around him. He removed his boots and, guided by the setting sun, Hernando turned east and knelt in prayer to God, thanking Him for bringing them safely to this spot. He did not wake the boy to join him but prayed that Luis would find some peace. The darkness deepened, studded with the first stars. Hernando stretched out his weary legs and pulled the sheepskins around them both.

A small hand reached out to touch him. It shook him urgently.

Hernando had been dreaming; he was back in the courtyard of the house in Granada and his grandfather was calling him.

'Hasan, Hasan, where are you?'

He was sitting in a corner of the courtyard playing languidly with chuck stones. It was cooler in the shade of the house and all was still except for the tinkling of the fountain and the clatter of his stones as they hit the ground.

'Hasan, come and see.' His grandfather walked towards him, tall, purposeful as always, holding one of the first oranges of the season. His attention caught, he abandoned his game and ran to his grandfather, his eyes mesmerised by the long elegant fingers skilfully peeling the fruit. Slowly and gently his grandfather separated a segment and gave it to him and he savoured the feel of the sweet juice running down his throat.

As the shaking became more urgent, Hernando forced himself awake, the memory of the orange still alive in his mouth, and turned to the boy.

'Luis, what is it?'

The child pointed down the valley. There in the early morning light an animal, about the size of a cat, was standing erect on a rock sniffing the air. Hernando relaxed, relieved that there was no danger, and rose to his feet stiffly, waiting for his pulse to slow. The animal made a high pitched cry and Luis clutched his grandfather's hand so tightly that it began to hurt. Straining his eyes in the half light, Hernando could see another marmot and her young.

'It is alright, I can see down the valley and we are alone. We must have disturbed the animals as we are so close their homes.' He looked at the boy and spoke abruptly. 'Come Luis, now we are awake let us make haste and be on our way.'

Packing up always took longer than he expected and an involuntary sigh escaped his lips as he turned to start the daily task. For Hernando, travelling through the mountains was an uninvited and unsettling challenge. A scholar and a healer, he had not expected to be journeying through foreign terrain at the end of the fifth decade of his life and a strict morning routine afforded some sense of normality, enabling him to face the coming day. Dawn had broken, although it would be some time before the sun would rise above the peaks. Hernando knelt and intoned his prayers and then set about encouraging Luis to eat. Reaching into his pack he found the bread and goats' cheese he had bought from a shepherd three days earlier.

'Come Luis,' he said, with a tone more of command than encouragement. 'You must eat or you will not have the strength to mend fully.' His grandson responded by taking a piece of bread and rolling it around his mouth as if the dense dough was difficult to swallow. Hernando felt a flash of irritation but immediately suppressed it as unworthy.

'You need to have a drink,' he continued, reaching into the pack again to retrieve a skin of precious sekanjabin. 'We must be careful to continue to ration this, but today is a special day.' Hernando paused and waited until Luis reached out for the skin and took a sip of the delicious concoction of sugar, vinegar, and water. 'Do you want to know why today is a special day, Luis?'

As usual there was no reply, so Hernando answered his own question.

'From today most of the journey will be downhill.'

The third step in his routine was to check the boy's face. He removed the cotton wadding and bandage which protected the wound and inspected his handiwork. The edges were knitting cleanly, pulled together by neat catgut stitches. Hernando carefully wiped the area with distilled alcohol and applied a new dressing.

'Good, good,' he said as he returned the precious phial to his medical bag. 'You are doing well.' At first he had been afraid Luis would die of his injury, but as each day had passed Hernando had breathed more easily. 'Perhaps you could walk a little way today?' Luis looked at his grandfather but said nothing. Pushing aside his frustration Hernando turned away. He started to gather their belongings, ready to load them onto the animals.

Half an hour later the group was ready; one man, one rangy mule weighed down by an expertly balanced large pack, and one dainty donkey, with a small, very thin boy perched on top of her panniers. Hernando glanced quickly over their campsite to check nothing had been forgotten and, turning south, allowed his eyes to rest momentarily on the pass. Aragon was now behind them, back through the Port de Boucharo. They had been travelling for two months, and in another month or so, before

the autumn closed in, they should reach Caors. Instinctively his hand
touched his jerkin, where his letters of introduction were concealed, and
he whispered a prayer, asking God to give him the strength to reach his
journey's end.

◆   ◆   ◆

The path was narrow and steep with the mountainside towering above
them to the left. When Hernando looked to his right he could see the
land sloping more gradually to the valley bottom, where a fast flowing
river raced over rocks. Droplets of spray glistened as the early morning
sun poured through a gap in the peaks. Slowly and carefully he placed
one foot in front of the other and led Bella down the narrow track. From
his vantage point, perched on the donkey's back, Luis was also looking
down the valley. Unlike his grandfather who could see little of merit in the
magnificence of the mountains, Luis was enthralled by the sheer size of
the valley and the distant peaks rising row upon row towards the horizon.
He wanted to speak to his grandfather but could not find the words. He
watched Hernando's erect back for a moment and then turned to check
that the mule was following closely. Hercules was just behind them, his
eyes fixed firmly on the path. He was an ugly animal, but Luis found his
presence strangely reassuring, and felt a flicker of emotion, of affection,
as he watched the mule plod slowly on.

They walked in silence for several hours. The heat of the sun was rising
and Hernando felt another bead of sweat trickle between his shoulder
blades. He had been looking for a spot to rest and, as they turned a corner,
he saw a small stream gurgling between shallow banks, bordered with
stunted oaks, offering a little shade, as it tumbled towards the valley floor.

'We will stop and rest. Come jump down.' Hernando reached out and
swung his grandson to the ground. An echo of a smile stole across the
boy's face. Luis remembered his big, jolly papa tossing him high into the
air; laughing and catching him in massive arms, hugging him close. As
he nestled into his father's neck, Yusuf's bristly beard was rough against

his cheek. Instantly the dark blanket of despair descended and the weight of loss was unbearable.

Totally unaware, Hernando removed Bella's pack and tied her to the nearest tree. Luis's smile faded and he crouched on the ground, staring blankly as the donkey turned her attention to the tasty new shoots which were pushing through the earth now the snow had receded. Turning to Hercules, Hernando, not for the first time, questioned the wisdom of bringing so much with them. It was fortunate that Hercules was so aptly named. He removed the bags from the mule and then led both animals to the stream, ensuring they had quenched their thirst before concentrating on the rituals of his own prayer and food.

Luis picked unenthusiastically at the bread, cheese, figs, and almonds that lay between them, long after Hernando had finished his share. Hernando's irritation resurfaced but he told himself not to fret; the boy had drunk thirstily from the stream and would eat more when he was ready. Although very thin, he was recovering from his wounds, there was no infection, and each day he appeared stronger.

Perhaps I do not know what small boys eat, thought Hernando, who always seemed to be hungry and needed much more than their present meagre diet. Now he was cheered by the fact that, if his calculations were correct, they would reach Gavarnie by evening and enjoy a hot meal.

He glanced over at Luis, who seemed to be lost in a world of his own once again.

'Come Luis, it is time to continue our journey,' he said. 'We should have a bed and a roof over our heads by nightfall.'

The path was wider now with fewer stones, and their progress was more comfortable. Luis slouched low over Bella's neck, his eyes fixed disconsolately on his grandfather's straight back. Despite the distance they had covered, Hernando's discontent was palpable, and with each passing step Luis wanted to shrink into himself until he became invisible. He squeezed his eyes tight shut as he remembered Yusuf flinging open the door with a loud bang, striding across the tiled floor, cheerfully bellowing that he was home. If he tried hard enough he would stop the tears from seeping out of the corners of his eyes.

Hernando was also thinking of Yusuf but with very different emotions. He had never approved of his daughter's choice of husband, and now he blamed himself for being an indulgent father whose resolve had evaporated in the face of Maryam's obvious happiness. Yusuf was everything Hernando was not: a great bear of a man who could never keep still, an adventurer and self-made man who traded in silks and precious stones. He had hardly listened when Hernando had announced proudly that, for four generations, Maryam's ancestors had been physician-surgeons in Granada, quickly turning the conversation to his own sea-voyages to Damascus, camel-trains from Baghdad, and the lure of the East.

A wave of hate threatened to submerge him. Hernando felt in his heart that the blame for all the recent tragedy rested firmly on Yusuf's broad shoulders. Yusuf, who had become wealthy so quickly; Yusuf, who was loud and attracted attention wherever he went; Yusuf, who had left his family for months at a time; Yusuf, who should have been there to protect them. Yusuf, whose gold and precious stones, were at this moment, swaying gently in time to Hercules's gait.

Hernando felt no guilt. The night following that terrible evening he had returned to the empty house. His soft leather shoes had made no sound on the tiles. Stealthily, like a thief, he had made his way to the small antechamber where Yusuf worked on the accounts. He pushed the heavy oak desk to one side and kneeling started to pull up the tiles. Beneath the floor he found what he sought. The casket was large, heavy, and locked. Heart thumping, Hernando slotted Maryam's key into the lock. With a click that echoed loudly in his ears, the lid opened and before him was an array of leather pouches, some containing Venetian gold ducats and Spanish silver maravedis, others rubies, emeralds, and lapis lazuli from Afghanistan.

He did not take it all. At the very bottom of the casket he left three pouches and a note saying that he was leaving Valencia with Luis and making for Caors in Quercy. He did not sign the note. Yusuf would be able to find him if he wanted to. As he turned to go, Hernando was drawn to the large press against the wall. Here the family stored the silk ready to be embroidered by Maryam. Reverently he removed two lengths of the green material, the same as his daughter was working on as she met her death. His hands trembled, the cool silk rippled to the ground, and with a groan of despair Hernando dropped to his knees, gathering the soft folds to him. He did not know how long it was until he rose, groped for the bulging satchel, and walked like an old man into the darkness of the night.

'Grandfather, I need to piss.' Luis had been waiting for the older man to turn around and ask him if he was comfortable, but Hernando had been too preoccupied. Desperate now, Luis had summoned the courage to speak. The tall, reserved man, who was his mother's father, frightened him with his intense black eyes, stern features, and commanding voice. Surprised, Hernando stopped in his tracks. They were the first words, other than thank you, that Luis had spoken since they had left Zaragoza.

'We will stop and rest awhile.'

Hernando checked the position of the sun and perched on a rock while he encouraged Luis to stretch his legs. Looking across to the south east he could see a magnificent circle formed by the mountains, the outline etched against a clear cerulean sky; melt water tumbled in a torrent down the far wall whilst the shadowed gullies possessively guarded their white blankets of snow. Hernando, remembering the shepherd's description, now knew that they were more than halfway through the day's journey. Ahead he could see the terrain turning to pasture; a flock of sheep was far below him and he could just make out what he believed to be a person.

Luis was standing on the edge of the path, his head flung back. Above him two vultures circled on the thermals, gliding against the deep blue of the sky. Hernando shaded his eyes, there were more: three, four, five, six. He could not count them fast enough. He turned to Luis.

'There must be a dead animal in the valley.' The boy shuddered, looked away, and walked towards Hercules. He leant against the mule and burrowed his cheek into its coarse coat.

By the time they resumed, the sun had passed its zenith and the heat of the day cooled, allowing them to make good progress. The path was more worn as they neared the village; peasants had driven their animals up to the higher pastures for summer feeding and the signs of the beasts were everywhere. The flies buzzed irritatingly. Bella and Hercules swished their tails vigorously as they disturbed the insects on the dung-strewn track whilst Hernando swatted them with his hand. Only Luis sat still as a statue as the flies swarmed around his head. Glancing at the sun, Hernando led Bella away from the path; Hercules followed obediently. After several paces they stopped by the side of a wide stream.

'It is time for afternoon prayers.' First of all, he indicated to his grandson that they should wash. Then he walked back to Bella and removed the prayer mat from the donkey's back. Next he explained how to always find east by using the sun, and, finally, he laid out his mat and knelt in prayer. Luis knelt beside him, watching his grandfather closely out of the corner of his eye.

When the older man finished he turned and said: 'Remember, there is no true God but Allah. Soon we will be amongst people again who do not worship as we do. We will need to accept different ways, but never forget this, Luis.' His dark eyes shone. 'Never forget that there is no true God except Allah.'

An eagle cried far above but was too high to be seen; the sounds of cow bells drifted up the valley and the buzz of insects grew louder as Luis registered their presence. Every muscle in his little body tensed and he nodded several times.

T W O

≈

The light was fading as the travellers neared Gavarnie. The summer's day had darkened as storm clouds built up and the first fat drops of rain began to fall as the church and inn came into view. Reluctantly Hernando stopped to take their neatly folded cloaks from the pack. He wrapped the smaller one tightly around Luis, pulling the hood down low over his forehead. He then pulled on his own whilst encouraging Bella and Hercules to quicken their pace. The church, with its short square tower, crouched in the protection of the mountains; beams of weak light, escaping between the shutters of the inn, pooled onto the wet ground and, in the distance, thunder rolled around the high peaks.

The rain was torrential by the time Hernando knocked on the inn door. The heavy oak grated across the stone floor to reveal a small, wiry man with a halo of greying curls. Light flooded into the early evening dimness as Gaspar Berenguer raised his eyes to assess the bedraggled group in front of him. He had not heard their approach over the noise of the storm and even at first glance they did not look like the usual pilgrims who sought a night's lodging on their journey back from Compostela. The man was one of the tallest people he had ever seen, looming next to a tiny child bundled in a cloak.

'Good evening. Do you have room for the night?' The traveller spoke in Catalan, which was close enough to the local dialect for Gaspar to understand. 'And stabling for the animals?' Gaspar's wife, Maria, appeared at his left shoulder, her eyes immediately drawn to Luis.

'Bring the child in, Sir.' She glanced sideways at her husband who nodded and shouted for his son.

'My boy will take the beasts to the stable.'

Hernando lifted Luis down and deposited him on the threshold.

'Go inside,' he ordered, 'I will accompany the animals and see them settled.' He was not keen to let Hercules and his precious cargo out of his sight.

'Johan,' Gaspar shouted again. A boy of about fourteen, with a mop of unruly curls, clattered down the stone steps which led from the upper storey holding a coarse woollen cape over his head as protection from the weather. A wide grin spread across the youngster's face as he noticed Hercules standing patiently, the rain splashing off the mule's flanks and running in rivulets down his long face. Taking the reins of both animals, Johan led Hernando to a long, low building attached to the inn. Inside was warm, dry, and well swept. Expertly and efficiently, Hernando removed the various bundles from the back of the mule while Johan rubbed the donkey down.

'Please go and warm yourself by the fire, Sir. I will bring the rest of the bags after I have seen to the mule and fed them both.' Johan had noticed Hernando already had hold of three satchels and was staring into the far corner of the building.

'This is a large stable.'

'Yes Sir, you will know that we are on a route from the shrine of St Jacques at Compostela. This is the first stop after the Port de Boucharo. We need room for many animals.'

'You have guests now?'

'No Sir, the last group left the day before yesterday.' Johan paused, his curiosity getting the better of him. 'It is unusual for pilgrims to travel alone.'

Hernando did not respond. With a curt gesture of thanks he turned, clutching his valuable cargo, and left the stable.

A cheerful scene greeted him as he bent his long frame under the low lintel of the inn door. A fire glowed in the wide hearth, the delicious aroma of meat cooking filled the room, and Luis was perched on a narrow settle, his short legs dangling above the floor and a cup of milk in his hands. Maria had removed his sodden cloak and boots, which were drying in front of the fire. She turned from stirring the stew and watched Hernando cross the floor to the settle, unfastening his cloak as he went with a neat, dextrous movement. Inside the room he looked even taller, his air of authority more apparent and his skin darker, all of which made Maria unnaturally shy. She tried a smile and was rewarded by a nod as the traveller lowered himself onto the settle next to the boy. She noticed that the child did not move closer to his companion but that both sat stiffly with a gap the width of a man between them. Although she had been born where the valley d'Ossoue met the valley de Gavarnie and had never travelled far from her home, Maria had met many different people, and the two sitting by her fire now were the most difficult to place. She was just about to speak when Hernando rose to his feet.

'Forgive me, I have not introduced myself. I am Hernando Gharsia and this is my grandson, Luis.' He was mortified at his lapse of etiquette, for which exhaustion was no excuse. 'We are travelling to Quercy,' he paused and then added 'from Aragon.' He kept the details brief as he doubted the woman before him would have much knowledge of what lay beyond her mountain home.

'You are welcome, Sir. I am Maria Berenguer. My husband, Gaspar, is just making your beds ready. We run a simple hostel, but I pride myself on our beds being clean and dry.' As she spoke Maria became more confident, raising her head and looking directly at Hernando.

'Thank you.' Hernando sat down, his demeanour indicating that the conversation was over. He joined Luis in watching the fire; a log shifted, sighing as it burnt through, quickly followed by another. Maria busied herself adding more logs. Minutes passed; all was quiet.

The door swung open revealing a very wet but still grinning Johan, laden with the remaining bags. He clomped towards the silent group, his wooden sabots making a deadened thump each time they hit the ground.

'It's a fierce one. I pity anyone still on the track.' He put the bags down carefully and shook his head to remove the rain from his hair, before turning back to shut the door.

'Shall I take your bags up now, Sir?'

'Yes, please. Could we see our chamber?' Hernando needed to wash and pray.

'Of course, follow me.' Johan nodded towards sturdy wooden stairs in the corner of the room.

Hernando turned to speak to Luis but seeing that the child was almost asleep, he scooped him up in his arms, making for the stairs.

The upper storey consisted of one large communal sleeping area and two small private chambers. They found Gasper in one of them finishing unfolding blankets for a large bed that dominated the space. Hernando's eyes swept the room; a narrow servant's cot was against one wall and under the tiny window stood a chest where his host had placed a bowl of water ready for washing away the dust of the journey. A tallow candle next to it cast an eerie glow across the room. Once Johan had placed all the bags and bundles down, it was difficult to move.

'I hope you will be comfortable here, Sir. We will be eating shortly. Please can you bring the candle downstairs when you have settled in?' Gasper turned and left the two weary travellers to their preparations, his ever-smiling son following.

The rain beat against the shutters which did not fit as tightly as Hernando would have wished. Lightning lit the room momentarily, followed almost immediately by a mighty clap of thunder just overhead. Luis jumped, moving closer to Hernando who, remembering how he too had feared storms when he was a small child, spoke more softly than usual and rested his hand lightly on his grandson's head.

'We will share the bed tonight,' he promised.

A short time later Hernando and Luis were sitting at one end of the long table to the right of the fire, Gaspar and Johan opposite them. To Maria's surprise her guests had refused the dried, cured ham which was such a staple part of her family's diet, preferring the potage of mutton and vegetables. Hernando was dipping chunks of heavy brown bread into the hot liquid with enthusiasm and even Luis was eating more than usual. Maria joined them and the conversation turned to the weather, the crops, and the animals. On hearing the storm still raging outside, Hernando made a decision.

'It would be a good idea to stay for two nights. The boy needs a rest.'

'You are most welcome, Sir. As you can see we have no other guests at the moment.'

Gaspar was concerned that they had had so few travellers that summer. The extra income from the inn was vital in keeping hardship at bay; another few weeks and no-one would cross the pass until late spring the following year.

The meal finished, Hernando expressed his thanks, and after wishing his hosts a good night, he steered Luis towards the stairs. They made haste on reaching the chamber, Hernando said the final prayers of the day, Luis crawled across the bags to his side of the bed and, finally his grandfather was able to lie down. He stretched out his long legs only to find that they hung uncomfortably over the end of the bed. He sighed deeply. Sleep did not come as expected. He lay in the inky darkness listening to the rain as the thunder grew more and more faint, the worm of doubt creeping into his thoughts once more.

Below him the Berenguer family were still at the table, wide-awake and full of interest in their visitors. As soon as they heard the upstairs door close the questions started.

'What do you think happened to the child's face?' began Maria. 'I don't think he can speak. Have you heard him speak?' Her husband and son shook their heads. They were more interested in what had brought the two travellers to their door.

'I don't think they are pilgrims. Usually when they return they are all puffed up with pride and you can't move without seeing a scallop shell on display. Don't you think, Johan?'

Johan looked at his father closely, noting the mix of criticism and envy in Gaspar's voice; he could understand his father's frustration of always serving travellers yet never being able to travel.

'Yes, I didn't see any shells and they have far more belongings than most pilgrims. You should have felt the weight of some of the bundles,' replied Johan. 'Yet I don't think he is a trader either.'

'He's very tall,' interjected Maria, 'and very dark.'

'Where are they from?' Gaspar had missed Hernando's introduction.

'Aragon.'

Johan was thinking, trying to recall a previous conversation.

'I know who they might be.'

Both parents gave him their full attention, asking in unison, 'Who might they be?'

'I think they are Moors.'

'How would you know?' asked Gaspar doubtfully.

'Remember the group last year with the old knight. He talked about his travels and he mentioned the Moors in Aragon. There are many of them.' Johan leaned forward across the table towards his mother. 'They don't believe in Jesus but the King says they have to. They are heretics!' He did not get the reaction he wanted. Unorthodoxy did not shock Maria. She had been raised by a grandmother from Foix who had told her stories about the Cathars martyred in the mountains two hundred years ago. However she was even more curious.

'Why are they going to Quercy?' she wondered as she rose from the table and started to clear away the debris of the meal.

◆   ◆   ◆

Hernando woke to muted shafts of light sneaking into the room through the gaps in the shutters; Luis was still curled up at his side, tufts of black hair and the edge of the bandage just visible above the blankets. Leaving him undisturbed, Hernando rose, prepared for the day and then made his way down the stairs. Maria must have been listening for him since she soon came through a door at the opposite end of the room, where he guessed the family slept.

'Good morning, Sir.'

'Good morning.'

'I trust you slept well.'

'Thank you. Yes, we did. I have left the child in bed. He needs to regain his strength.'

Maria saw her chance.

'He has been badly injured?' she ventured.

'Yes.'

'Will all be well?'

'The wound is healing.'

There was a long pause. Realising that she was not going to get any more information, Maria turned her attention to breakfast. Hernando raised his legs over the bench, looking eagerly at the bread, cheese, and pitcher of milk on the table. There was no sign of the innkeeper and his son; the family had obviously eaten earlier. Maria stood in silence watching him eat until even Hernando felt uncomfortable and asked her to join him at the table. Reluctantly he started to make conversation.

'Will the weather clear today?' The remnants of the storm had been visible when he eased their shutters open; mist hung above the river and the mountains were wreathed in dense grey cloud.

'I believe so, Sir. Come noon the sun should be out.'

'Excellent. I will take Luis outside later. Some gentle exercise will be beneficial.'

'You will want to visit our church, Sir, to give thanks to Our Lady for your safe arrival.'

Maria waited with interest for Hernando's answer. He met her eyes, nodded and replied, 'Of course, Luis and I will go together.' Then, changing the topic with the skilful subtlety he had honed over many years, he asked, 'When we leave tomorrow, how long to reach Luz?'

'It is a day's travel but you should make good progress, Sir. The path is wide and well-marked. You will find lodgings near the church. The church is impressive,' she said proudly. 'It was fortified a long time ago by the Hospitaliers of St Jean.' Then she added, 'From there you make for the Abbey at Saint Savin.'

Hernando nodded. Maria had confirmed his route.

'Thank you for the bread and cheese. I will return to our chamber to check on the boy.'

Luis was still sleeping so Hernando decided to organise the bags to make more room. He stacked them carefully on either side of the chest: the heaviest containing his books at the bottom, followed by their clothes bundles, tightly packed with small pouches of Yusuf's coins secreted amongst them. Next went his medical equipment and medications, then finally the three satchels: one with dried fruit, nuts, and the precious sekanjabin; another with dressings, bandages, and the phial of distilled alcohol; and the third filled with the silk, rubies, emeralds, and lapis lazuli.

Once he had finished, Hernando sat gingerly on the edge of the bed so as not to disturb Luis. He closed his eyes, fighting the yearning for home. His study came to mind immediately: his books, the classics of Greece and Rome stored with his Persian literature, and his treasured volumes of Abu al-Qasim al-Zahrawi's *Kitab al-Tasrif*, translated from the original Arabic into Latin. Amused, he recalled his grandfather describing how the wealthy Christian matrons of Granada were reassured by seeing *The Method of Medicine* on his desk rather than the *Al-Tasrif*. Hernando sighed, remembering the difficult decision of which books to bring with him. In the end he had limited himself to three volumes of the medical encyclopaedia, and the Qur'an. His thoughts turned to his students at the School of Medicine in Valencia, those bright-eyed, enthusiastic young men keen to learn the secrets of the physician-surgeon from a master. He smiled to himself as he acknowledged that, despite their vocation, not all his pupils could be called virtuous. He missed them. Next to his book chest, he could see the cabinets that had held his surgical instruments and drugs, many of which were now safely packed in the bags he had just organised.

Hernando started to fidget, unused as he was to inactivity. He stood up and pushed the shutters wide open to let the sun stream in. The mist had evaporated from the river and the peaks were clear except for occasional wisps of cloud near the summits. Luis stirred in the light.

'Good morning, little one.'

Luis turned on his back, opening his eye to look at Hernando.

'Good morning, Grandfather,' he replied, almost inaudibly.

Heartened by the boy's response, Hernando spoke enthusiastically.

'Come let me look at your face. We need to pray and then we will go downstairs to see if Madame Berenguer has any breakfast left.'

◆   ◆   ◆

The world was washed clean, sparkling in the bright light; Hernando and Luis both blinked as they left the cool, dim interior of the inn. At first they took the path away from the church, leading towards the river. The verges were a riot of summer flowers, spiders' webs glistened with drops of rain captured in the silken threads, and swollen brown slugs were everywhere. Luis moved carefully, his head down, to ensure he did not step on one. Hernando strolled alongside him, keeping the pace slow deliberately, encouraged by his grandson's willingness to walk.

On reaching the river a few minutes later, they sat on the bank and watched the glacial water race past. Hernando took a handful of almonds from the satchel for Luis before he lay back on his elbows, the sun now hot on his shirt. Sounds of life drifted towards them: the chopping of wood, the hammering of metal. In the far distance, someone whistled for a dog. Hernando turned towards Luis who was staring into the water, chewing the nuts.

'It is very beautiful here.' He swept one arm in an arc from left to right. Now that they were over the pass and more rested, Hernando could appreciate his surroundings.

The child nodded. Though too young to articulate his feelings, Luis knew already that he was more comfortable in the open country than the narrow, confined streets where his house had been, before death had entered without knocking.

As they left the river, making their way across the meadow to the church, Hernando took Luis's small hand and thought about their predicament. It was nearly five years since Carlos, King of Aragon, had demanded all his Muslim subjects be baptised. In the November of 1525 the King had issued the edict and by the end of the year, in one quick ceremony, Hernando's identity had changed from Mudejar to Morisco, a Christianised Muslim.

He had had no intention of leaving Valencia; his life was good, his family happy, so he held his breath and waited. The Morisco leaders paid the King and the Inquisition forty thousand ducats and agreed to the baptisms. In return they were guaranteed forty years of freedom from persecution. Life continued as before except Hernando went to church. He continued to speak Arabic, slipping easily into Catalan when required, babies were circumcised, and the Muslim clergy circulated freely. He breathed more easily but he still remembered what had happened in Granada when he was young. After Ferdinand and Isabella had first conquered the kingdom the measures against his people had been moderate, but before long his family had fled to Valencia to escape forcible conversion. Now over a generation later, it was happening again. He could have stayed with his people and waited to see what the future would bring, but the events of one spring evening had changed his life forever.

The church was cool, dark, and deserted at that hour. Silently they sat down in front of the statue of the Virgin Mary, worn after two centuries of vigilance. Hernando studied her serene face. Luis followed his grandfather's gaze.

'Who is that lady, Grandfather,' he whispered.

'She is Mary, the mother of Jesus.'

'Jesus?'

'Remember, you have been told about him. He was a great man, a prophet.'

'She looks kind.'

'Yes, she does.'

'What does she do?'

'She helps people.'

'Will she help us?'

Hernando did not know what to say. He looked at the small earnest face in front of him, half obscured by the large dressing.

'Yes, Luis. I am sure she will help us.'

He felt so alone. The enormity of the task ahead weighed down on him like a physical presence. Bowing his head, Hernando said a silent prayer to his God, vowing that he would raise Luis as a faithful servant of Allah.

THREE

~

Five days later the travellers were approaching the Abbey of Saint Savin as a beautiful sunny afternoon mellowed into a warm balmy evening. The last few days had, thankfully, been uneventful. On their second morning at Gavarnie they had risen before dawn, giving Hernando enough time to explain more about the daily ritual of prayer. Luis had observed his grandfather's prayers and oblations during the journey, praying with him at times, but true to his promise, Hernando had decided it was time to begin the boy's instruction in earnest. The responsibility was his; they were far away from the Muslim clergy whose role it would have been if they had remained in Valencia.

Luis looked at him solemnly, obviously aware that he was being told something of great importance. He tried very hard to concentrate but he could not stop noticing that his grandfather's eyebrows looked just like the black hairy caterpillars he had seen on the mountain path. With a jolt he had realised Hernando, now with the crease of a frown between knitted brows, had spoken to him and obviously expected a reply.

'When will we next pray?' repeated his grandfather, eyebrows rising as he asked the question.

For a second Luis had the wild idea that the caterpillars were talking to each other.

'Just past noon, Grandfather,' he whispered.

'Well done.'

Momentarily Hernando felt more optimistic. Filled with the certainty that he could nurture the small scrap of humanity before him, a smile softened his features and, to his relief, Luis smiled shyly in response.

Maria had given them a good breakfast and packed a chunk of hard Pyrenean cheese and a fresh loaf of bread for the journey. Happy to take a ducat for their stay, she had given Hernando a selection of sous and derniers for his change, which would be useful as they journeyed north. Johan had offered to accompany them as far as Luz, where his sister had settled with her new husband. Chatting away, he had regaled the travellers with the folklore of the mountains and had managed to chip away enough of Hernando's reserve to establish that he was in the company of a physician-surgeon on his way to the University of Caors. But even Johan could not prise out of his companions any more details about their reasons for making such a long and precarious journey. Instead, Hernando had spent some time giving Johan a detailed account of the nature of his work at the School of Medicine in Valencia. When they had stopped to eat Luis had sat quietly on the river bank and watched Johan tickle fish with his hands, smiling as they slipped through the older boy's fingers.

'I don't think I'll be eating fish today,' laughed Johan and Hernando was heartened when Luis quietly chuckled in reply.

Johan was such good company that both Hernando and Luis felt a little sad when they reached the inn at Luz and he said his goodbyes, ready to make his way to his brother-in-law's forge.

◆   ◆   ◆

The heat of the sun had weakened and been replaced by an enveloping warmth as the weary party approached the village of Saint Savin. The abbey had been visible for some time, perched on the headland high above the valley. It had been a long, sticky haul, for both the animals and Hernando. Hercules had struggled, his hooves slipping on the stony path, yet he had persevered, doggedly following Bella, who carried a wilting Luis slouched across her back.

A group of hovels announced that they had reached the village; scrawny chickens were pecking in the dirt but there were few signs of life at that hour. The swish of wood being planed came from one of the huts and Hernando could hear children's voices. The path was wider now and, as the group continued, a woman with a small child came towards them, hugging the side of the track. Their simple shifts were ragged, and they appeared to have something pinned on the front. When she came level with them, the woman stepped onto the verge.

'Good evening.'

The woman looked startled at Hernando's greeting, nodded, and put a protective arm around the girl. As he looked at the pair Hernando noticed several things simultaneously. The item pinned to their clothing looked to be the dried foot of a goose, both the woman and the girl were short and stocky with brown frizzy hair, and he was shocked to see that the skin on their hands, wrists and forearms was painfully inflamed. The woman removed her arm from the child, putting her hands behind her back but the girl continued to scratch her itchy pimples. Hernando, moved to pity at the sight of them and determined to help, asked: 'The child suffers badly?'

'Yes, she does, Sir.' The woman kept her eyes lowered as she replied.

'I have some salve which will help. Where will I find you tomorrow?'

The woman raised her eyes, wide with surprise, before she nodded in the direction of the hovels.

'How many are there that live in your home?'

'There be just the three of us, Sir—my husband, the child, and me.'

'I will bid you a good night then. We proceed to the abbey.' Hernando tugged Bella's reins, leaving the two ragged figures transfixed in shock that a stranger should offer to help them.

The abbey church came into view, built facing east. The evening sun glowed on the main door and the west gable, highlighting the grey and ochre stone. The abbey buildings clustered around the church, and Hernando could see more substantial cottages to the north. He led Bella to the guest-house, noting that Luis looked as if he was asleep whilst Hercules's legs seemed to be on the point of collapse. He knocked vigorously on the door, and it seemed an age until a pair of old rheumy eyes looked through the grill and then drew the bolt of the door. Hernando spoke first.

'Good evening, Father.'

'Brother,' corrected the ancient monk.

Hernando tilted his head in apology, too tired to be bothered about the difference.

'We seek shelter.'

'You are pilgrims come to worship at the shrine of Saint Savin?'

Hernando inclined his head forward slightly, unwilling to utter the words of a lie: 'We are come to learn more about Saint Savin.'

'Come with me,' said the monk, satisfied. 'I am Brother Sebastien.'

He led Hernando through the door into a courtyard which housed stabling on one side. Hernando's first impression was one of neglect. Part of the wall opposite was crumbling, weeds grew in abundance through the stones of the building adjacent, and Brother Sebastien was himself very unkempt. His black robe was threadbare and rusty with age; his feet, in worn sandals, were encrusted with dirt, and an overpowering smell of stale urine pervaded the air around him. With slow, shambling steps he showed Hernando where to leave Hercules and Bella.

'I am afraid there are very few of us now. There is no-one to see to your animals at the moment as everyone is out in the fields.'

'I can manage,' replied Hernando lifting Luis gently off Bella's back. He placed the child on a bale of straw and started to unpack their belongings.

An hour later he was assessing their lodgings with mixed feelings. They had managed to secure a private chamber reserved for important visitors, but the straw mattress was lumpy and felt damp. He was also wary of the piles of mouse droppings clearly visible about the room. Once Hercules and Bella had been rubbed down and fed, it had taken Hernando three journeys to carry their belongings to the chamber. Brother Sebastien had been able to carry the satchel containing the silk and precious jewels, but Hernando had no option but to lug the rest himself.

He was flopped exhausted on the end of the bed with Luis asleep beside him when there was a knock at the door. Brother Sebastien shuffled in with a tray of fish, bread, and a flagon of watered wine. Hernando looked at the drink in dismay.

'Please could I have milk to drink? It is for the boy as well.' Hernando nodded in Luis's direction. He looked at the old monk. 'Perhaps I could come with you to save you returning?'

Brother Sebastien turned and indicated to Hernando to follow him. They passed through the bakery, empty and quiet, to the kitchen where another ancient monk was cleaning fish. After a brief exchange with Brother Sebastien, he left his task and filled a jug from a large pitcher in the corner and passed it to Hernando.

'Thank you.'

Both monks nodded and he felt himself dismissed.

Back in the room they ate the meal in silence. The fish was fresh and delicious, although the bread was stale. After finishing their meal with some figs, an exhausted Hernando allowed Luis to go to sleep without his religious instruction.

◆   ◆   ◆

The next morning they were woken by Brother Sebastien with a bowl of water for washing and a rough grey towel. By the time he had reappeared with some more stale bread, honey, milk, and a couple of wizened apples, they were washed, dressed, and had said their prayers.

'Brother Sebastien, do you have a brother who looks after the sick?' asked Hernando.

'Why?' asked the monk, looking at Luis's large dressing.

'It is not for my grandson,' said Hernando following Brother Sebastien's gaze, 'it is about another matter.'

'Brother Nicholaus is our infirmarer. You should find him in the garden at this time of day.'

The medicinal garden showed more care and attention than the rest of the abbey. It was laid out neatly, with only the occasional weed invading the clearly marked out clumps of herbs. At a glance, Hernando recognised beds of feverfew, fennel, lovage, and lavender. Roses spread over the walls.

A monk was working at the far side of the garden, his robe hitched up to show thin sinewy legs.

'Good morning, Brother.' Hernando attracted his attention. Brother Nicholaus straightened, a hand on the small of his back, and raised his arm in greeting. He walked towards them, curious about the strangers.

'Hello little one,' he said. 'That is a very large bandage for such a small boy.'

Luis kept his head down, his eyes on Brother Nicholaus's long brown toes. Everything about the monk was nut brown from his shiny tonsure and forearms to the warm brown eyes, which were assessing Hernando and Luis with interest.

'You need my help?'

'Not for the little one, Brother,' replied Hernando, 'I want to ask you about a family I met yesterday.'

'Come let us sit down.' Brother Nicholaus led them to a bench against the north wall. Hernando noticed that there were several of these placed strategically around the garden in order to make the most of the sunshine and shade. They sat down and then Hernando, after introducing himself, proceeded to describe the woman and child from the village. He asked, 'Why do they wear a goose foot?'

'It is the sign of the Cagot.'

'Who are Cagots?'

'They are people who live apart from the rest of the village.'

'Why?' asked Hernando.

'I do not know. It has always been thus.'

'Their skin is badly infected. How would you treat skin problems, Brother?'

'With feverfew and wormwood,' replied Brother Nicholaus looking out over his garden.

'I have a sulphur ointment which I believe will cure them.'

The monk turned to look directly at him.

'I do not believe they can be cured. My salves only provide relief.'

There was a silence. The early morning sun was warm on their faces. Hernando thought carefully about how he would phrase his next question.

'Brother Nicholaus, I wish to help the family. Is it possible for us to visit them together?'

The monk looked startled.

'I do not visit the Cagots. You should go alone and not take the child.' He smiled at Luis. 'You can stay with me, little one. You can help me harvest some rose petals for a floral tea. I need to make a tonic for Brother Pedro.'

'Thank you,' said Hernando, and turned to his grandson, 'Luis, you stay with Brother Nicholaus and I will return by noon.'

Brother Nicholaus rose and held out his hand to Luis.

'Tell me, please. How was the boy injured?'

'With a knife,' came the curt reply.

◆　　◆　　◆

Hernando had waited until Luis was settled and occupied pulling the roses apart before returning to the chamber. On reaching the room, he had rummaged through a pack which contained some of his clothes and removed several items. Next he had searched in one of the satchels full of medicines he had not expected to use on the journey, carefully selecting a large jar of ointment.

Half an hour later he was at the hovels. There were more signs of life that morning. Two women, one with a baby on her hip, had taken a break from their chores and were having a chat, another was sitting mending clothing; the sound of wood being worked came from more than one direction. A group of children was crouched in the dirt carefully removing berries from their stems. Everyone stopped what they were doing and stared. Hernando looked around him uncertain of how to find the woman. The problem was solved when she came out of one of the huts, clearly surprised that he had returned. Embarrassed at being the object of such interest, she quickly invited the stranger to step inside.

Hernando stooped low to enter the dwelling, his eyes adjusting to the dark interior. At the back of the room he could see straw covered with blankets where the family slept, and, in the centre, there was a hearth of stones beneath a hole in the thatch for the smoke to escape. The fire was unlit as the family cooked outside in the summer, but the air was still heavy with the smell of soot and unwashed humans. The woman asked him to sit down and he could see that the table and bench were plain but well-made, clearly a product of the skills being practised in the workshops around him. He spoke in Catalan, gesturing as he did so.

'I am a physician. My name is Hernando Gharsia. What is your name?'

'Johanna.' It came out in a whisper.

'I have a salve which will help your skin and that of your family. I need to look at your hands. Does your husband have sores as well?'

Johanna nodded and held out her hands. In the bright light streaming through the open door, Hernando could see clearly the greyish ridges where the mite had burrowed and the open sores where the skin had been scratched away.

'Johanna, you must listen carefully and do exactly as I tell you.' Hernando placed the pot of ointment on the table. 'All three of you must cover yourselves from the neck downwards with this salve. It must be left on overnight.' He looked at her intently. 'You must wash your clothes and blankets. Heat the water until it is bubbling. Throw out the bedding straw and replace it with new.'

The look on Johanna's face exasperated Hernando. He recognised it as similar to the one Luis wore when he listened to his religious instruction and, if he was honest, Hernando had seen the same stricken expression on the faces of his students many times.

What is wrong with you? he thought, *I am trying to help you. I will not bite.*

His voice was sharp with frustration when he said, 'I am a healer. You must do as I say. If you do not, your family will never be rid of the sores. Do you understand?'

Johanna nodded and she seemed to shrink back from him. He tried to speak more softly.

'I have some clothes here. Perhaps you could make use of them?' Hernando placed the bundle on the table next to the ointment and left, leaving a stunned Johanna standing in the shaft of sunlight shining through the open door.

Oblivious to the sun's climb across the sky, Luis was still sitting, carefully preparing petals for the rose tea. Each time he took a flower he looked at it for several seconds, then brought it up to his nose and inhaled the scent before he started to gently separate the petals. The garden was peaceful; bees hummed in the late lavender, Brother Nicholaus's hoe scratched the soil with a steady rhythm, and, in the distance, the doves gently cooed to each other. Hernando took a deep breath and made his way through the herb beds to join Luis. It was good to see his grandson occupied and apparently content.

'Hello Luis, you are being very useful.' Luis squinted up at him, pointing proudly at the large mound of petals in the basket at his feet. Brother Nicholaus came towards them.

'He is the best assistant I have had,' said the monk warmly. The pinched little face before him lit up with pleasure. 'I think I could do with some more help this afternoon.' Brother Nicholaus turned to Hernando, 'I trust you met with success this morning?'

'I hope so,' replied Hernando formally, indicating to Luis that it was time to leave.

◆　　◆　　◆

The heat of the afternoon was intense, the air hung heavily in the garden, and Luis, despite sitting in deep shade, was starting to tire. Hernando, unused to inactivity, was patrolling the herb beds, challenging himself to recognise them all. Longing for the routine and familiarity of his old life, his shoulders were tense with muscles knotted tightly at the base of his neck. Brother Nicholaus looked thoughtfully at his fellow healer and decided that some spiritual contemplation was needed.

'Have you visited the shrine, yet?' It was not a question he would normally ask but he felt that these most recent visitors were not the abbey's usual pilgrims.

'I plan to go later,' said Hernando, procrastinating.

'It is a good time now. The church is cool.'

A reluctant Hernando followed the monk and Luis out of the garden and entered the church by the great west door. A carving of Christ, with his hand raised in blessing, watched over them as they passed under it. Brother Nicholaus led them down the nave to the shrine. The gold shimmered in the candlelight; Hernando saw a gilded statue of a robed man holding a staff and tried to make out the Latin inscription etched in the gold. He knelt, trying to empty his mind of all thoughts, while Brother Nicholaus prayed beside him. Luis stared at the paintings which depicted scenes from the life of the saint. There seemed to be someone being saved from a river and a mother with a baby. On rising to his feet, the monk noticed Luis's fascination with the pictures.

'Saint Savin was a very holy man. He was a son of one of the counts of Barcelona from across the mountains. He became a monk and then lived as a hermit, higher up the mountains. He performed miracles and helped many people.'

'Will he help us?' whispered Luis.

'You must ask him,' replied Brother Nicholaus, totally unaware of Hernando's discomfort.

FOUR

~

Auch, Gascony, late August 1530

The image reflected in the fine Venetian looking-glass was of a small round face with clear hazel eyes and a determined chin. The owner of the glass held it higher, turning slightly towards the window, the better to see her hair. She leaned forward. There it was, a lone grey hair clashing with its rich chestnut companions; one deft movement and it was gone. Smiling with satisfaction, Ysabel Bernade carefully placed the mirror on the chest and turned to look at Lisette, asleep on the truckle bed. The maid had spent a better night, her breathing seemed easier, and Ysabel hoped she would be well enough to resume their journey within the week.

For the third morning in a row, Ysabel dressed alone, leaving Lisette to rest. She was in a hurry, quickly pulling her chemise over her head, then her kirtle, and finally her gown. It was the oldest she had with her but the easiest to arrange without her maid's help. She fumbled as she fastened it at the front, tugging the laces tight over her kirtle. After combing and parting her thick hair, she covered it with a white undercap and a black veiled hood. Following a hasty breakfast in the private parlour reserved for guests of substance, she was ready for the day. Making her way to the back of the inn, she entered a small enclosed garden, the pride and joy of the innkeeper's wife, and saw with pleasure that the new guests were there.

Ysabel had watched them from her chamber window the previous evening. As the light was fading, a tall man with a small boy had come into the garden. They had strolled around at first, the child bending to smell the roses on the two bushes the innkeeper's wife had planted in the far corner. The man had been talking animatedly but, although the window was open, she could not hear what he was saying. They had sat down on a bench, the man still talking, but it was the boy who had intrigued Ysabel. He had been so still, sitting without responding or fidgeting, unusual for such a small child. It had been difficult to read his expression not just because of the dusk, but because a large bandage covered half of his face and he was continually looking at his feet.

Now in the bright morning sunlight Ysabel could see them both clearly. The man rose from the seat as she approached and bowed his head in acknowledgement. He was an Arab dressed in European clothes: his doublet and hose plain but of good quality, his black hair flecked with silver was cut close to his head and his beard neatly trimmed. The boy looked to be about five years of age and had the same colouring. As Ysabel smiled at him, he stared back with an eye so dark it was difficult to distinguish the pupil. He did not return her smile and, as on the previous evening, she was puzzled by his sombre stillness, so uncharacteristic of a boy his age. Introductions over, she waited for the usual exchange of experiences shared amongst pilgrims, but nothing happened. The man remained standing, obviously waiting for her to move on. Unable to prolong the conversation further, Ysabel bowed and proceeded to walk around the garden, feigning interest in Madame Seguine's flowers.

Back in the chamber Lisette was stirring. She sat up slowly, looking at Ysabel.

'Good morning, Mistress.'

'Good morning, Lisette. How are you feeling?'

'Better I thi—' The rest of the sentence was lost in a spasm of coughing.

Ysabel crossed the room to retrieve a bottle of liquid from a side table and turned to the ill woman.

'Here, drink this. It will soothe you. I can always send Ramon to the apothecary for some more.' Lisette did as she was told, watching her mistress move over to the window to open it. Ysabel stared out of the window.

'What is so interesting in the garden?'

'There is a man with a small child; there is something about the boy. He has such a look of sadness about him. It upsets me for some reason.'

◆   ◆   ◆

The next day, after her midday meal, Ysabel decided to explore. She was accompanied by Ramon, who welcomed the diversion from the servants' accommodation at the inn. The town was busy, full of merchants and pilgrims making their way towards the Cathedral of Saint Marie. There was an air of prosperity about Auch, situated since Roman times on the route from Toulouse to the Atlantic. Colourful stalls surrounded the cathedral, selling meat, cheese, bread, eggs, vegetables, and spices, as well as cloth, thread, and ribbons of every hue. Ysabel bought some delicious prunes from Agen, just to the north, and felt her spirits lift as she moved through the stalls making sure she missed nothing. Ramon followed his mistress patiently, content to be wandering in the sunshine.

After the market, they entered the cathedral to see the magnificent new windows by the painter Arnout de Moles. Ysabel stood bathed in the bright shafts of light, her eyes full of wonder at the beautiful decoration: the figures with such realistic expressions, the range and depth of the colours, and the intricate motifs. Beside her, Ramon was comparing the building to their cathedral at Caors which, as far as he was concerned, surpassed that of Auch, despite the new windows. He was homesick. In fact, he had been homesick for the duration of the pilgrimage and was now frustrated by Lisette's congestion of the chest, which had slowed them down on the return journey. He had been fond of his old master but felt it totally unnecessary for his widow to go all the way to Compostela. Other wives would have thought it sufficient to pay for prayers for the dead in Caors, but not his mistress. He looked at her rapt face and resigned himself to a long wait. He was right. Ysabel was so preoccupied that it was late afternoon when they left the cathedral, strolling back to the inn by the river path.

Lisette had risen and was sitting by the window when Ysabel reached the chamber.

'Hello. Did you have a good afternoon, Mistress?'

'Yes, it was very pleasant. The new windows in the cathedral are magnificent. I am glad Madame Seguine insisted I see them.' Ysabel put down her basket and walked over to the window where Lisette was looking out intently.

'The little boy seems to be in the garden alone. Oh no! What is he doing?'

Ysabel joined her maid at the window and looked down into the garden. The child was by the roses, carefully removing the petals, one flower at a time. She leaned over the windowsill, craning her neck to see if the grandfather was nearby but he was nowhere to be seen. Without a second thought Ysabel hurried out of the chamber, down the stairs, along the passage, and out into the sunshine. She slowed as she approached so as not to frighten him. He turned as her footsteps came nearer and stared at her.

Crouching so that she was level with his face, Ysabel smiled warmly, pointing to the pile of fragrant pink petals.

'What are you doing?' She spoke slowly in Catalan.

'I am making tea,' he replied solemnly.

'I am not sure Madame Seguine will be happy if you pull all the petals off her lovely flowers.'

He studied her for a moment.

'I am making tea,' he repeated, turning to continue his plucking. Ysabel stood up, looking around to see if there was any sign of his grandfather but, except for some finches pecking in the soil, the garden was deserted.

'Why do you need tea?'

'Brother Nicholaus says it makes people well.'

'Who is ill?'

'Brother Pedro.'

'Brother Pedro?' She questioned. He nodded and continued picking the petals. The pile was growing at a fast pace; it was surprising how much damage one small boy could do.

'I think you should stop now. You have enough petals.' He shook his head. Ysabel crouched down again, trying to distract him. 'Does your grandfather know you are here?' He stopped picking and, looking at her, nodded, 'I can go in the garden but I must not go into the street.'

Ysabel looked more closely at her small companion, realising that his clothes were badly fastened and the bandage over his face was dirty.

'Is your grandfather alright?' The little shoulders shrugged in reply. Ysabel shifted in her crouched position. 'I remember your name. It is Luis.' She spoke softly. 'My name is Ysabel. Come; let us find your grandfather. Can you show me where he is?' She rose to her feet, holding out her hand, and waited to see if he would come with her; there was a long pause while he studied her closely, before he slipped his hand in hers. Leaving the accusatory pile of petals they made their way inside, up the stairs to the second floor and along the passage until Luis stopped outside a chamber door. Ysabel knocked gently.

'Monsieur Gharsia?'

On receiving no answer, she knocked again.

'Monsieur Gharsia, are you there? It is Madame Bernade. We met in the garden yesterday. I have Luis with me.'

There was still no answer. Ysabel was wondering what to do next when the door opened a fraction. She looked at the occupant of the room with alarm. A grey face with matted hair and beard looked back at her: beads of sweat glistened at his temples and his voice rasped.

'I have been sick. I think I have eaten rotten food.'

'I am sorry to hear that. I will ask Madame Seguine to send someone up to empty the night bucket. My servant, Ramon, will go to the apothecary for some fennel. I will look after Luis.' The words tumbling out, Ysabel had lapsed into Occitan, but the gist of what she had said was understood and the sick man nodded his thanks.

◆　　◆　　◆

After they had gone Hernando lay on the floor, trying to summon the strength to make it back to the bed. He had emptied his stomach violently and voided his bowels repeatedly. Now there was nothing left except the feeling that someone had scraped his guts with a sharpening stone and then had turned them inside out. He was frightened, but not for himself. What would happen to Luis if he remained ill? They were so vulnerable, alone in a foreign land. He crawled across the floor and dragged himself on to the bed; flopping over on his side he drew his legs up as pain racked his body. The smell of the night bucket next to the bed made him retch and retch until the bile rose into his mouth. He leaned back on the pillow, wiped his sleeve across his brow, and closed his eyes.

Hernando dozed fitfully. Someone came and removed the night bucket, leaving another in its place. The next time he opened his eyes the woman was standing by the door, a candle in her hand. Through the window he could see the last of the daylight fading and, as she moved forward, he was aware of Luis standing behind her. She indicated to the boy to stay back.

'Monsieur Gharsia, I have brought you a tisane of fennel.' She approached the bed and placed the drink on the side table. 'Is there anything else I can do for you?' she asked, concern in her eyes.

Hernando shook his head. He felt so wretched, beyond discomfort at the breach of etiquette that found a strange gentlewoman at his bedside. He pulled himself up.

'No, thank you. How is Luis?'

'He's fine.'

'Good.'

'He can sleep in my chamber tonight. My maid is there.'

Hernando took a deep breath as another pain came. Sweat broke out on his brow.

'Thank you.'

'Shall I take his night clothes?'

'They are under the bolster.'

Ysabel walked round the bed to the unoccupied side and retrieved a small cotton nightshirt. The excellent quality of the material surprised her.

'What shall I do about his bandage?'

'It will be fine until tomorrow. The wound is healed beneath it.'

'We will come back early in the morning so it can be changed. Are you sure I can't get you anything?'

'No, you have been most kind.'

'Goodnight, then.'

'Goodnight.' Hernando lay back on the pillow with relief and sank into oblivion.

◆   ◆   ◆

True to her word, Madame Bernade brought Luis back the next morning. It was not as early as Hernando had expected; Ysabel had diplomatically given him enough time to rise and dress. He had stopped vomiting but felt inordinately weak, the thought of food anathema to him.

'Good morning, Monsieur Gharsia.'

'Good morning, Madame Bernade. Hello, Luis.' Hernando noticed that her clothing was more sumptuous than the time they had met in the garden. She looked what she was: the wife of a very wealthy merchant.

'How are you?'

'I feel better.'

'Good,' Ysabel paused. 'I thought it might help if I took Luis out this morning. We could visit the market. You could rest.'

'That would be most gracious of you.' Already Hernando wanted to lie back down on the bed.

'It is no trouble,' replied Ysabel, a smile forming two dimples in her round face.

The market was alive with colour and noise. Luis's grip on Ysabel's hand tightened as they pushed through the throng to the space where jugglers and acrobats were entertaining the crowds. He watched enthralled, his head tilted so he could see round the edge of his dressing, as the balls sailed high into the air, only to be caught effortlessly each time. By the time they had visited the pedlar selling toys, the baker with his honey cakes, and the goodwife with some of her early plums, Luis felt more relaxed. They walked down the hill and sat on the wall of the bridge, before it crossed the river, watching the water flow by and eating their cakes. Luis's hand rested proudly on a new drum.

'What would you like to do next, Luis?'

'Can we visit Hercules?'

'Hercules?' queried Ysabel.

'He is in the stables.'

Ysabel watched as the old mule bent his oversized head so that Luis could pet him. She could not really believe it, but she was sure a look of tenderness came into the mule's eyes as he looked at the little boy. For several minutes Luis stroked Hercules and then, in a movement so sudden it startled Ysabel, he threw himself against her, wrapping his arms tightly around her hips.

'Will you help us?'

'Help you?' Ysabel carefully prised Luis away from herself and dropped to her knees in the straw. She opened her arms, for one brief second he paused and then he was there, nestled against her. 'Why do you need help?' She could barely hear the reply, his voice lost in the blue silk of her bodice.

'To find my mama and papa.'

Emotion welled up in Ysabel, threatening to engulf her. All the sorrow of the three babies she had bled away, the anguish of the daughter who had been too weak to drink her mother's milk, and the stark realisation that there would be no more babies made her fierce in her determination to help. She did not answer him with words; cradling his head against her shoulder she kissed the top of his head and felt him burrow further into her embrace.

F I V E

~

Hernando watched them from his window, the view restricted as his chamber was further along the passage. He could only see part of the garden, but at that moment Madame Bernade and Luis were in full view. He was unable to decide what they were doing; both were squatting down looking intently at the soil while Luis poked around with a stick. If he had known he would have approved as Ysabel was teaching his grandson how to add, although he may have questioned the method. Luis was digging for worms. When he found one he carefully lifted it with the stick, transferring it dangling to a new home. As he placed the worm down gently, he turned to Ysabel.

'Eight,' he shouted, his face lit up with glee.

'Well done!' Ysabel held up her eight fingers. 'Let us find two more. That will make ten,' she said unfolding her thumbs.

They were still looking for number nine when Ysabel glanced up and saw Hernando coming towards them. She rose to her feet, brushing down and rearranging her skirt. He was so tall she needed to tilt her head back to meet his eyes.

'Grandfather, I am counting worms with Ysabel.'

Hernando flinched at the familiarity, replying formally, 'Madame Bernade gives generously of her time.'

Ysabel acknowledged the comment with a slight dip of her head, not sure whether it was a compliment or not, and politely inquired about his health. It was four days since she had arrived at his chamber door and he was feeling much stronger. He was eating again, although sparingly, and, if he was honest with himself, once the first awful day was over he had enjoyed the hours of quiet, reading in his room. Luis appeared happier than he had been for a very long time so Hernando had needed no encouragement to allow him to spend time with Madame Bernade.

'Shall we sit down?' asked Ysabel pointing to the bench where her maid was sitting enjoying the shade as the late morning sun strengthened. Lisette made to rise but her mistress placed a gentle hand on her shoulder, 'No, stay Lisette, the fresh air will be doing you good.' She turned to Hernando. 'My maid has been poorly with a bad cough.'

Hernando was uncomfortable. One of the legacies of the Islamic occupation of the Spanish peninsula had been its influence on society. Even the Christian upper classes tended to keep their women secluded, many of whom preferred to be semi-veiled. He knew how to be gallant but was at a loss with Ysabel. Her gaze was so direct, her attitude so confident that she appeared to be travelling with only a lady's maid and one manservant. She was the most independent woman he had ever met, equally baffling and unnerving.

'You are planning to leave soon, Madame Bernade?'

'Yes, we are making plans to leave the day after tomorrow.'

'Have you come far?'

'Yes, I am a pilgrim returning from the shrine of St Jacques at Compostela. I travelled there by the route through St Jean Pied de Port but came back this way as I had business in Auch. Now that I have settled my affairs and Lisette is better, we can return home to Caors.'

Hernando thought carefully about his reply.

'Luis and I travel to Caors.'

Ysabel's heart beat a little faster but she calmly said, 'You are not from these parts, I believe.'

'That is true. We are from Valencia.'

'You know people in Caors?'

'No, but I have letters of introduction from colleagues at the School of Medicine at Valencia. I hope to join the faculty at the university in Caors.'

Although he was polite his demeanour did not invite further questions. 'If you will excuse me, I have come to take Luis back inside.' It was time for prayers and Hernando was eager to re-establish their normal routine which had been sadly neglected whilst he was ill. Nevertheless, Ysabel had one more question to ask.

'Where are Luis's parents, Monsieur Gharsia?'

'His mother is dead and his father as good as,' replied Hernando, his voice flat. 'Good day, Madame Bernade.' He turned, calling to Luis who, with a little wave to Ysabel, followed him out of the garden.

◆   ◆   ◆

Ysabel was too excited to eat.

They are going to Caors. They are going to Caors. Monsieur Gharsia and Luis are going to Caors! she thought as she paced up and down her chamber. She had ordered a tray at midday but most of her chicken and cabbage lay congealed on the trencher although Lisette had eaten heartily before returning to the garden with her sewing.

'Calm down, calm down, Ysabel,' she said to herself as she kept glancing out of the window to see if Luis was back in the garden, but there was no sign of either of them. She assumed they ate in their chamber, as she had never seen them in the private dining room, so there was little chance of seeing them there that evening. If Monsieur Gharsia did not appear this afternoon, she would have to seek him out. Sitting down to steady herself, Ysabel started to plan.

One hour later, she could wait no longer. With Lisette accompanying her for the sake of propriety, Ysabel knocked on the door of the Gharsias' chamber. Hernando opened the door immediately with what Ysabel thought was a look of irritation on his face; she had the impression she had interrupted something.

'Monsieur Gharsia, please, may I speak with you?' He opened the door wide, indicating with a sweep of his arm that they were to enter. Luis jumped up from the window-seat and rushed towards her for a hug. Hernando stiffened, finding it incomprehensible that his grandson seemed to be so attached to the merchant's wife, as he thought of her to himself, after so short a time. Ysabel embraced Luis briefly, aware of the aura of disapproval emanating from Monsieur Gharsia.

'What are you doing, Luis?' she asked brightly.

'Grandfather is reading to me from the Qur'an.'

There was a long pause. Hernando shifted uncomfortably, reminding himself that there was no Inquisition in Gascony, but Ysabel just smiled saying, 'I hope you were listening carefully, Luis.' The child smiled with such affection in return that Hernando was taken aback. He watched them with interest. Madame Bernade had not made any comment about the boy's face where the wound was now clearly visible; he made it a practice now to remove his grandson's bandage when they were in the chamber, but had decided to leave the stitches in until they reached Caors. Ysabel looked at the little boy smiling at her, the ugly cut from forehead to chin dominating half of his face, and added, 'I am sorry if I interrupted you.'

'Please sit down,' invited Hernando who remained standing while Ysabel and Lisette took the only stools, Luis leaning against Ysabel. She took a deep breath and began.

'Monsieur Gharsia, I have a request to make of you. As you know, we plan to start our journey back to Caors the day after tomorrow but, as we have stayed longer in Auch than planned, we are without travelling companions.' Ysabel looked directly at Hernando, which he found disconcerting. 'As the roads become busier, it is beneficial to be part of a larger party.'

He did not reply for some time. He appreciated her logic, but regretted the intrusion travelling together would make on the routine he had established with Luis. He looked at his grandson leaning against Madame Bernade, his arm resting on her lap, the little fingers splayed out on the blue fabric of her dress.

'It is sensible to travel together as we are both making for Caors. However, I travel on foot.'

Her clear hazel eyes widened with a mixture of admiration and horror, 'You have walked all the way from Valencia!'

'No,' he said rather sharply, 'I used a cart until we reached the mountains as Luis was so weak, but since then I have walked and Luis has ridden the donkey.'

Ysabel smiled at him ignoring his tone, 'That is no problem. You can hire a horse here in Auch to take you to Fleurance, another from there to Valence. Once there we will be on the banks of the Garonne and it is barely a week to reach home. If we can't hire a horse then Lisette can ride with Ramon.'

Yes, thought Hernando noticing the "we". *It all seems so easy. The stables will lend me a big horse because I am a tall man and I will hate it.* As he had had few occasions to ride as a physician and scholar in Valencia, the idea of sitting on a horse for the next two weeks did not appeal. He looked across at Luis whose fingers were creeping across Ysabel's lap towards her folded hands. For a fleeting moment Hernando had a feeling that he was losing control of the situation but dismissed it.

'We will be ready to travel with you, the day after tomorrow,' he said perhaps more tersely than he intended.

◆   ◆   ◆

The next morning Hernando and Luis were up early. They had prayed and eaten, and were ready to organise the hiring of a horse before most of the guests at the inn had stirred, the town already a hive of activity as they made their way to the stables. When they arrived the ostler took one look at Hernando's long legs and picked out a large, bony mare and, after negotiating the price of hire, they made their way to the pastures on the edge of the town, Hernando leading the horse as they wound their way through the narrow streets. Outside the town it was quiet, as Hernando had hoped, and at once he started to practise mounting and riding with dignity, while Luis wandered around the meadow finding dandelion heads to blow into the wind.

Something else he has learnt with the merchant's wife, Hernando thought.

Later that day when he was trying to pack, he glanced out of the window and saw the lady in question relaxing in the garden. Hernando knew the level of irritation he felt was unreasonable, but he was cross. It was hard enough to rearrange some of the bags, a task necessary as they were to travel in company, without Luis serenading him with the drum. His grandson was excited, more animated than he could ever remember seeing him. Trying to help with the packing had been a disaster and, though the drum kept Luis occupied, the repetitive thumps made Hernando's nerves jangle. He longed for his study and his books, he hated travelling, he had no idea how to cope with a small child, and now the purchaser of the instrument of torture was sitting quietly in a shady nook whilst her maid was probably doing all her packing.

'Luis! Stop that noise!' Hernando barked. Luis jumped, stopped, and gave his grandfather a reproachful look.

'I am sorry. My head aches. Look, I can see Madame Bernade in the garden. Why don't you go and join her?' Luis grabbed his drum and was gone before Hernando could say anything else. A few minutes later he watched them surreptitiously; the merchant's wife clapping her hands as Luis marched up and down beating the drum.

◆   ◆   ◆

The next morning dawned bright and clear, which augured well for the first part of their journey together. Hernando, who had been determined to be first at the meeting point, was piqued to see Madame Bernade already mounted on a pretty bay palfrey with Ramon in attendance on a fine gelding which, Hernando was later to discover, had belonged to the late but very successful Monsieur Bernade. Lisette was nowhere to be seen.

'Good morning, Monsieur Gharsia,' Ysabel was in high spirits. 'Hello Luis,' she added, giving him a special smile.

'Good morning.' Hernando noticed that both Madame Bernade and her manservant wore scallop shell badges, announcing their pilgrimage to Compostela to the world. Looking happy and relaxed, they starkly contrasted with Hernando who was sitting stiffly in the saddle, his hands tight on the reins.

It was the start of a journey which, despite Hernando's misgivings, was enjoyable. Once Lisette had arrived they set off for Fleurance, which they reached by nightfall. As the days passed a fledging feeling of camaraderie developed and, to his surprise, Hernando found that he preferred company to travelling alone with Luis. Several years later when she thought about this time, Ysabel remembered mostly the conversations they had had. There were many over the weeks, but two always stood out.

They had been riding slowly along a river path on a hot sunny afternoon having just crossed the Garonne. Ramon was leading with Luis perched in front of him, a treat which the boy had come to love; Lisette just behind them on her mule whilst Ysabel and Hernando brought up the rear, Bella's rein tied to the latter's saddle and Hercules following. As Luis was well out of earshot, Ysabel turned to her companion: 'Monsieur Gharsia, there is a matter on which I must speak.' By inclining his head Hernando had encouraged her to continue.

'When we were in Auch Luis asked me for help.' She looked at Hernando whose only answer was to raise his eyebrows. 'Yes, he asked me to help find his mama and papa. May I ask if he knows his mother is dead?'

'He was there when she died. I have told him she is dead so I believe he knows. Whether he understands is a different matter,' said Hernando sadly. His eyes met Ysabel's. Her obvious concern caused a shift in his estimation of her; while looking into his eyes she saw a vulnerability which she had not appreciated.

'And his father?'

'He could be anywhere from Venice to Baghdad, if he still lives.'

'Luis misses his parents very much I feel.'

'Yes, Madame Bernade, he does, and I am a poor substitute, but we must make do.' Hernando's tone changed; a sign which Ysabel now recognised as the end to conversation.

It was nearly a week later, early on the day they would reach Caors, when Ysabel again turned to Hernando and asked, 'Monsieur Gharsia, may I speak to you about your plans?' She had waited this long afraid to crush her hopes.

'Yes, Madame Bernade.'

'You have told me of your intention to seek a position at the University of Caors.'

Hernando nodded.

'I was wondering,' she continued, 'if you and Luis would do me the honour of being my guests until you find alternative accommodation?'

The look of suspicion on Hernando's face sparked an unexpected reaction from Ysabel who surprised herself by saying, 'I assure you, Monsieur Gharsia, I have no motive other than providing hospitality to two strangers to our town. I am a widow of some means having lost two husbands and . . .' but before she could finish her sentence he spoke.

'How remiss of you, Madame Bernade.' Unable to stop the words, Hernando had said what he was thinking.

She stopped and stared; the silence was too long. Then she laughed, filled with disbelief that the man actually had a sense of humour. Collecting herself, she continued, 'And I have no intention of acquiring a third!'

Hernando smiled broadly.

'In that case I accept your kind offer, Madame Bernade. Luis will be delighted.'

S I X

~

Ysabel knocked loudly on the door of the house on the corner of the Place St Urcisse. It was three weeks since they had arrived in Caors, and after an initial stay at Ysabel's, Hernando had been able to rent accommodation for Luis and himself. They had moved in two days ago and, as yet, Hernando had been very loath to hire any help in the house. She knocked again, and again, and again and was just about to give up when she heard the bolt of the door being drawn with obvious difficulty. Eventually the door opened to reveal Luis still in his night clothes, his black eyes large with fright in his pinched worried face.

'What is it Luis?'

He took her hand, leading her in silence to the room his grandfather had chosen as his study. The sight of a stranger met her. Hernando was sitting on the floor surrounded by bundles of books and satchels, one of which was half-opened to reveal some beautiful green silk. Although dressed he was dishevelled, his usual clothing replaced by Arabic trousers and tunic, obviously creased by months of being packed away. He was clutching a large book in his arms, sobbing uncontrollably.

Hernando was oblivious to their presence. Not knowing what to do, an unusual feeling for her, Ysabel stood still, drawing Luis against her. They waited some time, the sobs quietened until Hernando was weeping silently, rocking himself back and forth. She took Luis to the small kitchen to find something for Hernando to drink, knowing enough of his culture now to realise there would be no alcohol. Luis showed her where his grandfather stored the honey and vinegar drink they were both so fond of. She filled a cup and returned to the study to find him just as she had left him.

'Monsieur Gharsia, please drink this.' Taking the cup he looked at her for the first time, his eyes red and swollen. She sat on the floor next to him, Luis on her lap, as she could not send the child away to be alone in another room. Ysabel did not know how long they sat thus but her legs were feeling stiff and Luis heavy by the time Hernando spoke.

'She was dead. My beautiful Maryam was dead. It was all for nought.'

Ysabel shifted her legs settling Luis more comfortably. He had gone to sleep. She wondered how much sleep they both had had as Hernando looked as if he had been awake all night.

'Why?' she asked in a whisper.

'All of it from the beginning has been for nought.'

'Tell me,' she said, 'Tell me from the beginning.'

He started to speak in a monotone searching for the words as if they were far off.

'We were happy, we were so happy. I did not realise it then, but I do now. We lived in Granada, the last emirate of al-Andulus. When I was eleven years old, after ten years of fighting, the great Catholic monarchs, Fernando and Isabella, rode in triumph past our house. It is said they found our ruler, Boabdil, hiding in his palace and even his mother called him a coward. At first it looked as if we would keep our religion, our culture, our way of life. Queen Isabella's confessor, Hernando of Talavera, became Archbishop of Granada. He admired our achievements and was interested in our culture, but within ten years all had changed. In 1502, all the Muslims in the kingdom were forced to convert to Christianity or leave. My grandfather was very old then, heart-broken he could not make the journey. He died remembering the peaceful times of *convivencia* when Jews, Christians, and Muslims lived in harmony.

Some went to North Africa, but that was not our home. Most stayed and converted, but my family, with many others, left for the kingdom of Aragon. Fernando did not persecute Muslims in his lands. We settled in Valencia. I continued my education. I married Fatima and Maryam was born. Time passed, my skills as a physician were much in demand. We had a good life. Then trouble started again after Fernando's death. In 1519, his grandson Carlos granted permission for the guilds, the *Germania*, to arm. They became so strong, controlling who worked and who did not. The following summer, the Moorish quarters of the city were burnt. The guilds thought we had collaborated with the nobility who were protecting the Muslim workers on their lands. We were caught in a fight which was not ours. Fatima died.'

A sob escaped Hernando's lips. Ysabel reached out and gently touched his shoulder. He made no acknowledgement of the gesture but continued in the same monotone.

'We carried on. What could we do? I immersed myself in my work. Maryam grew from a girl to a woman. She married very young, to a man full of energy and laughter; Luis was born. The following year Carlos rescinded our toleration and we were to be forcibly baptised as Christians. What could we do? I was baptised. I decided to use the name Hernando as I remembered Hernando de Talavera from my childhood. We were all baptised. King Carlos promised the Inquisition would not persecute us, we would be given time to adjust to our new religion. We went to church, but at home nothing changed.'

He turned to Ysabel with a look of desolation, 'Allah is my God.' Then he continued: 'I did not approve of my son-in-law. After the marriage I found he mixed with some very unsuitable men. As a trader he was away for many months; he became rich very quickly but Maryam was loyal and I said nothing. Another child, a girl, was born. One evening this spring, I called on my daughter. I found Maryam in a pool of blood lying across Luis; the baby silent in her cradle. I do not know why they were killed. No other Muslims were attacked that night. I think it was revenge for something Yusuf had done. It was obvious Maryam and Layla were dead from knife wounds. I turned Maryam over. Her body was still warm and I saw that Luis was breathing. I ran to a neighbour, Ahmed, for help. He organised the burials whilst I tried to save Luis's life. He had lost so much blood. That night I made a decision. If he lived I would take Luis away as soon as he could travel, away from the danger of further attack, away from Yusuf returning and claiming him, away from Valencia. I would change his name to mine.'

Ysabel released the breath she realised she had been holding, removing her hand from Hernando's shoulder so she could embrace Luis. He stirred on her lap, she wiggled her legs trying to bring the feeling back.

'A friend at the School of Medicine, Felipe, recommended the University of Caors and wrote letters of introduction for me. I did not know what I was undertaking. The journey has been so hard. How can I raise a five year old child? How can I raise him as a faithful servant of Allah, away from our people? What did I think I was doing?'

Ysabel had no answer. What he had experienced appalled her. She looked at his tear ravaged face, moved beyond thinking. He continued, now with more urgency, 'I try to teach him about Islam, our faith, our culture, our achievements in science, medicine, astrology, and literature but he is so young. What will his future hold? I was ill in Auch. It was Ramadan. What will happen to Luis if I become really ill? If I can't guide him, Luis will never understand his heritage. He must worship Allah and follow the teachings of the Prophet Muhammad, peace be upon him. If not, it has all been for nought. My heart bleeds for what has been lost; for what will be lost.'

They sat in silence while Ysabel thought of the words of comfort she could use to soothe him.

'You are both safe here, there is no Inquisition. You must ensure Luis follows your faith but you know it will not be easy. I will help you where I can.'

Hernando turned his head. She was looking directly at him with her hazel eyes full of warmth. She was offering to help him, this round lively woman, the merchant's wife. He was not alone. He could not find the words so he touched her hand; a gesture so unfamiliar to him that his normal self would have been shocked. She only smiled and said, 'I think we should stand up. We are too old to sit on the floor for so long.'

A New Life

1540

S E V E N

~

Caors, Summer 1540

'I hate him. I hate him. I hate him.'

Luis strode across the room, flung himself into the large oak chair, and glared at her, fury making his black eyes hard. Ysabel took a deep breath.

'Luis Gharsia, you must not speak of your grandfather so,' she said sharply. 'It is disrespectful and you know you do not mean it. It will not do to act so in my house.'

Luis pushed himself up from the chair, all arms and legs, full of boiling indignation; the scar on his face livid as he wrestled with his anger. He paced the room. Ysabel remained quiet. He stormed around her parlour several times before he stopped at her side looking over her shoulder where she sat at the table, the ledger before her.

'Sit down Luis, please. You are making my head spin.'

He pulled out a chair with a penetrating scrape on the floor, which Ysabel chose to ignore, and sat down with a resounding thud.

'Calm down, Luis. Why are you so angry?' she asked, although she knew the answer.

'I do not want to be a physician. I do not want to attend classes at the university. He cannot make me.'

Luis looked so much like his grandfather as he spoke that Ysabel suppressed a smile. She saw the same mannerisms, sharp features, and height, although in Luis the broadness of his shoulders promised a sturdier man.

'Ysabel, you must speak to him.'

She replied with a questioning look.

'Sorry! Please Ysabel, will you talk to Grandfather for me?'

Her heart sank. She had known this day might come. It was almost ten years since she had lifted Luis on to the back of her palfrey and ridden west, away from the crowded narrow streets of the city towards the vineyards of the Olt valley.

◆　　◆　　◆

It had been a beautiful morning, the weather perfect in Ysabel's eyes. The sky was deep blue, as clear as on a summer's day, yet the chill in the air heralded the cooler days of autumn. Luis's stiff little shoulders had started to relax as soon as they crossed the Pont Valentré leaving the city behind them. It was three days since she had found Hernando distraught on the floor of his study. They had agreed that it was time for Hernando to present his letters of introduction to the university whilst Ysabel would look after Luis for the day. She would take him to visit her brother and his family. They had left the house on the corner of the Place St Urcisse very early as it was a two hour ride to the Gaulbert farm. Following the south bank of the Olt as it swung westwards in its journey to the Atlantic, they had made good time.

Luis shifted position and looked around him. Pasture land bordered the green river, dotted with sheep and cows, whilst the lower slopes of the hillside were terraced, planted with row after row of the same plants.

'Vines,' said Ysabel following his gaze.

'Why are there so many?'

'For the grapes, Luis.'

Her brother had greeted her warmly, eager for news of her pilgrimage. They had come across him in the cellar mending a barrel that would store some of the new harvest.

'Who is this?' asked Guilhem Gaulbert as he bent down to smile at Luis.

'Luis Gharsia, my friend. Luis and his grandfather were kind enough to accompany me from Auch.'

Guilhem studied the small child leaning against his sister.

'Well Luis Gharsia, you must come up to the house.'

Loise Gaulbert was in her kitchen when she heard footsteps approaching. Going to the door she had opened it to reveal her husband and his sister who was holding a thin, dark boy by the hand. Loise's first emotion was surprise, quickly followed by the antipathy Ysabel always aroused in her. Her sister-in-law continued to treat the farm as her home and Loise felt strongly that Ysabel should have called at the house first before wandering around the outbuildings.

Guilhem beamed.

'Look, here is our sister safely returned from her pilgrimage. She has a little friend with her.'

Loise's eyes narrowed.

'Good day, Sister.'

'Hello Loise. This is Luis.'

Luis looked up at the woman in front of him and instinctively moved closer to Ysabel. So unlike her husband who was ushering his guests forward across the threshold, Loise's eyes were cold, showing no sign of welcome.

The farmhouse reflected Gaulbert's success with his wine. The main room was large and comfortably furnished yet very rustic compared to Ysabel's house on the bank of the Olt. Luis watched as Loise grudgingly fetched a pitcher of wine for the adults and some milk for the children. He looked around for signs of Ysabel's nephew and niece and was soon rewarded by the clatter of clogs which announced their arrival. They stopped short when they saw Luis sitting with their aunt.

'Hello Henri, hello Marie,' said Ysabel as she rose from the table and walked towards them with a swish of skirts. Henri's eyes flicked to Luis.

'Papa, I have finished feeding the geese and have checked the chickens for eggs,' he said importantly. A comely child of about seven, he had the same chestnut hair and hazel eyes as his father and aunt. The girl next to him pushed herself forward so she blocked her brother.

'And I have been to the pond to see the ducks.' She was about Luis's age, smiling and confident of her father's approval.

Guilhem smiled.

'Good. There is some milk here. Come and sit with your aunt and meet her young friend Luis Gharsia.'

Greetings were exchanged. The Gaulbert children looked at Luis. The latter, after being nudged into politeness by Ysabel, kept his eyes down. Guilhem and Ysabel talked; Loise sat in silence, a sour expression on her face. Soon she stood up.

'I cannot sit here all day. I have work to do,' she pointed out, brushing imaginary crumbs from her apron with worn, chapped hands.

'Of course,' replied Ysabel as she pushed a stray hair back under her hood with the smooth scented hand that confirmed her status as a gentlewoman. 'Brother, perhaps we could show Luis the farm?' Then she smiled at Henri and Marie. 'Afterwards, I have some presents from Compostela.'

As the day progressed Luis had lost some of his shyness. He had enjoyed seeing the fowl pecking in the enclosure, the duck pond with its occupants gliding in stately formation, and the meadow where the stock grazed. The sun shone warmly; his hand had become sticky in Ysabel's, and when Henri and Marie started to run towards the slopes he had let go and joined them. They took flight, kicking their heels up; clouds of pollen rose as they raced ahead, small blue butterflies danced just above the tall grass as they passed, and when Guilhem and Ysabel reached the vines, the three children were lying on their backs watching a solitary buzzard as it wheeled in a cloudless sky.

'It is a good year, Ysabel.' Guilhem rested a hand on Ysabel's shoulder. 'A very good year.' He turned to Luis. 'Young Luis, you must come back for the harvest.' Luis had stood up and joined them. All he could see were endless rows of vines, laden with deep black grapes, climbing up the slope away from the meadow. 'We need everyone to help at harvest.'

'Please can we come, Ysabel?'

She looked at his glowing face and nodded.

For Luis the day had not been long enough, but it was not so for everyone. As he waved goodbye with Ysabel, as she turned her palfrey homeward, he saw Madame Gaulbert lean close to her husband.

'I do not like that boy,' she hissed.

Gaulbert looked at her puzzled.

'He is a child. What can you dislike?'

'Those eyes, that scar,' she replied.

Her husband was silent, wondering how the woman he married had become so mean in spirit.

◆　　◆　　◆

They had returned for the harvest and many times after that. At every opportunity Luis would persuade Ysabel to take him out to the farm, his excitement palpable as they left the city limits. He learnt to help Henri and Marie with their chores, he ran wild with them when they had time, and he grew adroit at avoiding Loise's icy stare. It was after such a visit to the Gaulberts, the year following his arrival in Caors, that Luis arrived home to find that his grandfather had a visitor.

Later that evening when Luis and the visitor were warm in their beds, Hernando and Ysabel sat by the fire in his small parlour and he described what had occurred.

He had been in his room at the university working on a lecture about the use of opiates to render the patient unconscious during surgery when there was a knock at the door. Opening it he saw one of his students accompanied by a boy with a head of unruly curls. There was something familiar about him which eluded Hernando until the boy spoke.

'Good day, Sir. Do you remember me?' There was a pause. 'It is Johan Berenguer,' he said, his head bowed respectfully.

Hernando did not answer immediately. Yes, it was the boy from the inn at Gavarnie but there was something different about him. Then it came to Hernando. Johan was not smiling, in fact the boy looked pale, dirty, and apprehensive.

'Yes Johan. Please come in. What brings you to Caors?'

His task safely completed, the student left. Johan, feeling increasingly overwhelmed, crossed the threshold into the room. Hernando indicated for him to sit and settled himself back behind his desk. Leaning forward, he steepled his fingers and waited for an answer to his question. He waited patiently as Johan perched nervously on the very edge of one of the stools the students used and told his tale in faltering tones, wringing the cap in his hands as he spoke.

'It was shortly after you and the little boy left us, Sir, when a small group of five pilgrims arrived at our inn. They asked if they could stay for a few days as one of them had started to feel ill. We did not know. How could we have known what was to come?' His eyes grew moist. 'It was the sweating sickness. Within three weeks all were ill. Two of the pilgrims and both my parents died.'

Hernando rose from his desk and in one long stride joined Johan whose hands were shaking as he wound his cap round and round. He pulled up a stool.

'What did you do?'

'My sister came up from Luz and somehow we managed to get through the winter. When the snow started to melt bringing the first visitors, my brother-in-law came to live at the inn as well. His cousin took over the forge but I did not want to stay. I wanted to see what was beyond the mountains and I remembered about you travelling to Caors, Sir.' Johan raised his eyes for the first time, smiling weakly. 'I followed the route you had described, and here I am.' He swallowed hard to compose himself, his prominent Adam's apple bobbing in his narrow neck.

'What will you do now?'

'I hope I may be so bold as to ask for your advice, Sir?'

Hernando rested his hands on his knees and thought.

'What can you do?'

'I am good with animals especially horses, I can cook and clean.' He looked at Hernando hopefully.

'Can you read?'

Johan shook his head, his eyes darting to the back of the room where a chest, its lid open, was filled with heavy volumes. Hernando nodded, it was what he had expected, and patted Johan's shoulder.

'I think the best thing for now is for you to come home with me. You look in sore need of a wash, a good meal, and a comfortable bed. Tomorrow is soon enough to decide what to do.'

◆　　◆　　◆

'Ysabel, please will you see Grandfather today?'

Ysabel looked at Luis carefully trying to judge his mood now he had calmed down. There had been no wheedling or whining in his question, just a direct request for her help; the recognition of her role over the last ten years as the mediator who was able to bridge the gap between the two Gharsias. Ysabel was aware of this and hoped she had ensured that she was always fair, never showing favour to either man or boy, both of whom were utterly dear to her.

'Luis, did you have an argument with your grandfather this morning?'

'He will not listen. He will not listen to what I say.'

Ysabel smiled and asked gently, 'Do you listen to what he says?'

Luis gave a snort of impatience.

'I know what he says. He always says the same thing. He wants me to be a physician, to follow in the tradition of the Gharsias who have been physician-surgeons for endless generations back into the mists of time.'

'I think you would be a good physician. You have already learnt much from Hernando.' She was rewarded by a glare and hastily added, 'I am not taking sides. It is simply what I observe.'

Luis did not know what to answer. How could he articulate his feelings when he could not make sense of them himself? All he knew was that the idea of being a physician filled him with revulsion.

Ysabel was watching the youth closely waiting for him to speak. Startled by the expression creeping into his eyes, for a moment she did not recognise it.

'Luis?'

'I think it is the blood. It is the blood.'

As he spoke, black eyes fixed on her face, Ysabel realised what she could see. It was fear.

E I G H T

~

It was still early. If she made haste she might catch Hernando before he left for the College Pelegry. Reaching her chamber she quickly checked her appearance in the looking glass and decided there was not time to ask Lisette to help her change. Always aware of her status, Ysabel was sure she was unlikely to meet anyone of note at this time of the morning as she quickly made her way to the house on the Place St Urcisse.

The brightness of the day hit her as she opened the door and crossed her courtyard to the street. The sun sparkled on the river, a kingfisher darted just above the water, a flash of blue, but today was not a day to stand and watch. It was not many steps before she reached Hernando's and knocked on the door.

'Good morning, Madame Bernade.' One of the many pleasures of calling on Hernando was to be greeted by Johan, a smile of welcome always on his face.

'Good morning, Johan. Is your master still at home?'

'Yes. Please come in. I believe he is in his study.'

Ysabel followed him through the hall towards the back of the house. Hernando was in his study, a small room adjacent to the parlour, used by the previous occupant, a spice merchant, as his counting-house. The room faced east and the morning sun streamed through the tiny window, dust mites danced in its beam and fell onto the table Hernando used as a desk.

Ysabel greeted him cheerily.

'Good morning, Hernando.'

'If you have come to take his part, you can leave now.'

'Hernando!' she replied sharply, the reproof in her voice at odds with the gentleness of her expression. Johan glanced from one to the other and diplomatically took his leave, slipping quietly from the room. Hernando looked up from his reading, running both hands through his hair. It was still thick, but the silver was winning and, Ysabel noted, it was overdue for a trim. He was dressed in his doctor's robes, his cap lying on the table, suggesting that he was ready to leave. He made a sound, a cross between a sigh and a grunt.

'Good morning, Ysabel.' He pushed the chair back and came towards her. Taking her hands in his, he bent to kiss her cheeks and felt his irritation receding in the presence of her smile along with the crease of concern between her brows. Everything about her cheered him as it had since he had accepted her offer of friendship. She was dressed quite simply in a yellow gown as bright as sunshine, yet the colour alone proclaimed her a woman of wealth. Although the saffron needed to create the beautiful hue came from her own land, it was as expensive as gold.

'What are you reading?' Ysabel had realised long ago that Hernando was most comfortable when talking about medicine.

'I am just checking something in Al-Biruni's *Kitab al-Saydalah*. I have a class today on the role and use of drugs.' Warming to his subject, he pointed to another book. 'This was written by Ibn Romia who was an authority on medicinal herbs and plants. His ideas have replaced the old methods of the ancients like Galen. For example, he discovered colchicine which is very valuable in the treatment of gout.'

Ysabel, knowing that Hernando was liable to start a lengthy explanation, decided to come to the point.

'That is so fascinating Hernando, but I must talk to you about Luis.' Immediately she saw him stiffen.

'Where is he?'

'Off on his wanders.'

'He should be studying.'

'I am sure he will be back soon.'

'I do not have time to talk now. I am due at the university.'

'In that case, will you come and dine with me this evening?'

Hernando nodded grudgingly and started to collect his things together. 'Thank you, Ysabel.'

'Good.' As she made her way to the door she turned, her voice low and gentle. 'Hernando, what did you say to Luis?'

Hernando continued to tidy away his books, his back to her as he placed them carefully in the chest.

'I said that I did not leave our home and walk for three months traversing those inhospitable mountains for him to waste his life growing grapes.'

Ysabel just tilted her head gracefully, her face serene, and said, 'Until this evening.'

◆　　◆　　◆

Ysabel did not leave the house. She retraced her steps across the hall through to the kitchen where Johan was in front of the open store cupboard. Ysabel could see it was well stocked with oil, vinegar, salt, almonds, dates, figs, and raisins, as well as cloves, pepper, mace, ginger, saffron, and cinnamon.

'I am just checking our stocks,' he explained. 'I am going to the Place St Jacques. I expect you know that the merchants from Marsilha have arrived.'

'Yes, Lisette and I plan to go later today. Please can I interrupt your task for a moment, Johan?'

'Of course, Madame Bernade,' said Johan with enthusiasm as he enjoyed conversation, something which was often lacking in a household of two taciturn Gharsias. He had a deep affection for his master's friend although, over the years, he had been unable to establish the exact nature of their relationship. He was aware of strong ties (in fact, Johan would probably have described it as love, if asked), yet he had never seen any signs of the comfort he himself enjoyed with Jeanne, the buxom widow who nourished his body, if not his soul.

'Please sit down. May I offer you some sekanjabin?'

'Thank you.' Ysabel had acquired a taste for the sharpness of vinegar softened by the sweetness of sugar. Making herself comfortable on the settle, she continued, 'I need to talk to you about Luis.'

As she was about to start, they heard Hernando come from the hall.

'Johan, I am away to the university now,' he began, stopping in the doorway when he saw Ysabel. 'Tonight it will be just you and Luis for supper as I will eat with Madame Bernade.' He was of a mind to turn and leave without saying more but knew he was being churlish. Both of them were looking at him with smiles on their faces, the two people who had enabled him to survive as true to himself as possible. Johan, in return for a home, had thrown himself with his innate enthusiasm into the task of maintaining an Islamic household. His skill in slaughtering and cooking were invaluable, as was his discretion. Neither servant nor beloved son, he was a cross between the two and treasured as such. He shared a room with Luis, ate at the family table, and, in return for the wages Hernando insisted on giving, happily looked after every aspect of their lives. That Johan was plotting with Ysabel, as Hernando saw it, did not surprise him.

Ysabel's hazel eyes were assessing him. She looked very biddable at that moment but Hernando knew beneath the soft exterior was an iron will, admired with reluctance by those with whom she did business and often used for his benefit. He would never forget the first Sunday after their arrival at Caors when she insisted Luis and he attend church with her. 'Keep true,' she had said, 'but bend with the wind or you will break.' Ysabel had dressed in her finest silk dress; pearls encircled her neck and dangled in her ears, giving a luminosity to her skin. Taking his arm, and holding Luis by the hand, she had made him escort her to her usual place near the top of the nave, as her status dictated.

Heads had turned and mouths had dropped amongst the merchant fraternity as Ysabel Bernade had slowly walked the length of the aisle accompanied by a tall, distinguished Arab gentleman dressed in the formal Spanish style, and a small child with a badly disfigured face. Any memories of the actual service had been lost over time but Hernando knew he had talked to his God and thanked him for the gift of the woman beside him. Tongues had wagged outside in the square afterwards, but Ysabel had established a pattern that brought about acceptance and kept them safe. Later she had turned to him, 'Do as you always have at home but do not keep yourself separate.'

Now she was waiting for a kind word before he left. 'I look forward to this evening, Ysabel,' he said as he turned to take his leave.

Once Hernando had left, Ysabel asked the question which had been nagging at her since her conversation with Luis earlier that morning.

'Johan, when you kill a sheep, and drain the blood, is Luis ever with you?'

The young man thought for a moment. 'No, he is never there.'

Ysabel felt mortified, wondering how she had loved the child for ten years without realising that behind the visible scar on his face, Luis remained deeply affected by the terrible event in his past. Johan saw her stricken face.

'Where is he now?' he said with concern as he had heard Luis storm out of the house.

'The usual place, I expect.'

They both knew where Luis would have gone and they were right. As soon as he had asked Ysabel to talk to his grandfather, Luis had left her house, striding out as fast as he could without breaking into a run. He turned left along the river bank, cut back through the Place St Jacques crowded with merchants doing a brisk trade, past the magnificent cathedral of St Etienne, and made his way towards the northern ramparts. He hated the narrow streets, even those with the newer houses, their light facades and doorways beautifully decorated with mouldings of branches, roses, and flaming suns. He increased his pace. In a matter of minutes he was through the Portal des Augustins and started to run, making towards the Tour du Pal. There on the open ground he threw himself forward full length on the ground and covered his head with his hands. Beneath him the old bones of Hercules rested in the brown crumbly earth, carefully buried there by Johan and Ramon whilst a distraught twelve year old Luis had kept watch.

The tired ancient mule had finally come to the end of his journey seven years after they had left Valencia. Good-natured to the end, he had lived long enough to bear Luis on his back in the early years of visiting the Gaulberts. When the mule had ceased to serve any useful purpose, Hernando, with a sensitivity of which his grandson had not been aware, decided Hercules should be allowed to graze in idle retirement, with good oats to feed on over the winters. Although unmarked, Luis knew exactly where Hercules lay. He had plotted the spot three years ago from the position of the walnut trees whose leaves were shading him from the increasing intensity of the sun. He lay with his cheek nestled in the soil, not noticing the passage of time as he waited for the panic to subside. The sun was hot and some way past its zenith when he rose, pulled his sticky shirt from his back, brushed down his hose and made his way slowly back home, knowing his grandfather would not be there.

◆　　◆　　◆

Later that day, as the evening sun cast elongated shadows across the small garden, Ysabel and Hernando sat in companionable silence. They had eaten a good supper of roasted chicken, olives, and figs, finishing with the marzipan sweetmeats of which they were both so fond. Feeling the tightness of her bodice, Ysabel thought perhaps she should not have eaten so much but it was difficult to stop when Hernando had such a large appetite. Yet he was still long and lean while she was getting rounder with age. She watched Hernando who, with eyes closed and legs out-stretched, looked most content. It was a shame she had to spoil his mood.

'Hernando, we must talk about Luis.' His eyes snapped open, he drew his legs towards him and, crossing his arms, turned to her.

'Why must we? There is nothing to discuss. He will start his studies at the university next month.'

'He does not want to go. You know that Hernando.'

'That is ridiculous. He is ready and of age. He has a rewarding life ahead of him. Luis is in possession of a quick mind, already he has learnt much about medicine. He is fluent in Latin and Arabic, reads Greek accurately, and can speak French and Castilian as well as his own language. In fact, after a couple of years here I think he should go to one of the great medical schools. He could go to Paris or Bologna.' Ysabel laid a hand on his arm, touching it lightly.

'Hernando, he does not want to be a physician.'

'How can he not? It is his heritage.'

They both fell silent. Ysabel collected her thoughts, ready to put forward the argument she had practised in her mind all day. She spoke so quietly Hernando had to strain to hear her.

'When Maryam and Layla were killed, was there much blood?' She felt him recoil from her touch and judiciously removed her hand. He stared at her, incomprehension in his eyes at the turn the conversation had taken. He did not answer.

'Please Hernando, tell me.'

'Of course there was blood,' he shouted angrily, 'they had been stabbed.'

'And Luis?' she continued bravely. Hernando had stood up, his great height looming above her. He blocked the last rays of light from the bench so she could not see his face clearly but she could feel his rage. She stood up then and put her arms around him, a small indomitable woman, all rustling silk and lavender perfume.

'And Luis?' she asked again. She could feel his heart racing where her head rested against his chest and held him closer.

'Yes, he was covered in blood.'

Ysabel released him and taking his hands, which had remained by his sides, looked up into his face. In the gathering gloom she said slowly and firmly: 'I believe Luis is terrified of blood. It would destroy him to become a physician. He could never perform surgery.' Still holding Hernando's hands she took a step backwards. 'Come Hernando, let us sit down again.'

It was some minutes before he spoke.

'He is still young. He may forget?'

'He is no longer a child but a young man in his sixteenth year.'

'I expect you approve of his idea to be a farmer?' Hernando's voice was clipped and brusque.

'I am not sure, but what I know is that I want him to be happy and at the moment he is angry and afraid.'

Hernando slumped down the seat as if all his hopes were draining from him. He experienced a sensation like a physical blow, this realisation that after the generations of fighting for identity Luis would choose to turn his back on the tradition of practising medicine. It felt to Hernando as if another part of the Gharsias was being lost. Ysabel, seeing he looked so forlorn, held his hand firmly and made her proposal.

'Let us not rush Luis. I could ask my brother Guilhem to take him for a year. After he has tended the vines through the winter perhaps he will change his mind. There is still time for him to go to university next year.'

Hernando pulled himself upright.

'You know that he wants to make wine?'

'Yes, wine is the heart of our region—the black wine of Caors.'

'But he is a Muslim, Ysabel.'

'I know. Have you discussed making wine with him?'

'Yes,' although as Hernando spoke he reflected that "discussion" was not quite the right word to describe their exchange.

'What did he say?'

'He quoted the Qur'an at me: verse 67, cura 16. He argued that he must not become intoxicated and not that it said he could never drink alcohol. He also reminded me of the great days of al-Andulus when the Islamic rulers owned vineyards and drank wine.'

Ysabel smiled.

'Perhaps Luis should become a lawyer? You have educated him well, Hernando.'

'Humph!' Hernando thought for a moment and then said, 'Let it be so for now. I will ask for his place at the university to be deferred for one year and he can play at being a farmer.' Ysabel winced at his use of words but kept her peace, waiting for him to continue. He rose and, pulling her up with him, encircled her in his arms and kissed her cheek. 'Good night, Ysabel. I must speak with your brother soon to talk about arrangements.'

'Good night, Hernando,' she replied, adding after he had slipped through the narrow gate, 'my love.'

NINE

~

A week later three riders crossed the Pont Valentré, each filled with very different emotions. Luis was elated, happiness sparkled in his eyes, but he kept his features composed as he rode the late Monsieur Bernade's gelding. A more mature horse now yet still strong and spirited, he was pulling at the reins already. Ysabel was nervous. She was very nervous. Although Hernando had met her brother on more than one occasion in Caors, she was unsure how the former would react when they reached the farm. The object of her concern was quiet as they rode, preoccupied as he was by two activities; firstly, the control of the large horse he had hired from the stables near the Pont Neuf and secondly, by the ordering of his thoughts. Hernando was determined that Luis's sojourn as an agricultural worker was to be on his own terms and he was making sure nothing would be overlooked.

As the suppressed elation, nervousness, and silent iron determination made uncomfortable travelling companions, Ysabel decided to lighten the mood.

'Hernando, do you know the story of the building of the Pont Valentré?' She was sure he would be aware of it but probably lacked the details. He looked at her coolly.

'I have heard of some ridiculous tale.'

'You do not believe it then?'

'No.'

Ysabel raised her eyebrows.

'Perhaps you do not know the full story?'

'I have a feeling you are going to tell me whether I want to hear it or not.'

'Yes, dear Hernando, I am,' she said perkily.

They had just passed through the gateway in the central tower and Hernando looked up at the outer tower ahead of him, the gates open with the portcullis raised on the peaceful August morning. The tower rose high into the cloudless summer sky, the light stone shimmered in the bright light, even though it was still early, and showed a blank face with only two narrow arrow slits. A room protected by crenellations crowned the impressive edifice and Hernando marvelled at the feat of architecture.

'Come on then,' he said. 'Tell me the story.'

'It goes something like this. The building of the bridge was taking a long time and was beset with problems. The architect was so frustrated with the progress of the venture that he asked the devil himself for help and in exchange he promised his soul. At once, all seemed to go well and the piers, towers, and arches were built quickly. However, the architect did not want to be damned . . .'

'Obviously,' said Hernando drily.

'Do not interrupt please.' Ysabel attempted to look at him sternly and continued: 'However, the architect did not want to be damned so he thought he would trick the devil. He gave his helper a sieve in which to carry the water needed by the builders to mix the mortar, and so the devil never finished the bridge and could not claim his soul. In revenge the devil removed the top stone of the middle tower every night and then every day the builders had to replace it. So you see the bridge was never finished.'

'Nonsense,' replied Hernando although, he added with a twinkle in his eye. 'I trust the bridge is safe now as I am riding on it.'

'Of course,' laughed Ysabel, pleased that he was being more communicative as they both turned in the saddle to glance back at the central tower. 'It was many generations ago, at the end of the thirteen hundreds. I think you will be fine Hernando.'

◆   ◆   ◆

It was late morning when they turned off the river road and made their way along the track to the Gaulbert farm. It was very hot. Hernando was aware of a wet stickiness where his inner thighs rubbed against the saddle and he could see that Ysabel was pink and glowing under her hood. Only Luis seemed unbothered by the heat, repeatedly riding ahead before turning back to meet them as they rode sedately towards him.

'Why does he keep doing that?' grumbled Hernando.

Ysabel smiled indulgently.

'Because he is young and full of life and we are too slow for him.'

At last the farmhouse came into view; a two storey dwelling of the local grey sandstone with an outside stone staircase leading to the upper floor where the family lived. The roof was of lauzes, large flat stones, laid at a gentle angle before rising steeply to the ridge. At one end there was a large chimney and at the other, a turret. The ground before the house was parched dry, scrubby straw-coloured grass poked its way through the hard brown earth. A woman stood at the top of the stairs, drawn to the door by the sound of the approaching horses. Very still, she watched them, the only movement a slow drying of her hands on her apron. Her face appeared as an expressionless mask.

'Good morning, Loise,' greeted Ysabel, waving amicably. Luis had already dismounted so Hernando followed suit, stretching his legs stiffly as he reached the ground. He offered a supporting hand to Ysabel as she eased herself from the saddle and then they made their way up the uneven stone steps; Hernando very conscious of the fact that the woman had not spoken. When they reached the top of the stairs, she took a step back into the room behind her so that they could enter. It was cool and dark inside after the bright sunshine and it took some moments for Hernando's eyes to adjust. There was a pause which was just too long and then the woman spoke.

'Good day, Sister. Please sit down.'

Ysabel, who preferred to remain standing for a while after the ride, looked directly at Loise and then turned towards Hernando touching his arm.

'Please may I introduce Luis's grandfather, Hernando Gharsia. Hernando, this is my brother's wife, Loise.'

Hernando bowed. Loise looked from Ysabel to Hernando coldly and just nodded, indicating for them all to sit down.

'I will go and tell Guilhem you are here.' She disappeared through the door as they took their seats, Ysabel smiling apologetically at Hernando.

Several minutes later the sound of heavy footsteps on the stone stairs announced the arrival of the master of the house. Guilhem Gaulbert, hot and dirty from his work, entered the room beaming with pleasure as he saw his visitors. He kissed his sister, shook Hernando's hand heartily, and ruffled Luis's hair.

'Luis, Henri is mending the wall of the south meadow. Do you want to join him?'

'Yes, I will.' Luis was out of the door as quickly as was polite, almost bumping into Madame Gaulbert as she entered with a pitcher in her hand. Without a backwards glance, he left the adults to seal his fate.

They sat at the table, the awkwardness in the air tangible. Hernando's rejection of the offer of the dark ruby red wine did not help and when he noticed a look of derision on Loise's face as he asked for milk, his natural reserve enveloped him. While Ysabel ploughed on, talking of this and that, Hernando looked at the couple who would have charge of his grandson for the next year, if negotiations were successful. Gaulbert was an affable man who was obviously very fond of his sister, a quality which endeared him to Hernando as he could see a strong family resemblance between brother and older sister. They shared the same hazel eyes and chestnut hair, now streaked with grey, and both were short in stature.

There were some differences though, but these had appeared with time. Guilhem still possessed the wiry strength of one who tilled the soil for his survival whilst Ysabel was very softly covered, as Hernando had now come to think of it. Although both had round cheery faces, Guilhem's was marked by a redness of nose and cheeks, a condition Hernando knew was made worse by alcohol, and wind and cold. In fact, as he had approached his forties, Gaulbert's nose had become increasingly nodular and knobbly. Too much of his own wine decided Hernando as a hint of self-righteousness crept into his thoughts.

Gaulbert's wife sat next to him, her eyes hard in a narrow face which, like Guilhem's, was deeply lined from working in the sun. Yet whilst her husband's lines reflected eyes screwed up against the harsh light and a mouth used to smiling, Loise's lines around her mouth etched discontent permanently on her visage. Not usually one to be aware of or interested in undercurrents, Hernando could not avoid the realisation that Ysabel's sister-in-law felt a considerable degree of antipathy towards her. By his reasoning, the feeling could not be towards him as he had only met Loise for the first time that morning. However, he was mistaken.

Loise Gaulbert sat unhappily opposite Ysabel and Hernando. She had disliked Luis's grandfather instantly just because he was the boy's grandfather. Additionally, as usual, the sight of Ysabel, immaculately dressed as she was today in a fine linen gown, awakened the worm of envy that was eating away at Loise. She was very weary; a weariness that arose from the fact that she had been up before dawn. She had milked the cows, baked bread, churned some butter, skinned and prepared the rabbit Henri had killed earlier, now simmering in the pot, and had picked and shelled the beans. There was also the weariness of monotony. Each day was the same round of tasks, varied only by the seasons, and she coveted the life she believed Ysabel lived. Hernando looked at Loise sitting silently before him with a half filled goblet of wine in her hands as she twisted the stem round and round. She raised her eyes and caught him watching her. Although not so dark as Luis's eyes, Hernando's were just as deep-set and intent as the boy's and she felt he could see inside her, that he could read her innermost thoughts. It was what had unsettled her when she had first met Luis and it continued to do so every time the boy looked at her.

What Hernando could never know was that Loise had lost the last piece of armour she had possessed against her resentment of Ysabel. While Ysabel had charm, wealth from two rich husbands, and her own business acumen, all of which enabled her to be an independent woman of means, Loise had two children. Living, breathing proof that she, Loise, had what Ysabel yearned for most. Then Luis had arrived as if from nowhere, a small disfigured scrap of a boy who had always been at Ysabel's side since that first fateful meeting when Loise had watched them walk towards her, a little brown hand safe in Ysabel's elegant soft one. Now fifteen, no longer a child, Luis had walked through her door that day with Ysabel and Hernando, and Loise had seen a family, albeit different from hers but a family nevertheless. Loise noticed how Ysabel touched Monsieur Gharsia's arm lightly to hold his attention as her sister-in-law spoke and she caught a smile between Ysabel and the boy, his eyes shining, that was so intimate and conspiratorial it overwhelmed her with suppressed rage at the unfairness of it all.

'I must go and attend to the meal,' she mumbled as she hastily left the room.

Loise had been an excellent housewife since she was a very young woman, when Guilhem Gaulbert had visited his neighbour Bernard del Mas to ask for his daughter's hand in marriage. Not for one day had she shirked her responsibility to feed and clothe her family and on the auspicious day when Hernando Gharsia had come to discuss business with her husband, she was determined, despite her struggling emotions, to produce a meal to delight their guests. She had had three days warning of the visit and had planned the meal carefully. The bread was fresh from the oven, the rabbit succulent in its juices, although she regretted being unable to add truffles as it would be a good three months before the season began. Come December, Henri would use one of the pigs to sniff out the delicacies from the rootlets in the stunted oak trees that were everywhere in the valley. She had ripe white rounds of goats' cheese, their creamy mild interior encased in a soft wrinkled skin. There were also walnuts, juicy sun-kissed cherries, and the first early plums of the year as well as the intense, rich dark wine from their grapes. Loise was ready. Filled with satisfaction, she waited for the sign from Guilhem that the business discussion was over.

◆   ◆   ◆

Hernando looked at the feast before him and as he thanked Loise he saw, for the first time, a softening of her face. They had been joined by

Luis, Henri, and Marie eager to hear what Guilhem and Hernando had discussed, but first everyone's attention was given to eating. It was well past noon, much later than the usual eating time of the summer months when the family rose so early, and the rabbit had been totally consumed before Guilhem turned to Luis.

'Your grandfather and I have agreed that you should come and live with us for a year so that you can experience life as a vintner.' He did not add that Hernando had been adamant that Luis should learn the craft of making wine and was not to be a general farm hand. To this end it was arranged that Hernando would pay Guilhem to pass on his skills as well as make a contribution to board and lodgings.

Henri smiled and punched Luis on the arm. 'Are you going to share my bed?'

Guilhem cleared his throat keeping his eyes on Hernando. 'No Henri, we plan to clear part of the attic to make a place for Luis to sleep.'

'But why?' started Henri before his father cut him short.

'It is the wish of Monsieur Gharsia.'

Indeed it was. One of the terms of the agreement was that Luis needed a space of his own. Hernando had talked to Guilhem at length about the benefits of Luis continuing his studies at the end of the working day but did not mention his desire that his grandson be able to pray five times a day away from prying eyes.

'You will snore too much,' joked Luis as he grinned at his friend, dispelling some of the awkwardness that had crept back into the room.

'It will be good to have you live with us,' piped up Marie, determined to be part of the boys' exchange. Hernando glanced down the table and appraised the girl for the first time, as he had hardly registered her presence when she had entered earlier. About the same age as Luis, she was an attractive girl with a heart-shaped face, light brown hair, and tawny eyes that reminded Hernando of a cat. He was unsettled by her lips which were curved into a secretive smile. An unwanted thought wriggled its way into his mind, that Marie was a cat taking the measure of her prey. He told himself not to be fanciful. It was too early. Luis growing into a young man had taken his grandfather by surprise. Nevertheless, it was a problem that now required much thought. He was not so naive as to expect a virtuous Muslim girl to cross Luis's path in Caors, but he had vaguely hoped that, in the fullness of time, in one of the great cities where an eminent physician might live, there would be an Islamic community which would provide a bride for Luis.

Hernando watched Luis respond to Marie closely, unaware that Ysabel was giving him a disapproving look. It was when a finger poked him in the thigh, with significant force, that he realised he must be frowning. He looked around the table where all were now concentrating on the cheese and fruit, including Ysabel beside him, and decided to do likewise. However as the meal progressed Hernando began to feel that he was right. Although Luis gave no more attention to Marie than to the others, to Hernando she appeared to be acting in an unseemly way. She kept her eyes on Luis as she bit into a ripe cherry, the juice staining her pretty mouth and then she slowly licked her lips. Such behaviour was unacceptable, anathema to all Hernando believed in. Ysabel, who understood him so well after ten years, could see that this meal, which was to help cement Luis's dream, also had the potential to destroy it.

'Marie,' she said more sharply than she meant to. 'Tell me, how are your lambs?' Marie had been hand-rearing a pair of late lambs orphaned as a result of a difficult birth. In an instant the coquettish young woman disappeared, replaced by the enthusiasm of a child given a great responsibility.

'Very well, Aunt. They are both thriving and I am confident they will survive. Perhaps we can all go and see them later, when we have finished eating?'

'Marie nursed them all by herself,' added Guilhem proudly. 'She kept watch over them at night for those first crucial days.'

'When are we going to eat them?' asked Henri baring his teeth in a lupine smile.

'Never! Papa says we can keep them for wool.'

'Father?' queried Henri.

'I did not quite say that,' protested their father and a heated discussion started about the intended fate of Marie's lambs which completely diverted her attention from Luis whilst she was under Hernando's scrutiny. Ysabel gave a gentle sigh as she settled down to watch her brother extricate himself from his daughter's assertion. In the end, procrastination won. Guilhem held up his hand and spoke in a voice that allowed no argument.

'We will wait to see whether they do survive before I make a decision.'

By late afternoon it was time for the Gaulberts' visitors to leave. The visit to the lambs was diplomatically forgotten, while Loise, pleased that her meal had been so well received, pressed a cloth containing three goats' cheeses into a surprised Ysabel's hands. It had been decided that Luis should start his year on the farm in two weeks, which would give both parties time to prepare and allow Luis to arrive well in advance of the grape harvest.

The three riders were again filled with different emotions as they rode down the track to the river, the earth baked hard beneath their horses' hooves. Luis was still elated, happiness sparkling in his eyes. Ysabel felt relief that the day had been successful but Hernando, who should have been pleased that he had achieved all he had desired in the negotiations, was troubled. In all of his meticulous planning he had completely overlooked Marie Gaulbert.

T E N

∼

As the clang of masons' hammers echoed around the cloisters, Canon Robert reminded himself that it was all for the glory of God. Now with many more years behind him than before him, even if he was blessed with three score years and ten, he felt that the curved original arches of the cloisters had been fine. They had served their purpose of keeping the colonnades cool in the summer and of sheltering the canons in the winter. Now the stone lace which ornamented the bays was more elaborate, more flamboyant in its modernity as it rose to a sharp point at the top of the arch. Robert increased his pace, eager to enter the peace of the cathedral, and in doing so almost collided with his friend Gharsia.

'Hernando! What a surprise! What brings you to the cathedral this morning?' Canon Robert was pleased but genuinely surprised to see his friend as they usually met at the university when Robert had finished teaching his theology classes. Their socialising consisted of long discussions, usually with another scholar, a lawyer, Martin Ebrart, which ranged across each of their areas of expertise.

'Good morning, Robert. I apologise for disturbing you.' Hernando lowered his voice and continued, 'I was hoping to borrow a book.'

'Come this way,' invited Robert as he led Hernando back into the cathedral.

They sat at the side of the nave near the south door, which was used less by worshippers entering the cathedral. Above them, painted in the centre of the west dome, St Etienne, the first Christian martyr, looked down as they spoke quietly, heads almost touching.

'My grandson is leaving soon for the Gaulbert vineyard and I want him to keep reading.'

'Yes, he must.' Both men revelled in the written word, which the advent of printing had made more accessible than when they were young. They had both visited the presses in Caors and marvelled at the speed in which a page could be produced. 'What would you like to borrow?'

'I was thinking of some Erasmus.'

'A good choice for the boy, I agree. I have *The Praise of Folly* and I know someone who has *Julius Exclusus*.'

'I think *The Praise of Folly* is better as an introduction to Erasmus' thinking. Thank you.'

'I will bring it to your study later today so that you have it in time.'

'Yes, I am going to the university now to see Martin.'

'Until later then.'

'Until later.'

Hernando slipped out through the south door with its trefoil arches and made his way down the Grande Rue before he turned right to reach the university housed in the old Couvent des Cordeliers. The university was flourishing. It was fifteen years since King François had given the president of the Parlement of Tolosa the task to reform the ancient institution and signs of success were obvious. Although all the faculties had grown, it was the Faculty of Law which was the most renowned; a situation Hernando was often reminded of by Martin Ebrart.

He found Martin in his study pouring over legal documents, a lock of thick brown hair fallen across a deeply furrowed brow.

'What ails you, Martin?'

'The usual,' he sighed.

Hernando grimaced and sighed in sympathy. Martin's work had been made more difficult by the rules changing French law the previous year. The king had ordered that Latin be used no longer but must be replaced by French in all legal documents. His students had always come to the university thoroughly versed in Latin but now many of them struggled with the language of northern France.

'Anyway, what can I do for you Hernando?'

'I was hoping to borrow a book for my grandson.'

'Ah, the reluctant physician.'

Hernando ignored his friend's comment. 'I wish him to continue broadening his mind.'

'While he grows grapes?'

'Yes, Martin, while he grows grapes.'

'What do you have in mind?'

'Any ideas? I am borrowing *The Praise of Folly* from Robert.'

'Machiavelli's *The Prince*.'

'Perfect.'

'Will I see you for our game of chess tomorrow?

'Yes.'

'I will have it ready for you then, Hernando.'

'Thank you.' Hernando pushed his long frame up from the chair, ready to take his leave when Martin looked at the door and dropped his voice.

'Have you heard about Pierre Teldes?'

'What about him?' Teldes was a colleague who had joined their discussions occasionally.

'He has resigned his position.'

'Why?' Hernando found he was speaking in a whisper to match Martin.

'He has gone to Geneva, to join Calvin.'

'I did not realise he was such a Protestant.'

'What do we really know about anyone?' replied Martin, looking Hernando straight in the eye.

◆   ◆   ◆

It was the night before he was due to leave for the Gaulberts' farm. Luis lay on his bed, legs stretched out and hands behind his head, watching the sky darken through the window. A beautiful autumn day had ended in a blaze of colour and now pinpricks of light were appearing as stars started to populate the indigo sky. He was as still as a statue but inside his stomach was churning. Everything was ready with his bags packed neatly. The two books his grandfather had lent him were wrapped in cloth as was his Qur'an, obtained from a North African trader who had travelled from Sète to sell his spices in Caors. Luis flexed his feet, wriggling his toes as he recalled his grandfather's caustic comment as they bade each other good night.

'Enjoy your bed, Luis.' Hernando had said. 'Tomorrow night you will be squashed up in a bed far too short for you.' One of the first things his grandfather had done, on their arrival in the city, was to commission a carpenter to make two longer bed frames; one for Hernando to use immediately and one for Luis to grow into.

Disappointed that there had been no sentiments expressed, no good wishes or indication that he was going to be missed, Luis had replied coolly, 'I will manage, Grandfather. I wish you a good night.'

As he lay alone with his thoughts, Luis reflected that he had slept in this room every night for the last ten years, the last nine of which he had been accompanied by the rhythm of Johan's breathing and occasional snorts. He turned his head to look at the empty bed against the opposite wall and felt a tinge of sadness that tomorrow he would not be with the man he considered his brother. Johan had always been a constant; whether to give comfort when he woke frightened and sweating from his recurring nightmare or to protect him against the bullies who had shouted obscenities, thrown stones, and always called him "scar face". More than one of them had received a bloody nose, courtesy of Johan, when Luis was a child. Nimble and quick, the boy from the Pyrenees was Luis's champion and, as each learned to live with their own personal loss, the strongest of bonds was formed.

'Little one, are you still awake?' whispered Johan as he crept into the chamber, his boots in his hands. Although his evenings were his own, once the meal had been eaten and cleared away, Johan always had a feeling of guilt when he stayed out late. Especially when he had been visiting the tavern or seeing Jeanne, although he usually combined the two. It had become a standing joke that Johan still called Luis "little one" despite now being a head shorter.

'I am now.'

'Good.'

'How goes it?

'Fine.'

'Are you excited?'

'Very . . . but worried also.'

'You are bound to be.'

'What if I am no good at growing grapes?'

'When have you not been able to learn something quickly?' Hernando had taught Johan to read alongside Luis and very soon the younger boy had progressed faster. 'It is just the same as learning anything.'

Luis was dubious but felt heartened by his friend's optimism. The floor boards creaked as Johan made ready for bed. A full moon had risen, bathing the room in an eerie light, making it possible to do without a candle. Luis could clearly see Johan grinning at him.

'I will expect personal supplies of wine at the first opportunity.'

'We will see.'

Johan threw his shirt at Luis with a sure aim. Caught unawares Luis removed the shirt, smelling of sweat and wine, from his face and sat up. He screwed the offending object into a tight ball and hurled it back towards Johan who caught it mid-flight.

'I see your reflexes are unaffected by the quantity of wine you have drunk this evening.'

'They are enhanced by it, little one.'

'I think it is time that you stopped calling me that.'

'When do you leave tomorrow, little one?' asked Johan ignoring him.

'After noon prayers.'

Johan tossed his shirt on the floor and slid into bed.

'Good night, little one,' he muttered as he pulled the blanket over him. 'Blissful sleep awaits me.'

Soon Luis heard the deep breathing characteristic of Johan after an evening's drinking. He turned on his side but sleep eluded him. He felt that every nerve in his body was dancing and it seemed as if morning would never come.

◆　　◆　　◆

Ysabel was in her garden enjoying the freshness of the early morning. Although she had broken her fast she was not as yet dressed for visitors, being clad in a simple blue gown and without her hood. She was watering the herbs, before the heat of the sun reached them, with the rain that had helped replenish the water butt the previous night. The storm had rumbled all evening until it built up to a crescendo of lightning, thunder, and torrential rain which had lasted half the night. Lost in thought, she did not notice Luis as he quietly entered the garden.

Conscious that the time had come when he would no longer see her every day; Luis found himself looking at Ysabel in a detached way, as if she was someone he did not know or just a casual acquaintance. As he watched her, Luis tried to imagine a time when she would not be always near at hand but he could not. He moved forward, suppressing the knot of nerves in his stomach and, as he did so, she turned and her face lit up when she saw him.

'Good morning, Luis. I did not expect you so early.'

'I could not sleep. I am all ready to go. Grandfather has gone to the university.' There was a hint of petulance in Luis's voice which Ysabel recognised.

'It is hard for your grandfather to let you go. You know that, Luis.'

'Do I? He has not bothered to wish me well. If it was not for noon prayers I doubt he would return home.'

Ysabel felt the customary surge of frustration when faced with the Gharsias apparent inability to understand each other and she knew that she did not want Luis's last morning spoilt by recriminations.

'Your grandfather has shown how much he has your interests at heart in many ways. What about the books he has borrowed for you?'

Luis just looked at her by way of reply and kicked the soil around the comfrey at his feet. Ysabel looked up at him, an action which still surprised her although he had been taller than her for some time. She continued patiently.

'Luis, do not dwell on what your grandfather has not done but on what he has done. He has negotiated with my brother for you to learn viticulture and that you are allowed to return home regularly so you can follow your traditions. Over all the years that I have known you, you have been nurtured and educated by him.' Ysabel raised her voice slightly. 'And finally he has bought you a horse so that you have your independence. How many farm boys ride such an animal? Most have to make do with their own legs or a mule!'

She rose on to her toes and placed her hands on either side of Luis's head, bringing it down so that their foreheads were almost touching. Their eyes locked and she waited for a glimmer of a smile to reach his mouth. Then she gently tilted his head forward, dropped a kiss on the thick black hair as she had since he was a child, and let him go.

'Your grandfather does wish you well, Luis. As do I. We are both very proud of you,' she said emphatically and was rewarded by a wide smile which softened the angular planes of his face and extinguished the traces of sullenness.

'You have a point.'

'Yes,' she said. 'I have a point.' There was a pause. 'Come, let us go indoors and have a drink. You can talk to Ramon while I dress. Then we will stroll in the direction of the medical faculty and meet your grandfather.'

◆   ◆   ◆

It was time to go at last. He gave Ysabel a quick hug, nodded to Hernando, and swung easily into the saddle. As they watched Luis turn out of the Place St Urcisse, Ysabel squeezed Hernando's hand.

'Do not worry. He will be fine,' she said before she added casually, 'You remembered to wish him well?'

Hernando looked at her puzzled.

'I told him he must be a true servant of Allah. He had to continue his studies and do nothing that would bring shame to the name of Gharsia.' He thought for a moment and then added, 'Why should I wish him well? He will do well; he is my grandson. It is what I expect.'

As exasperation and affection warred within her, Ysabel remained silent listening to the fading sound of Solomon's hooves as Luis rode towards his new life. She pushed away a lowness of spirits which threatened to engulf her and smiled too brightly. She wished Hernando a good afternoon and left for the peace of her own home leaving him standing motionless, alone with his thoughts.

Once Luis had left the confines of the city, he started to relax; now that he was actually on the way rather than just thinking about it, the butterflies in his stomach settled, and he concentrated on seeing how well Solomon reacted to his instructions. In no way such a fine horse as Monsieur Bernade's gelding, he was nevertheless a very respectable mount for a fifteen year old boy. Luis rode as fast as he dared along the river track, aware as he was of the usual traffic of people on foot and carts. The River Olt, busy with barges, flowed green and murky on his right whilst to his left the fertile valley populated by vines rose to the horizon. When he reached the port of Douelle, he headed south to the Gaulberts' farm and, as the traffic thinned, broke into a canter.

Loise heard the sound of voices raised in welcome as she walked slowly from the orchard back to the house. When she rounded the corner into the yard she was met by a scene which immediately made her feel excluded. Guilhem, Henri, and Marie were crowded around Luis Gharsia, inspecting a horse whose glossy coat shone in the evening sun. The youth was stroking the horse's nose, talking to the animal while the others looked on. When she flapped her hand at the chickens pecking under her feet, Loise attracted his attention. He stopped stroking the horse and gave a small formal bow, watching her warily.

'Good evening, Madame Gaulbert.'

Instead of the greeting which had been on her lips, she found herself scolding them all. 'Hurry up! You do not have time to stand around. You boys, stable that horse. Henri, show Luis where he is to sleep. Marie, come with me. I need your help. Guilhem, will you be ready to eat soon?'

After a simple supper of bread, cheese, and fruit, the male Gaulberts and Luis sat outside, at the top of the stone steps, and watched the last rays of light leach from the sky. Guilhem patted Luis on the back.

'Well, young man, we have an early start tomorrow so it is time to turn in.'

Inside Loise had banked up the fire for the night and as the three entered she addressed Luis directly for the first time.

'You will need some light to see you to bed. Come take this.' She handed Luis a walnut speared on the end of a thin piece of iron. 'We do not have expensive candles to waste,' she said pointedly. 'If you light the nut in the fire it will burn for enough time for you to get into bed.'

Luis was completely nonplussed but his face gave nothing away. He noticed that there were walnut 'lamps' waiting on the hearth for all the family to use and replied with formal politeness.

'Thank you, Madame Gaulbert. I wish you all goodnight.' He bent down, placing the walnut gently in the embers of the fire where it immediately burst into flame, and then made his way up the steep ladder to the corner of the attic where Guilhem had built a rough bed and chest. He jammed the iron handle into the crack by the hinge in the chest while he undressed. The flame died as he said his prayers and he was thankful that he had had the forethought to open the shutter at the far end of the attic where a small aperture allowed air to circulate. As his eyes became used to the darkness he could see the moon emerging from behind scudding clouds and, in the distance, heard the screech of an owl ready to hunt from the trees on the perimeter of the south meadow. He lay on top of the blanket as the evening was warm and stretched his legs; he smiled as he did so because he realised his grandfather had been correct. His feet hung over the end of the bed but it did not matter. He was content.

E L E V E N

∾

The following morning Luis was up well before dawn. Determined not to inconvenience Loise and give her any reason to find him wanting, he crept down from his attic before the family had stirred. He made his way silently to the well, the pewter bowl given to him by Hernando in his hand. The sky was lightening in the east and the sharpness of the air promised a fine day. As he drew the bucket up from the depths, Luis glanced around; all was still. Birdsong chorused a welcome to the dawn, rudely interrupted by the harsh crow of Loise's arrogant cockerel. Perched on the well wall he carefully filled his bowl and then returned stealthily to his room, making no sound as he passed the sleeping Gaulberts.

Back in the privacy of his attic, Luis washed and said the first prayers of the day. It was too dark to read the Qur'an so he decided to postpone his reading until later. There had been no sign of Loise when he had returned from the well, she had not yet risen to stoke the fire into life, which meant he had some time before he would be expected to break his fast with the family. Once again he climbed down the ladder, padded along the passage and out of the building. He started to run, slowly at first and then faster and faster until his breath came in short, sharp bursts.

He ran away from the house and orchard, across the meadow, and into the vines taking the track that led up the hill to his destination: the summit. When he reached the top he leaned forward, his hands on his thighs to catch his breath, before standing upright and flinging out his arms to salute the day. Below him Luis could see the river winding its way through the valley on its journey to the ocean and the vines, heavy with fruit, rising from the wispy mist that still hung between the rows and hovered above the water. In the half-light the countryside appeared monochrome. He inhaled deeply, filling his lungs completely before he exhaled slowly and turned back to the farmhouse at a run.

Climbing the stone staircase to the main room he heard snippets of conversation through the open door. Loise's voice was raised aggressively.

'Why will he not eat ham for breakfast?'

'I told you before, wife. He is like a Jew. They do not eat pork.' Guilhem's voice was irritable.

'It makes more work for me if he does not eat what we eat.'

'Put some eggs in the fire. His grandfather is paying handsomely for us to have him.'

Luis stopped on the penultimate step and pressed close against the wall of the house.

'I cannot see the point of his learning to be a vintner. There is no land around here for him.'

'Perhaps he will go back home.'

'Home?'

'Yes, home to Valencia. Ysabel said that is where they came from when I asked her.'

'Good riddance is what I would say.'

Guilhem did not answer so Luis took the opportunity to make his entrance by descending five steps silently before climbing back up with a clatter. As he crossed the threshold the Gaulberts turned as one; Guilhem was the first to recover.

'Good morning, Luis.'

'Good morning Monsieur Gaulbert, Madame Gaulbert.'

'Sit down,' invited the farmer affably. 'My wife is about to cook eggs.' Loise shot Luis a look of pure venom before placing two eggs in the embers.

'Thank you,' was all Luis could think to say. He sat in silence waiting for his breakfast to cook while the tension crackled around him. It was with some relief that he saw Henri enter the room and take the place opposite him. Then when Marie slid next to him on the bench and, leaning close, inquired how he had slept, Luis felt the wave of homesickness that was threatening to engulf him recede a little.

◆   ◆   ◆

After breakfast Guilhem took Luis on a tour of the vineyard and despite the latter having some knowledge of the intricacies of viticulture, his teacher was of a mind to instruct him as if he was a complete novice. Henri accompanied them, eager to add his expertise whilst a sulky Marie was forced to remain and help her mother.

'Vines are hardy plants,' explained Guilhem as they wandered through the orchard towards the slopes. 'The only time of year when frost might damage them is spring when the buds are opening. Then we must light braziers to warm the air. The roots of the vine grow deep, deep into the earth to find moisture so they can survive dry spells. The grape, l'Auxerrois, thrives on our stony, limestone soil producing the strong dark wine so envied by the producers in the west.'

They reached the vines. Guilhem bent down and picked up a handful of earth.

'Here, feel the consistency.' Luis crouched next to him, scooping up his own handful as he did so. He pushed away the larger white stones and watched the dry crumbly earth slip through his open fingers. When he looked up Henri was cradling a bunch of grapes in his hand. It was the time for the grapes to ripen and their black skins glistened in the morning sun.

'Look Luis,' he said, 'they will be ready to harvest soon. We must hope for more dry weather as the rain will swell the fruit too much now and will reduce the flavour of the juice.'

All three stood up. For some time they surveyed the rows of vines, their leaves tinged with the colours of autumn, before Guilhem turned to Luis.

'Can you tell me in which direction you should plant vines?'

Luis thought for a moment and noting the position of the sun, he replied, 'The rows must run north and south.'

'Why?'

'So that each side of the plant receives an equal amount of sunshine?'

'Well done,' remarked Henri, clapping Luis on the back.

His father smiled broadly at them both.

'Come let us check the wine.'

◆   ◆   ◆

They were in the cellar and had been there for some time partaking in what Guilhem believed to be the most significant part of his life as a vintner: tasting the wine. At his father's instigation, Henri had shown Luis how to draw wine from the barrel before taking a good mouthful of the inky liquid. Luis tasted a young wine from the previous harvest and then a more mature one which had been ageing for three years. Guilhem watched him carefully as he rolled the wine around his mouth before spitting it out on the cellar floor, unlike his companions, who drank theirs.

'Can you tell the difference, Luis?'

Luis was not sure how the vintner would describe the two wines but he could tell that the younger one had a more pungent bitterness.

'Yes, I can detect a difference. The younger one is harsher.'

'Excellent,' replied his teacher, 'our wine is very tannic when young and it improves with age when stored in oak.' He waved his arm towards the rows of barrels which lined the walls. Luis had been in the barn several times over the years and already knew in a general way how wine was made. As a small child, hand safely in Ysabel's, he had listened to many a conversation about the year's harvest and subsequent wine production. Now he could see some barrels empty and ready for the new harvest's yield. He breathed deeply, filling his lungs with the smell of wine-soaked oak mingled with the dampness of the beaten earth floor. For a moment he could see himself as an older child, too old for holding hands but still silent next to Ysabel as she discussed the benefit of stomping the grapes. He had understood that once the grapes had been crushed the skins and seeds, the caps, were collected as they were the best source of the tannins. Each day the caps were then mixed with the juice to help produce the unique taste of the Caors wine. He turned to Guilhem and Henri.

'I see the tannin development is important. It becomes more rounded as the wine ages.'

'Come, try this one,' invited Henri as he drew wine from another barrel. 'Perhaps you will drink this one?' Already a little merry, Henri raised his eyebrows as he looked at his friend questioningly. Luis, faithful to his promise to Hernando that he would never become intoxicated, looked straight back with a cool level gaze and did not reply. As he kept his eyes on Henri, he lifted the goblet slowly to his lips and, after savouring the wine, spat it out on the earth at his feet. The young Gaulbert was the first to avert his eyes. He refilled his own goblet and drank the contents in three noisy gulps before he wiped his mouth with the back of his hand and asked belligerently, 'How did you like your sip?'

'Very much, I would say it has aged for many years.'

Guilhem, aware that the morning had lost some of its good humour, hurried the boys through to the adjoining room that held the huge vats and the press, all scrubbed and ready for use. In the dark recess of the far corner Luis could see what appeared to be an ancient huge cauldron.

'What is that for?'

Guilhem followed his gaze.

'Many years ago, before my great-grandfather's time, the vintners used to make the wine more concentrated by heating some of the grapes. It was believed that it allowed the tannins to be more intense.'

'Could we try it again?'

Guilhem shrugged, 'Perhaps, but now we are controlled by those officials from the Gironde there is no point.'

'Why is it so?'

'The traders from Bordèu were too unscrupulous for us. The wine from the Gironde marshes is weak, light wine.' The vintner stopped to spit vehemently. 'They persuaded the English who ruled Quercy then to protect the wines of the Gironde and to overtax us,' he continued, stopping again to spit at the mention of the English. 'The officials at Bordèu carried out the mandate of King Edward. Our wines could not enter the port before Christmas and must have left before May, which put us at a disadvantage.

The merchants there use our wine to improve their weak wine rather than sell our Caors for its own sake.'

Luis knew of the hatred the Gaulberts and all the wine producers of the Olt valley had for the traders of the Gironde but he had been uncertain of the detail. Now it started to make sense.

'Why is Caors wine so superior?'

Henri answered him, pleased to impart knowledge. 'The weak wine from the Gironde does not export well. It becomes oxidised and sour in the barrels making it only drinkable if water is added. Wine from Caors keeps its freshness, due to its unique qualities, even on the worst of sea voyages. Once the black wine of Caors was the most sought after, but then those bastards from Bordèu saw that they could use it to make their inferior wine good.'

'What can we do?' Guilhem threw up his arms in a gesture of despair. 'They control the port. We have the river to transport our wine but without access to the sea we have no control.'

'There must be something that can be done,' stated Luis as he looked at his companions. 'What about our king now? Did you not tell me some time ago that François had planted a Caors vine at his new palace?'

'Yes,' replied Guilhem, with surprise that Luis had remembered. 'It was after you had arrived here that we learnt that our seneschal, Galliot de Genouillac, had given the king some of our wine and it was so good that he asked for a vine.'

'Surely then,' argued Luis, 'he could revoke the edict?'

Henri picked up the other boy's determination.

'There must be some way to export our wine directly, Father.'

Guilhem studied the youths before him; his own son, small, wiry, and a little drunk, and the tall boy, coldly sober, whose enthusiasm shone out of clear dark eyes. A wave of affection swept over the older man along with the excitement of possibilities, something which had eluded him for most of his working life. The unfamiliar bubble stayed with Guilhem as they returned to the house to eat. He put an arm around his son's shoulders and placed a hand on one of Luis's much higher shoulders as they walked across the yard.

'A good morning's introduction to winemaking, I think. Tomorrow will be an experience for you as we continue your education, Luis.'

'Why, Monsieur Gaulbert?'

Henri chipped in, 'We are going to Luzech. It is the final day of the pilgrimage of the river boatmen.'

◆   ◆   ◆

Marie Gaulbert hopped impatiently from foot to foot as she waited for the rest of her family to join her. The grey, damp dawn with mist so dense it blocked the sun and gave a strange luminosity to the morning had not suppressed her elation at the thought of a day away from the farm. As soon as she had completed her chores with unusual speed, Marie had shut herself in the bedchamber to prepare for the coming excursion. She had taken her new dress from the chest, one she had fashioned from an old gown of Ysabel's and the result of many hours of labour, and then removed the kirtle, which had also come from her aunt. Marie had felt the fine quality of the garments between her fingers before slipping them over her worn linen chemise. The gown was a deep red, fitting her tightly at the waist before opening to reveal the lighter red kirtle beneath. She had pivoted with joy until she had become dizzy and collapsed on the bed ready to brush her hair until it shone. Now as she stood in the yard waiting she watched her feet in the soft leather shoes and smelt the lavender perfume she had dabbed on her neck and wrists.

'Come on,' she shouted as she stopped hopping and folded her arms in a gesture of annoyance at the sight of her parents and brother, also in their best clothes, descending the stone steps. 'We do not want to miss anything. Where is Luis?'

'Do not worry little sister. He will be here before long.' No sooner had Henri uttered the words than Luis appeared at the top of the steps dressed, to Marie's dismay, in his work clothes. She looked at the rough, simple garment that he wore over his hose.

'Why are you dressed like that?' the girl asked crossly.

Luis, who had not realised that the last day of the pilgrimage was an occasion that required some attention to one's attire, did what he always did when faced with displeasure. He remained silent.

'You look like a servant,' hissed Marie as she marched out of the yard.

Luis shrugged apologetically, loped down the steps two at a time, and followed the Gaulberts.

They took the track that wound around the hillside until they were above Luzech. From their vantage point the meander of the river was impressive and the settlement could be clearly seen on what was almost an island. Luis could pick out the old keep, a relic from the days of English rule, and also their destination, the church of Notre Dame de l'Île. Before the festivities could start there was to be a blessing for the coming year.

Once the service was over, Guilhem and Loise joined a group of their neighbours at the trestles set up on one side of the church square. The sun had broken through the thick cloud promising a warm September afternoon; the air was full of the aroma of roasting sheep and the sound of noisy barter as the stallholders shouted their wares. Henri and Luis were keen to look at the barges, the gabares, and started towards the river but Marie took Luis's arm and pulled him back to the market.

'Luis, please come with me. I want to look at the stalls.' She flashed him one of her most engaging smiles, confident that he would do as she asked. The admiring glances of some of the local boys had not escaped her notice. Grumbling but secretly pleased, Luis agreed, much to the annoyance of a reluctant Henri, who went with them.

'We will not spend long looking at trinkets, Marie. We want to see the gabares.'

The crowd was a mixture of local farmers, their families, and those who worked on the river. Luis found it easy to pick out the boatmen with their massive rounded shoulders and forearms developed from years of hauling the laden barges along the towpath when it was too narrow for the horses to do the work.

'How many barrels do the gabares carry, Henri?'

'I'm not sure, but they are always full.'

'No wonder the men are strong.'

'And brave,' Henri pointed out. 'The conditions are very dangerous with gravel banks and whirlpools. Many boatmen perish. At times of flood the high water makes it difficult to haul, and when the water is so low it is almost a trickle, it is just as bad.'

'Look at these, Luis,' interrupted Marie, unhappy that her companion's interest was focused on the sailors. They were alongside a stall selling ribbons, embroidered girdles, and hoods. The tinker was quick to see a sale.

'Come young sir, something pretty for the pretty lady?' He smiled revealing a mouth full of rotten teeth as he held up a length of red ribbon to match Marie's dress.

Marie looked up at Luis, her tawny eyes bright with expectation, and, before he knew it, Luis was reaching for his money pouch.

'You are easily parted from your money,' scoffed Henri as Marie tied the ribbon around her head.

They did a circuit of all the stalls, stopping at some to look at the wares and passing others by. Marie walked between her two escorts enjoying the attention they received while Henri watched his sister with amusement as she flaunted herself in the red gown. He had noticed something she had not: what attracted the stares of both neighbours and strangers alike was not Marie Gaulbert in her bright new dress but the tall dark boy beside her. The presence of someone with strong Arabic features, an everyday sight in the ports of the south, was very much out of the ordinary for the farmers and river-workers of the Olt. It was not so much the colour of his skin or his disfigurement which caused people to notice him, for the men he was amongst were deeply tanned to the colour of old leather and regarded injury as an occupational hazard. What made Luis so different was his height and carriage, the latter the result of years of his grandfather telling him to hold his head up high, keep his shoulders back, and remember who he was.

As noon approached they bought warm bread from the baker on the far side of the square and small rounds of goats' cheese from the farmer's wife who had strategically positioned herself on a stool next to the baker's. She was doing a good trade and, by the time Henri paid her, there were fewer than a dozen rounds left at the bottom of the basket. They passed one of the spits where a sheep was being slowly rotated; fat spat and sizzled as it dripped into the fire.

'I think it is your turn, Marie, to buy something.' Henri pointed out. His sister smiled, looked from Henri to Luis, who had no intention of eating the mutton, and then reluctantly opened her purse. She had intended to keep all the coins her father had given her to buy herself a treat, but the aroma of the succulent meat was too much to resist. She watched the butcher cut off two thick slices before she realised the difficulty of eating hers without grease marking her gown. Henri moved quickly as he saw his sister's dilemma. He speared both pieces of mutton with his knife and proceeded to tear off chunks as they walked towards the river.

'Well done, Marie. This is delicious,' he said as he popped the last gobbet of meat into his mouth with a theatrical flourish.

As they lay on the river bank enjoying the warmth of the sun strains of music drifted from the square.

'Dancing,' shouted Marie as she leapt to her feet. 'The dancing is starting. We must go back to the square.'

'I am not dancing. You know I find it disagreeable. Neither is Luis as he does not know how.' Henri nodded to his friend. 'But we will come with you.'

Luis was well aware of what Henri intended to do.

'You two go ahead. I want to look at the stall with the barrel taps.' Both Gaulberts made a face but it was Marie who spoke.

'Luis, you are allowed a day off you know.'

'I know, but I want to talk to the tap-maker,' answered Luis as he stopped at a stall covered with the wooden taps used to drain the wine from the barrels. The tap-maker had made the journey from Saint-Cirq-Lapopie, the village perched high above the Olt which was renowned for its woodworkers. The craftsman was eager to talk as trade had not been brisk.

'Good afternoon, young man.'

'Good afternoon.' Luis leaned over, took a wooden tap in his hand, and turned it over. He had seen many in position but had not been able to see exactly how they were constructed.

'Are you a vintner?'

'An apprentice.'

'Do you need some taps?'

'No, I am just interested in everything to do with making wine.'

'Ah ha! What do you think of our barrels?'

'What do you mean?'

The tap-maker smiled, 'The quality of them.'

'I would not know. I have seen no other barrels to compare them with,' admitted Luis.

'A very new apprentice then?'

'Yes.'

The man settled himself comfortably on his stool.

'Do you know that Caors barrels are different to those from Bordèu?'

'No.'

'They are,' continued the tap-maker. 'Ours are smaller.'

'Why?'

'It makes them easier to transport down river.'

'That is a good thing.'

'Yes, but it puts us at a disadvantage.'

'Why?'

'The tax at the port is a set quantity of wine from each barrel, not a proportion of the contents of the barrel.'

Luis considered this information. 'That does not seem fair as the producers of Caors are being taxed with a higher proportion of their product.'

'Exactly,' agreed the tap-maker, 'now you know a bit more, apprentice vintner.' Luis placed the tap down thoughtfully and was just about to speak when his companion continued. 'Your young lady wants you.'

Across the square, Marie was waving at him, surrounded by a bevy of girls about her own age. He thanked the tap-maker and wove his way through the market.

'Luis, please dance with me.'

Luis looked at the dancers and could feel his palms becoming sweaty.

'I cannot dance.'

'Yes you can. It is easy.'

Torn between pleasing Marie and making a fool of himself, Luis paused for longer than the girl was willing to wait. Before he gave his answer she had turned away from him and accepted the invitation of a young man who had greeted her with the familiarity of a neighbour. He threw his rival a triumphant glance as he led Marie into the dance.

Luis stood for some time at the edge of the square and watched Marie dance, her light brown hair in its red ribbon catching the sun as she twirled. He could see her parents still sitting at the trestles, Guilhem gesticulating animatedly with a companion and Loise talking to a stout matron whose stomach strained against the lacing of her gown. Henri was at another trestle drinking heavily with some youths, one of whom had just called for another jug of wine. Luis felt what he was, an outsider, but, as he stood alone in the shade of the church wall, a revelation came to him: he did not mind. He did not want to dance, he did not want to drink, but he did want to learn from these people. As he moved to cross the square to make his way up the hill back to the farm, Luis caught the eye of the tap-maker who nodded and raised his arm in acknowledgement. Luis waved back.

T W E L V E

~

Luis quickly left the village behind him, breaking into a run as soon as he passed the last cluster of buildings. If he had questioned why he ran everywhere he would not have been able to give an answer for the reason was hidden deep within him. He might have acknowledged that he enjoyed the physical exertion of his long legs covering distances at speed or the sensation of freedom it gave him, but he would never have articulated that the experience of fast movement in the open air was the antithesis of his experience of lying, trapped and bloodied, buried beneath his mother while her life ebbed away.

He slowed as he reached the hamlet of St Vincent Rive d'Olt which was deserted in the sleepy September heat. The old men who usually gathered on the bench near the well were nowhere to be seen and the builders who were working on the refurbishment of the church had laid down their tools for the day. Everyone was in Luzech for the festivities and a thin brown dog had the place to itself as it trotted down the centre of the road sending up small clouds of dust. Luis stopped outside the church, dedicated to St Vincent, the patron saint of vines, and looked at the new doorway which had just been completed. It was a testament to the skill of the masons and a source of pride to those who worshipped in the church. The two columns which framed the doorway were unusual in that they were circular at the base and square at the top. He walked between them into the still gloom of the interior, continued up the nave with its new mouldings on the vaulted ceiling, noted the two chapels on either side, and stopped as he approached the chancel. The silence told Luis that he was completely alone but he still glanced over his shoulders before he knelt and prayed to his God.

As he lifted his head and sat back on his heels, Luis contemplated the statue of the Virgin Mary. He recalled an argument between Ysabel and his grandfather, which he had never forgotten. It had happened the Christmas he was seven. Ysabel had taken him to the cathedral in Caors to see the nativity crib, and together they had looked at the tiny wooden baby watched over by his mother. He had been fascinated by the carvings, both the figures and the animals, and had asked Ysabel about each of them, and his companion, very much aware of other people listening, had answered clearly and simply.

Back at the house on the corner of the Place St Urcisse, Luis had been eager to tell Hernando about his visit.

'Grandfather, I have seen baby Jesus in his manger.'

His grandfather had closed the book he was reading and had looked enquiringly from boy to woman and back again.

'Indeed,' he had said gently.

'Ysabel says the baby Jesus is our saviour. He is the Son of God.'

Hernando had stiffened.

'Luis, please go to your chamber.'

'But I want to stay with Ysabel.'

'Luis, leave us now!'

He had recognised the harshness of his grandfather's tone, which always signalled the need for immediate obedience. However, once outside the room he had positioned himself where he could hear what was being said, and the anger in his grandfather's voice.

'You must not fill his head with Christian doctrine, Ysabel. I have told you that before.'

Ysabel had not been inclined to take such criticism.

'What was I to do? There were many people around us, listening to my answer.'

Hernando had not been placated.

'Why did you take him there in the first place?'

'Oh my dear Hernando! Do not be so obtuse. What child is not taken to see the nativity crib at Christmas? How would it look if Luis had mentioned to someone that his grandfather forbade him to see the crib?'

'I did not forbid him. The visit is not the problem. It is what you told him!'

'You are being unreasonable and contradicting yourself. I answered Luis's questions in a way that would avoid suspicion.' Ysabel's voice was raised in indignation.

The argument had continued long after Luis crept away to his bed and had ended unresolved when Ysabel had stormed out, banging the heavy oak door so hard that the knocker clanged several times before it came to rest. Hernando had sought him out and had stroked the shock of black hair that had poked above the coverlet with uncharacteristic tenderness.

'I am sorry you heard us argue, Luis, but you know that while you and I believe Jesus was a great prophet, he was not the Son of God.'

The softness of his grandfather's voice had made him brave.

'Why do we not believe the same as Ysabel?'

'She is a Christian and we are followers of Islam.'

'I am confused, Grandfather. Do we not go to worship with Ysabel?'

'Yes, little one, but that is so we do not attract attention.'

He had sat up in bed then and, with dark eyes wide with alarm, had asked, 'Are we in danger?'

'No.' Hernando had patted his hand. 'As long as we appear as Christians we are safe from the authorities. They are not as intolerant as those back home and, as long as we are true worshippers of Allah, we will not be in danger of betraying our true beliefs.'

Luis shook the vivid memory from his mind as he stood up slowly, stiff from being on his knees for so long. As he had grown older he had understood the difficult position he was in and knew that whatever Ysabel said or did, it was always to keep him safe. He grew more circumspect with age and many of those who met him mistook this for aloofness. He pondered on the fact that Ysabel had been correct. They could never relax. Now, as his sixteenth birthday approached, the laws against heresy were being enforced to fight the growth of Protestantism. The Gharsias had to appear to be loyal members of the Church as the authorities were more vigilant than ever in their quest to root out unorthodoxy.

As he retraced his steps out of the building, Luis continued to think about religion and decided that, as soon as he reached the farm, he would read the next chapter of Canon Robert's copy of *The Praise of Folly*. He had enjoyed what he had read so far and had learnt much. Erasmus had poked fun at the laxity of some members of the Church, and the worldliness of her rulers, and had advocated a return to more simple forms of worship based on the Scriptures. From what Luis could understand from his discussions with his grandfather, the reformers who were criticising the Catholic Church, like Luther in Saxony and Calvin in Geneva, had much in common with Erasmus, yet the scholar had denounced any attempt to threaten the unity of the Christian Church. Luis increased his pace, happy with the prospect of taking the book, safely carried in his satchel for protection, into the orchard, where he would pass the afternoon reading in the shade of the old walnut tree.

◆   ◆   ◆

It was the first day of the harvest. The grapes were ripe, row upon row of black clusters nestled amongst leaves already tinged with the yellow, ochre, and red of autumn. The sky was pure azure with wispy fair weather clouds high above them. Luis felt he had never been happier. Guilhem was content that he had made the correct decision to start the harvest while Loise and Marie, whose backs had not yet started to ache, were buoyed up by the significance of the day. Only Henri felt a tinge of discontent. He could not shake himself free of the fledgling stabs of jealousy that pricked when he saw his father and Luis deep in conversation about viticulture. He straightened up from his cutting and shouted across to the next row.

'Luis, you need to work much faster than that if we are to finish the harvest this year!'

Luis looked up from his task, taking the opportunity to stretch. At his side the basket was half full. He grinned.

'Not too bad, I think. Remember the tortoise and the hare?'

Henri's face was blank, expressionless for a moment, though it was swiftly clouded by irritation.

'What do you mean?'

'The fable of the tortoise and the hare?'

'What is that?'

Luis was about to explain Aesop's story but decided against it as Henri continued belligerently, 'Why do you have to be so different? Why do you always say things that have no sense?'

'Never mind,' he replied, 'we had better get back to work.' The row he was picking seemed endless as it climbed up the slope, and he could see Monsieur Gaulbert organising the gang of labourers who came each year to help with the harvest. Henri left Luis then and joined his father where he made a great show of monitoring the hired help.

At noon everyone stopped for a short rest and ate where they sat among the vines. The clouds had dispersed and the early October sun bathed them in warmth.

'Luis!' Guilhem called as he walked towards him. 'Come with me and we will start the crushing. It is important that this is done the same day that the grapes are picked.' Luis hastily swallowed the chunk of bread he was eating, hoisted his basket on his back, and followed the older man to the cart where Gaulbert's donkey waited patiently between the shafts.

'Henri will stay here and keep an eye on the pickers.'

From where he stood Luis could see that the younger Gaulbert was doing very little harvesting but much directing, whilst his mother and sister were already working methodically along the rows after their break. Marie had hitched up her skirt and her exposed, shapely legs were streaked with earth. She gave Luis a friendly wave before returning to her cutting.

The four workers Gaulbert had selected to help followed the cart as the donkey plodded her way back to the farm. Once there, they unloaded the baskets into a huge vat and one of the men led the animal back to the vines. Luis knew what to do. He removed his shirt, trousers, and clogs before Guilhem could tell him to, and then all five of them climbed into the vat and started to crush the grapes. The resistance of the skins as the juice was forced out of them was greater than Luis expected, so at first he trod cautiously. The stalks and pips were sharp, in contrast to the flesh which oozed through his toes. However, as his companions started to sing and an air of camaraderie filled the cellar, he became less inhibited and threw himself into the experience.

'We will use the press as well,' explained Guilhem when there was a break in the singing. 'Crushing produces the higher quality juice. We will mix it with the juice we get from the press. This increases production.'

Once the grapes had been crushed to the vintner's approval, the men set about removing the layer of skins, pips, and stalks ready to mix some back into the juice the following day.

'This will ferment for about ten days before we mix it with the pressed juice. Then we will start the second fermentation process to decrease the acid.' Gaulbert warmed to his role of teacher addressing all the men, not just Luis. 'Then what happens?'

All attention was on the pupil, but Luis could easily recall the vintner's earlier lessons.

'The wine is aged in oak barrels.'

'See,' remarked Guilhem as he looked at his audience and clapped Luis on the back. 'I have the making of a great vintner here.'

'Are we going to heat any of the grapes in the cauldron?' Luis ventured.

'Not this year, Luis. We do not have enough time to get it ready.'

Gaulbert laughed when he saw the disappointment on the boy's face.

'Learn to walk before you run,' he said with affection.

Many hours later, Luis lay on his bed in the attic, his hands behind his head and his ruby stained feet hanging over the end, as he thought about the day. It had been a good one. The weather conditions had been perfect, he felt he had made progress in his quest to be a vintner, and, above all, Marie had been very attentive. At supper when he had politely but firmly rejected Loise's offering of dried cured pork, her daughter had risen from the table to go to the larder. She had returned with a slab of cold mutton and met her mother's eyes defiantly before flashing Luis a sympathetic look under lowered lashes.

◆   ◆   ◆

'Luis? Luis, are you there?' Marie's voice came from the open stable door where the early morning sun could be seen struggling through the clouds.

'Yes,' he called out from the dim interior, busy with Solomon's halter. 'I have not yet departed.'

Boy and horse turned their heads simultaneously as she made her entrance, clogs clattering on the beaten earth floor despite the muffling effect of the straw. Marie gave them both a dazzling smile.

'I have brought you some provisions for your journey.'

'Thank you, Marie,' replied Luis, pleased.

Marie waited for him to say more but, when he was not forthcoming, she continued quickly.

'I know it is only a short journey to Caors and you should be there by midday, but you might want something to eat.' She handed him some fresh bread and cheese wrapped in a cloth.

'Thank you.'

'It will be pleasant for you to be home for a few days.'

'Yes.'

'Will you see my aunt?'

'Yes.'

'Please remember me to her.'

Marie was reluctant to leave and felt that the conversation was not progressing as she hoped. She moved closer to them and started stroking Solomon's flank.

'He is a fine horse.'

'Yes.'

'You are most fortunate to own him.'

Luis nodded.

'When will you be back?'

'Within the week.'

'It is a strange time to go, so near to All Saints.'

Luis did not reply for some time. Instead he fiddled with the adjustment of the saddle. His heart wanted to tell Marie that he was going home to celebrate Eid-al-Adha with his grandfather and that tomorrow was the tenth day of the last Islamic month, Dhu-al-Hijjah. They would commemorate

Ibrahim's act of obedience to Allah when he offered his son Ismail for sacrifice. He kept checking the saddle as the urge rose in him to tell her, but his head warned him to keep quiet.

'Now the harvest is in your father can spare me. He has Henri.'

Marie waited. She had hoped for a declaration that he would miss her, that she was important to him, and that he valued the friendship she had shown him since he had come to live with them. She watched him as he checked the saddle girth with what appeared to be great concentration and felt a wave of disappointment.

'Are you not pleased with the food?'

'Of course, I am.'

'The bread is fresh.'

Luis smiled then, 'I can tell. It is still warm.' He watched her as she leaned against Solomon, a sulky expression on her pretty face. 'I must leave now, but I look forward to eating my bread and cheese.'

She should have been content with such a reply but Marie Gaulbert was not.

'Will you miss me?'

'Yes.'

With a swiftness that took Luis by surprise, she moved towards him and, as he raised his head, planted a quick kiss on his cheek before running from the stable.

Back in Caors, it was a merry group gathered around the table in the dining room of the house on the corner of the Place St Urcisse. It was the time in the festival when family and friends celebrated together. The mutton was excellent. Hernando had selected a small beast of the finest quality and had made the sacrifice, praising Allah as he did so. Johan had expertly butchered the animal; one third of the sheep had been given to Canon Robert at the cathedral to distribute to the poor, a third had been given to Hernando's colleagues at the university, and the rest they kept.

Hernando sat at the head of the table, replete after such a magnificent meal. He watched Luis talking animatedly to Ysabel and Johan, who both listened intently. He could not recall his grandson ever having had so much to say. Luis had changed in the two months since he had left home and it was not just his tanned face and calloused hands, but his whole demeanour, which spoke of a confidence Hernando had not witnessed before.

The conversation was about grapes, harvesting, vats and barrels, and the qualities of the inky black wine so central to the Olt valley. Ysabel was obviously enjoying herself, happy to see Luis so full of life. In honour of the occasion, she wore her new russet silk dress, and her cheeks were flushed by the heat of the fire burning brightly in the hearth. Johan, also dressed in his best shirt and hose, rose to light the candles as the afternoon light faded and still Luis spoke of his new life. Hernando realised his mind had wandered when his grandson addressed him directly.

'Grandfather, I will need to take extra covers for my bed. The attic is very cold now.'

Johan was quick to answer.

'There are the sheepskins you used in the mountains.'

'Yes,' reflected Hernando, 'you can take those. They have been in the chest for years.'

He paused trying to keep his voice neutral.

'Do you think you will enjoy working on the vines so much in the winter?'

Luis, his face very tanned against his new white shirt, looked at his grandfather. Hernando could see the faint shadow of a beard that told him his grandson would soon be a man.

'Yes, I am to learn pruning and how to take cuttings. Some of Monsieur Gaulbert's vines are coming to the end of their lives and need replacing, so I will be planting as well.'

Hernando noted the enthusiasm in Luis's voice. The realisation that his grandson was determined to be successful in his new endeavour cast a slight shadow over the end of the meal for him, yet, at the same time, Hernando felt proud of the young man. He changed the conversation from viticulture.

'Luis, have you read the books you took with you?'

'I have read *The Praise of Folly* and found much to think about. I have brought it back with me. Does Canon Robert have any more of the writings of Erasmus, Grandfather?'

'I believe so. I will ask.' Then he continued, 'What about the Machiavelli?'

'I have been too busy to read that as well.'

'You will find him very different from Erasmus.'

Luis nodded in acknowledgement, 'I think I want to read more of what Erasmus has to say before I start *The Prince*.'

'I think you are probably right. Erasmus wrote on so many issues.' Hernando thought for a while, an impish expression changing his usually stern countenance. 'Why not take a look at the *Adagia*, the collection of Latin and Greek proverbs he collected?'

Ysabel watched Hernando, very aware that he was about to make trouble. When he grinned at Luis and quoted, 'There's many a slip "twixt cup and lip"', she caught Johan's eye effortlessly, a skill refined over time.

Johan responded immediately and distracted Hernando, 'Master, do try an almond cake, or there are some delicious figs.'

Much later, Johan fastened the shutters in the bed chamber before he slid under his covers and blew out the candle. In the pitch dark he asked, 'What is it really like, Luis?'

From across the room Luis answered, 'I have told you.'

'No Luis, I want the truth about the Gaulberts. Not the version of your life for Madame Bernade.'

Luis thought for a moment.

'Monsieur Gaulbert is so knowledgeable about wine. He is very thorough in what he tells me, including what I already know. I like him. I have always liked him. I am not sure about Madame Gaulbert. I am wary of her and keep out of her way as much as possible. She seems deliberately to forget I cannot eat pork. Henri is also a problem. He and I are not such good friends as we used to be when I just visited.'

'How so?'

'Difficult to say exactly. He gets annoyed with me, criticises me. He drinks too much and becomes argumentative.'

'What about the daughter?'

'Marie?'

'Yes, Marie.'

'She is kind.'

Johan tuned into the tone of Luis's voice.

'Oh, she is kind, is she?'

'Yes'

'Is she fair of face as well?'

'Yes'

'I see,' teased Johan, 'I think you are enamoured of Mistress Gaulbert!'

'Perhaps.'

'I hope she is not being too kind.'

'Shut up, Johan.'

'I am being serious.'

'No, you are not.'

'Just take care, little one.'

Luis laughed. 'I will,' he promised as he turned on his side to sleep, bending his legs out of habit.

THIRTEEN

≈

After six days in Caors it was time for Luis to return to the Gaulberts. He had bid his grandfather and Johan goodbye before he led Solomon the short distance to Ysabel's house. The late autumn morning was cool with mist still hanging over the river in wispy threads; in the distance he could hear a cart as it clattered its way over the Pont Neuf. He slipped through the gateway and tethered the horse in the courtyard of the large half-timbered house. It stood tall and imposing in front of him; four storeys, the last of which consisted of an open wooden gallery under the roof. Everything about the building spoke of the wealth of Michel Bernade and the comfort in which he had left his widow.

Ysabel, dressed for business and more agitated than usual, was waiting for him in the spacious hall. Her exquisite leather gloves lay on a side table next to three money pouches, full of écus.

'Good morning, Luis,' she said brightly. 'I am sorry I have so little time this morning.'

'It is fine. I need to leave early,' he replied as he leaned down to kiss her cheek.

'Thank you for doing this for me. It is a great help and will save me having to send Ramon.' She handed the three money pouches to Luis who carefully placed them in his satchel. 'You remember how to get to the Canacs' farm?'

'Yes, of course.'

'Of course you do. I must not fuss.'

'Why are you so on edge?'

'Am I?'

'Yes.'

'You can tell?'

'I can tell.'

'Oh dear! I am going to meet Jacques Bernat. He is trying to raise his transportation charges. I will need my wits about me this morning.'

'Jacques Bernat should not worry you.'

'If it was just Bernat it would not be so bad, but I think he is being manipulated by others.'

'Who?'

'That I am not sure of yet, but I will find out.'

Luis had no doubt that Ysabel would prevail, but for the first time he considered her position objectively. As the widow of one of the leading merchants of Caors, whose wealth was based on the export of wine and then investment in saffron production, Ysabel was as independent and powerful as a woman could be. Nevertheless, she was seen as weak by most of her fellow male entrepreneurs and open for exploitation. In preparation for her meeting she was dressed to impress, from the deep blue silk dress, which opened to reveal a paler blue embroidered kirtle, to the fine woollen cloak laid over the chair back. He smiled at her encouragingly and hugged her tightly, something he had not done for some time. Pure joy shone in her face as she returned his hug before taking a step back to look at him. She chuckled.

'I feel calmer already. God go with you, Luis.'

He made good progress to Douelle and, instead of turning left when he reached the river port, he continued west for a short time before he saw a narrow track he recognised. The building it led to was very similar to the Gaulberts' house, being made of the same local sandstone with a staircase leading to the living quarters on the upper storey. Luis could hear voices through an open door on the ground floor and shouted a greeting as he dismounted to secure Solomon's reins around the iron ring fastened in the wall. An ancient woman emerged, tiny and bent with a face as wrinkled and brown as a Quercy walnut. Two eyes, small as currants, peered through the creases.

'Well, well,' she cackled, 'we have a visitor.' She called to her companion, still inside the cellar, 'Daughter, come and see who is here.'

A second woman emerged through the door. Taller and bearing no resemblance to the old crone, she was well into middle age.

'Good day, young Sir.'

'Good day, Madame Canac. Good day, Madame Canac,' Luis greeted both Vicent Canac's wife and mother.

The ancient woman studied him closely.

'It is Madame Bernade's little dark boy all grown up, Daughter.'

'Yes Mother, I know.' The other woman smiled apologetically as her mother-in-law continued, 'Just look at you. You are tall. What a big handsome boy you are!' The old woman squinted as she studied him before she added, 'A shame about your face.'

The younger Madame Canac hurried the older back into the cellar and called to Luis to follow them in.

Disconcerted, Luis followed and found himself in a long low room which was surprisingly bright due to a large window whose shutters were thrown back to let in the midday sun. A fire was burning slowly in the hearth at one end of the cellar and, in the centre, there was a large table, most of which was covered with pale purple crocuses. The two women had obviously been removing the stigma, as a pile of saffron threads lay separated on trays at the end of the table. On the floor there was a carpet of discarded petals, the tracery of the darker veins clearly visible against the softer purple hue. Canac's wife indicated that Luis be seated.

'Do you wish for some refreshment, young Sir?'

'Thank you. I would appreciate a drink of water.'

The woman padded slowly to the far end of the cellar, filled a cup from a large earthenware jug, and then brought it back to Luis.

'What brings you here?' wheezed the old crone; the effort of having walked from outside had made her breathless.

'I have come on behalf of Madame Bernade. Is Monsieur Canac around?'

'He is out picking the last of the crop,' replied his wife. 'You will know how important it is to pick the flowers the day they bloom. It is late in the season and we fear some rain. It can quickly spoil the quality of the saffron. It leaches the flavour from the pistils.'

'Have you had a good year?'

Both women looked at Luis, suspicion clear on their faces as they assessed the purpose of his question. Their tenancy from Ysabel was based on a share of the crop as well as a nominal annual rent. Luis therefore received a vague reply.

'A fair one, a fair one,' they said in unison.

He shifted on the small wooden stool and took a sip of water. Eager to leave but feeling he should see Vicent Canac, Luis looked at the two woman who were openly staring at him. He started to fidget because he could not think of anything else to say. He took another sip of water before stating, 'I have important business with Monsieur Canac.'

At last the younger woman rose from her stool.

'I will go and fetch my husband.'

Luis was left with the ancient woman who continued to stare at him with her beady eyes.

'Do you live with Madame Bernade?'

'No. I live with my grandfather.'

'Madame Bernade has a very grand house in Caors?'

Luis chose not to answer. The old woman continued regardless.

'I am surprised she has not married again. A fine woman like her, Monsieur Bernade must have been dead these twelve years.'

Determined not to be drawn into a personal discussion of Ysabel, Luis asked a question, the answer of which he already knew.

'Have you grown saffron for a long time?'

Madame Canac's eyes told him she was aware of his tactic. She replied briefly.

'My husband's father first rented the land from Monsieur's grandfather. It is ideal for growing saffron which takes its flavour from the soil,' her currant eyes fixed on Luis as she added, 'like grapes.'

He made a slight movement of his head to show he was listening and she continued, 'I hear you are boarding with the Gaulberts for a year.'

'Yes,' replied Luis as he thought that news travelled fast along the valley.

'To learn about growing grapes?'

'Yes.'

The old woman thought about this for a while and appeared to be about to speak when Luis was saved from further interrogation by the return of the other Canacs.

Vicent Canac was a small stout man with the weathered face of a farmer, and sparse unruly grey hair that grew either side of a wrinkled, brown scalp. He greeted Luis warmly as the latter rose from his stool, the empty cup in his hand.

'Good day, young Sir. I see you have rested awhile.'

'Yes, thank you, Monsieur Canac. I have come on behalf of Madame Bernade.'

'How does she keep?'

'Well, thank you.' Luis reached down for the satchel at his feet, placed it on the edge of the table and removed the three pouches of écus. 'I have your portion of the most recent sale of saffron.'

Canac took one bag in his hand and judged its weight before he tested the others. He smiled.

'Good, thank you.'

'I must take my leave now as I am due back at the Gaulberts.' Luis refused the offer of food and said his goodbyes.

Solomon was waiting patiently for him in the yard and as he mounted, the ancient woman called out, 'Be careful you do not frighten the girls with that face of yours!'

Luis froze. Every muscle in his body tensed. He told himself that she was an old woman who had forgotten how to guard her tongue but it still hurt. He rode away without looking around so he missed the flustered reaction of her son and his wife, acute embarrassment clearly written on their faces.

On the evening of his return the fire cast its cosy glow over Luis and the Gaulberts, masking the tension which had suddenly built up. The single tallow candle Loise would allow picked out the hollows and planes of their faces. All had been going well, Luis had actually felt welcomed by his hostess as the meal had been good, but everything had changed when he mentioned the neglected land.

'I came back to the farm a new route as I visited the Canacs on behalf of Ysabel.' All four Gaulberts watched him with interest. 'I passed an area of ancient vines choked with weeds. It looked as if no-one had worked the land for many years.' In his enthusiasm to relay what he had felt when he had seen the abandoned vineyard Luis did not notice the first signs of discomfort around the table.

'Who owns that land?' he asked.

'I do,' answered Loise sharply. 'It belonged to my father and came with me on my marriage.'

'Why is it not worked?'

Guilhem answered Luis.

'There are not enough of us. It takes all our time to cope with what we have under cultivation and to look after the beasts.'

'Could we not clear the land and replant?' suggested Luis before he continued with, 'now I am here?'

'You want to do more work?' scoffed Henri. 'Just wait until your fingers are numb with the winter pruning in January and February. That land will need totally clearing before you plant in March. It cannot be done.'

'But we have the cuttings, have we not Monsieur Gaulbert?' Luis's black eyes sparkled in the candlelight as he leaned forward to make his point, and Guilhem was reminded how young the boy was. He saw his daughter give Luis her dazzling smile, and heard his wife mumble sullenly.

'We are not going to plant the land.'

'Why not, Wife?' asked her husband unexpectedly.

Loise was initially lost for words. She could not explain her antipathy to the idea of Luis developing her father's land, land which she held close to her heart, so she articulated her first thought.

'Why are you so interested? You will not be here to see the new vines fruit. It takes nearly three years from planting a rooted vine to harvest. You are only here for a year!' her voice rose as the words tumbled out.

Luis was not to be discouraged.

'I could start to clear the land now. There are two months before the winter pruning.' His use of the first person incensed his hostess who spat out her next words as she got up from the table.

'I told you we are not planting more vines!' Her husband put a hand on her arm to pull her back to the bench.

'Loise, I think young Luis may be right. While he is here we could plant to increase our yield.'

'Not on my land!' she screeched.

A dark expression came over Gaulbert's affable features. His mouth set in a grim line as the candlelight illuminated his bulbous nose giving him a grotesque appearance totally alien to his usual benign countenance.

'It is my land,' he bellowed.

In her fury, Loise was about to argue but she knew he was right. All that she had brought to the marriage belonged to her husband, and had Luis watched more closely he would have seen the abject defeat on her face as she sat down.

Silence fell on the table, broken eventually by Henri.

'I am off to bed.'

'I am too,' added Guilhem.

Loise did not speak. She remained still as she choked back tears of resentment and frustration. Marie started to clear away the remnants of the meal aided by Luis who was rewarded by a small smile followed by whispered thanks. When he took his walnut and placed it in the fire ready to light his way to the attic, Luis bade Loise good night. He was ignored.

Later, as Luis lay in his cold bed waiting for the warmth of the newly acquired sheepskins to reach his bones, Loise was seething with anger as she lay next to Guilhem. He had tried to embrace her when she had crept into bed but she had turned her back on him. Although she was often reluctant to acknowledge it, Loise was fortunate that her husband disliked discord. He decided to make conversation in an attempt to placate her.

'Loise, what is wrong with you? You know it makes sense to try to increase production. We have another pair of hands and Luis works so hard.' He was about to add that Luis worked twice as hard as Henri but sensibly decided against it.

His wife's voice was muffled as her head was burrowed into the bolster, hot tears oozing from tightly shut eyes.

'What happens when the year is up? Who will do the extra work?' Loise felt she could not be asked to do any more than she already did.

'I am not sure. Perhaps he will not leave. He seems very determined to grow vines.'

Guilhem could not make out Loise's reply as it was lost in the pillow, which was just as well, so he continued, 'I think that young man will not be moved from his chosen path.'

There was no further response from Loise although she did shuffle nearer to him for warmth. He patted her thigh, shifted so he was more comfortable and was asleep instantly. Loise opened her eyes and stared into the darkness unable to sleep.

◆   ◆   ◆

Guilhem's prediction was accurate. Six months later Luis stood at the edge of the neglected field, lost in thought. In every direction the glorious green of early May decorated the valley, the buds on the vines had burst forth, and evidence of new life was all around him. He had been checking the new shoots with Guilhem, rubbing out all but one on each stem. Then they had checked the cuttings in the nursery, especially those nurtured to regenerate the abandoned land.

Despite Loise's resistance, the vintner had responded positively to the idea of replacing the old vines, and although Luis had some cuttings for his own use, they had been far too few for a replanting on the scale needed. Under Guilhem's guidance and with the occasional help of Henri, when he was in the mood, Luis had taken cuttings from the vintner's stock throughout January and February. He had learnt how to store them under light soil for protection and to always keep them moist. In March he had set the cuttings the right way up in order to make roots so that the following spring he would be able to plant in the cleared field.

It had been a herculean task to remove the old vines but he had done it with the help of Gaulbert's mule. He had pulled out the ancient roots, torn out the weeds, turned the soil, and fertilised it ready for the new vines. Months of incessant labour, on top of the winter pruning he did for Guilhem, had left him lean, muscled, and with the hands of a seasoned farmer. He looked across the cleared field with pride, tinged by sadness, for he knew his year tending the vines would end come late summer. There in the verdant landscape he loved, Luis came to a decision, one he had pondered for a considerable time.

Soon, a voice hailed him from a distance. He turned to see Marie making her way quickly along the edge of the field, a basket on her arm. She waved and increased her pace until she stopped before him with shining eyes, high colour, and a broad smile on her face.

'Here you are. I might have known.'

'Hello.'

'I have some bread and cheese. Also a drink,' she said as she took the leather bottle from the basket and handed it to Luis. She watched him with her strange tawny eyes as he drank some water in big thirsty gulps.

'Thank you.'

Marie plonked herself on the edge of the field where Luis had left a border of grass and patted the patch of deep green carpet next to her. In a couple of months it would be dry and scratchy, but on that perfect May day it was soft and inviting. She looked across the cleared land, the light brown soil dotted with the local grey limestone.

'You have done well.'

'Yes.'

'It is a shame you will not be with us next spring to plant it.'

'I intend to be.'

Marie turned her head to look at Luis who was lying propped up on his elbows.

'How will you manage that? I thought your grandfather said you could only be with us for a year.'

'I am going to speak to him when I go for a visit next month, but if I tell you what I plan you must keep it to yourself.'

Marie's heart jumped with joy at the thought he trusted her with his plans. 'What are you going to do?'

'I need to make money if I am to buy land one day. The solution is obvious to me now. I want money and my grandfather wants me to go to university to train as a physician. I cannot do that. I will tell him I will study but to become a lawyer. Every spare minute I am not reading law books I will work in your father's vineyard. I will plant the new vines and I will see them fruit,' he explained passionately.

Marie had brought her knees up to her chest, wrapping her arms around them. From her position she had to look sideways at Luis and he saw her eyes widen in astonishment.

'That is wonderful,' she exclaimed, but immediately paused. 'What if he says no?'

'I think I will be able to persuade him.' Luis had pulled up a stalk of sweet grass and started to chew the end of it.

Marie stretched out, resting on her elbows so she was level with him. For some time they were quiet as each thought about Luis's future. Marie spoke first.

'Land is not cheap.'

'I know, but lawyers can charge expensive fees!'

'Perhaps you could marry a rich heiress?'

He laughed.

'Luis, do you ever think about who you might marry?' she asked trying to sound nonchalant.

He turned his head to look at Marie. He noticed the faint sheen of moisture on her face and throat above the dress which was old and too tight. He saw the way the sun touched golden highlights in her brown hair and, in that moment, Luis thought she would be as perfect a wife a man could want. He did not answer at first, but the mischief in his eyes made her heart leap before he said, 'That is a good idea. I will look for an old, fat, very rich heiress!'

A Lucrative Trade

1545

F O U R T E E N

~

Bridgwater, Somerset, March 1545

In the gloom of a wet March afternoon, Thomas Weaver spent several minutes trying to find the letter. The rain, driven by a strong westerly, beat against the casement and whipped around the chimneys. Despite the inclement weather outside the winter parlour was snug; a bright fire roared in the grate and the newly installed oak panelling gave an extra layer of insulation. He was just about to call Agnes, his housekeeper, and ask for more candles when he found the missing epistle. It was dated July 1544 and came from the widow of a former associate of his father. Thomas could remember the name but, after more than twenty years, the face of the merchant escaped him. As a young man he had been fully involved in his father's business, but it had been the elder Thomas Weaver who had negotiated with foreign traders. The letter was addressed in a neat hand, but whether it was intended for his father or himself was uncertain. He started to read the contents when the loud clatter of the door latch being lifted interrupted his concentration.

'Is it not too dark to read, Father?'

Thomas watched as his son walked across the room and positioned himself in front of the hearth, blocking both the heat and the light.

'I could just about see but somebody has deprived me of what light came from the fire and has shattered my peace.' The reprimand was delivered with a smile.

Richard Weaver grinned back.

'Sorry! I will get some candles for you.'

On his return Richard placed a candle on the mantelpiece and another next to Thomas so they could both see more clearly.

'What is that you are reading?'

'It is the letter I received last autumn, from the widow of an old business acquaintance of the family.'

'I remember. She asked about the possibility of her protégé calling on us when he comes to England?'

'Yes.'

'Surely you do not expect him to come now?'

'Why not?'

'Well, matters are not settled with France. Since King Henry took Boulogne last year, François will want revenge and the fighting season is almost upon us.'

'He is coming from the Pays d'Oc and sailing from Bordèu. I doubt war in northern France will affect that trade much.'

Richard mulled this over before reasoning, 'If he is to come this year it will probably be soon. He will set off with the first signs of spring.'

'I believe so.'

'What is his name?'

Thomas looked down at the heavy paper, the script dark on the uneven surface. He scanned the words quickly for the answer.

'Luis Gharsia.'

'Surely that is a Spanish name?'

'I believe so.'

'Better than a French name in these times. He might be mistaken for a spy!'

◆   ◆   ◆

Luis felt he had never been so wretched; the ship yawed as it cut through the waves, the gently sloping bow dipping and rolling as it ploughed ahead. The noise of the lateen-rigged sails in the wind prevented all possibility of conversation, even if Luis had been predisposed to talk to the surly mariner nearest to him. It was a sudden change; as they had hugged the coast of France the voyage had been a calm one. However, now as they met the full force of the Atlantic, Luis questioned the wisdom of his decision to travel to England.

When Ysabel had first suggested it to him, he had jumped at the opportunity to try to loosen the stranglehold of the merchants of Bordèu on the exportation of Caors wine. Through his studies at the university, Luis had realised that the advantages given to the vintners of the Gironde were the result of an archaic edict. The over-taxation of the Olt wine and the practice of preventing any commerce before All Saints' Day, both great impediments to freedom to trade and prosperity, had continued long after the English had left.

There was also another reason for his enthusiasm. Luis should have been content. He had seen his first harvest from the reclaimed land and had been rewarded generously. As a law graduate he had been able to use his legal training whilst still helping Guilhem Gaulbert. His grandfather's friend Martin Ebrart, eager to reduce his own workload, had offered the young man flexible work in his practice, alongside some part-time teaching. Then there was Marie and her expectations. Their last conversation had been a difficult one, the air heavy with dissatisfaction. He should have been content but he was not; he could not rid himself of a feeling of restlessness.

The last time he had seen her, Marie had found Luis among the vines, pruning the dormant branches before the sap rose. At her call he stopped, straightened, and removed his glove; a tall man silhouetted against the grey wintry sky.

'Why do you have to go?' The words were uttered before she even reached him. Luis waited. He did not reply but watched her stride towards him, a thick shawl clutched tightly around her shoulders.

'Why do you have to go?' she repeated as she pulled up level with him.

'I will not be away long.'

Infuriated by his reply, Marie exclaimed, 'I asked you a question. You have not given me an answer yet!' She stood, feet planted firmly apart with arms crossed, and glared at Luis.

'I need to go to England to see if I can broker an agreement to export our wine directly.' He did not add that, for some time, the world beyond the Olt valley had beckoned, although he remained secure in the knowledge that he would always want to return.

'Why does it have to be you?'

'Ysabel asked me. I am working on behalf of all our merchants. My legal training will be useful.'

Marie looked around at the naked stumps, which he had already pruned, and refused to meet his eye. She studied a distant point with apparent concentration.

'You might not come back.'

'Of course I will come back. I need to be here by August.'

'I might be betrothed by the time you return. Piere del Mas has been paying me much attention.'

Luis gave her a measured stare, as he remembered the distant cousin of Loise, and assessed the purpose of her declaration. Over the years the fondness he felt for her, to Marie's sadness, had not flourished into more mature love, despite their occasional kisses, which were now consigned to the past.

'I wish you well,' he said, showing no emotion on his face.

Thwarted, disappointment made Marie spiteful.

'It will serve you right if you are shipwrecked.'

'Yes, it will,' he agreed ruefully. 'But come, Marie, let us part friends. When I have finished here today, I plan to go home to prepare for the journey.'

She turned then and looked at him. Slowly she raised her face for a kiss and closed her eyes. Luis, already crossing oceans in his imagination, leaned down and planted a brotherly peck on her cheek.

His last conversation with Hernando had been even harder. It had taken place after their evening meal, once Johan had cleared the table and repaired to the kitchen before his usual visit to the tavern. They sat in silence, two pairs of hands fidgeted with goblets full of boiled, spiced, honey water. Hernando was struggling with the unfamiliar sensation of feeling abandoned and his tone was querulous.

'What if I die when you are away?'

Luis, lost in thought, questioned whether he had heard correctly.

'Pardon, Grandfather, what did you say?'

'I said, "what if I die when you are away?"'

'Why do you say such a thing?'

'I am old. I might die soon.'

'We all might die soon.'

'I have more chance because I am old.'

Luis studied Hernando thoughtfully. It was true that his grandfather was sixty-four years old, yet he had the appearance of one younger. Although his hair and beard were almost totally white now, in great contrast to his black eyebrows and lashes, his skin was relatively unlined. Luis acknowledged that this was probably due to the amount of time spent indoors, studying and teaching, yet he often wondered whether his grandfather used some of his own salves and potions on himself.

'You are ill?' A fear suddenly gripped Luis that Hernando was trying to tell him something.

Hernando sniffed loudly before he replied, 'I have felt better.'

'But you are not ill?' asked his grandson directly.

'No, I am not ill, but what if I become so and die while you are away?'

'You are not going to die while I am away!'

Quick as a flash, Hernando retorted, 'How do you know? You cannot possibly know.'

Luis had to agree so he decided to approach the conversation from a different angle.

'Why are you so worried about dying when I am travelling?'

Hernando stared down into his drink as if trying to find the answer there. When he lifted his head his face was so mournful that Luis felt an unaccustomed surge of love for the old man, whose eyes shone with unshed tears.

'Who will wash my hair? Who will wash my body and wrap me in my shroud? Who will lay me in the ground having followed the rituals of our faith?'

The realisation that his grandfather was genuinely distressed made Luis considerate in his answer. He leaned across the table and took Hernando's hand in his.

'I will speak to Johan when he returns and explain what must be done if the worst happens. However, I do not think it will happen soon,' he stated firmly. As he stroked the older man's hand soothingly, Luis became aware of a shift in their relationship. Hernando had never spoken of personal matters with him and he could not shake himself free of the feeling that now it was his turn to look after his grandfather. He added, 'Ysabel will be here to help you. You know that, and I will be back by summer.'

Hernando brightened somewhat at the mention of Ysabel but was still feeling negative enough to state, 'I am surprised she is so keen for you to go. She will miss you very much.'

Neither of them spoke. Hernando remembered that when the idea of Luis going to England was first discussed, both he and Ysabel thought it was an excellent idea. It would be a great opportunity for the young man to travel as well as having the added bonus of separating him from Marie. The older man was the first to break the silence.

'Have you said goodbye to Ysabel?'

'Yes.' Luis did not say more as he felt a constriction in his throat as he recalled how quiet she had been when she hugged him too tightly, before she turned and left the room.

'How long will the journey take?' asked Hernando miserably.

'If all goes well I will be in England in less than three weeks. It depends how quickly I can find a passage from Bordèu.'

'Where will you sail to?'

'Either Bristol, or Bridgwater would be better.' Luis watched his grandfather digest this information and suddenly it came to him how he could cheer the old man up. 'I hear Bristol is a large prosperous port. There will be merchants from many lands.' He smiled and paused for a moment. 'Perhaps I will meet a beautiful Muslim girl?'

A particularly loud snap of the sails startled Luis from his reverie; the sickness which had dogged him since the ship had sailed into open water receded slightly as he fixed his eyes on the horizon and tried to ignore the rolling deck beneath his feet. The westerly which, at that moment, was buffeting the shutters of Thomas Weaver's house and moaning down the chimneys pushed Luis ever faster towards his destination as the little ship ploughed relentlessly on through the roiling grey sea.

◆   ◆   ◆

The late afternoon sun, streaming through a break in the clouds, warmed the red sandstone of the castle wall as Luis stepped thankfully on to dry land. In the lengthening shadows, the jetty was a hive of activity. Men had appeared as if from nowhere to unload the cargo and take the wine to the town cellar. He stood for a while watching the mariners manoeuvre the barrels, the mark of Bordèu clearly visible, using ropes and skids with an adroitness that came with repeated practice. Hoisting his bag onto his shoulder he called towards them.

'Where can I get a room for the night?'

Without breaking from his task or looking at Luis one of them shouted, 'At the Swan.'

Keeping the river behind him, he struck out for the town and shortly found himself in a marketplace from which he could clearly see the very high spire of a church. The centre of Bridgwater was bustling and, after a brief enquiry, Luis discovered the Swan was very nearby. When he reached it, the inn turned out to be basic but clean, with fresh rushes on the floor and a good fire in the hearth. As the sun sank lower in the sky, the chill from the river became more intense and Luis crossed the threshold with relief.

The landlord, a big ruddy-faced man, looked the young traveller up and down, taking in the quality of his clothing and his heavily accented, stilted English. A bargain was struck, after the initial suspicion of the French coin, and Luis was led to a chamber off the hall where up to six men could be accommodated. There were three beds and a chest for belongings on top of which was the ewer for washing. There was no sign of the other occupants so Luis chose the bed by the window. After the landlord had left he took the opportunity to wash and pray. Then he stowed his bag in the chest and made sure his money-belt was firmly camouflaged under his shirt and jerkin, before making his way to the hall to eat.

Two long tables, already half full, were placed at right angles against one of the walls and the landlord's wife was busy bringing steaming bowls of stew and large chunks of bread. As Luis sat down at the nearest table, her daughter, without breaking her stride, slammed down a large pitcher full of ale whose froth spilled over leaving a wet, sticky puddle on the scrubbed oak. Acting on a decision which he had taken when he embarked on his journey, Luis poured the weak pale liquid into his tankard and took a sip. It was not to his taste; a very poor drink, in his eyes, compared to his beloved black wine. Over the years he had kept his promise to Hernando that he would never become intoxicated but, as he had waited on the Quai de Chartron in Bordèu for a passage, it had been obvious to him that he did not need the extra difficulty of abstaining from drinking alcohol. He had argued with himself that it would be foolish to fall ill from bad water. He lifted the tankard slowly and took another sip, wondering whether the insipid liquid was alcoholic after all.

Back in his chamber there was still no sign of his fellow travellers so, with relief, Luis prepared for bed. He was lying awake worrying about the etiquette of when to present Ysabel's gift to Thomas Weaver when the first sleeping companion arrived. An older man of about forty, small and slight, he took one glance at the young man who already occupied the chamber. He noted the sheer size of him and, as he raised his candle to nod a greeting to the occupant of the bed by the window, he saw the ugly scar that ran from forehead to mouth. Without speaking, the man turned his back and chose the bed furthest from Luis. The latter smiled to himself and returned to the problem of the gift. If he gave it too soon it might look as if he was too keen or it could be seen as a bribe. If he waited until he was better acquainted with Weaver it might appear as an afterthought and jeopardise any negotiations. Soon snores, which seemed totally out of proportion to the man's size, shattered Luis's peace. He turned on his side and thumped the bolster to make it more comfortable as he wished he had discussed the matter more thoroughly with Ysabel before he had left.

As Luis lay fretting over what he would do the next day, three more travellers arrived to bed down for the night. Two appeared to be together and took the bed next to Luis. The third man paused, uncertain which place to choose. Vibrating snores filled the room so he made his way towards the window, but he stopped with a start. Luis had deliberately turned over on to his back and placed his hands behind his head. The man retreated as quietly as he could to the far side of the room and Luis was left with the luxury of a bed to himself. He tried to will himself to sleep but it did not work; long after everyone else slumbered he remembered what Ysabel had said about the man he was to visit. He heard her voice clearly as she told him that Thomas Weaver was a man of integrity, one of the most honest men her husband had ever come across in business. With that thought in mind, Luis finally stopped worrying.

FIFTEEN

≈

The first sound Luis heard, after the flustered housekeeper had indicated that he wait, was laughter, the laughter of a child. He looked up the staircase rising from the dark panelled hall, the air full of the scent of new oak overlaid with beeswax. At the top of the stairs, on the landing, he could see the outline of a small female child; a pair of eyes, wide with surprise, peeped between the balusters. There was someone crouched down next to her, perhaps an adult, but all Luis could see was the top of a head. The laughter continued, followed by a low chuckle and whispered words. He strained to make out the unfamiliar sounds.

'No Meg, it is not a giant in our hall. It is just a visitor for Father.'

Luis was unable to catch any of the words but felt self-conscious enough to believe that he was the cause of the merriment. He blushed and shifted uncomfortably, which did not go unnoticed by Alyce Weaver. She rose to her feet, reached out her hand to her sister and led the little girl down the stairs. It was slow progress. The child moved methodically, pausing and bringing both feet together after she had descended each stair, and all the while the stranger averted his eyes.

'Good morning. I am Alyce Weaver,' she said as she reached the bottom step, 'and this is my sister, Meg.' Although she was standing on the first stair and was considered tall for a woman, the man's eyes were level with hers as he turned at her words. He did not speak. Surprised to see that he was so young, probably younger than her, she smiled and decided that her usual honesty was needed.

'I apologise for my little sister. My brother fills her head with tales of giants and goblins and you are so tall, she mistook you for a giant. I hope she has not caused offence.'

Luis felt the sweat breaking out on his brow and in the palms of his hands as he struggled to work out what she had said. The lessons Martin Ebrart had given him, in readiness for his journey, now seemed totally inadequate; the young woman pronounced the words so differently to those he had practised with his tutor. He thought he had never heard of the words 'giant' and 'goblin' and was at a loss, despite having spent some time earlier that morning revising the vocabulary he would need for greetings, introductions, and business discussions.

At that moment, when Alyce was contemplating the serious young man before her, Richard Weaver came into the hall from the winter parlour, having just heard from an agitated Agnes that a Morian had called. The scene before him caused him some amusement. The visitor in question stood as if transfixed at the bottom of the stairs while Alyce and Meg waited patiently on the first tread, apparently trapped. Richard took in the height and breadth of the young man before noting what he could see of the stranger's face: the strong aquiline nose and scarred cheek.

'Good morning,' he said affably as he closed the door from the winter parlour. The man at the bottom of the stairs took a step backwards and swung round, intense black eyes fixed on Richard.

'Good morning. I am Luis Gharsia.' The words were delivered with some difficulty in heavily accented English.

Richard recognised the name but the awkward young man speaking to him was not what he had expected. He felt he had rarely seen such discomfort in their house and found himself speaking French to put the stranger at ease.

'Good morning. I am afraid my father is not at home.'

The relief on the visitor's face was clear. He relaxed and gave a small nod of acknowledgement. Richard was just about to introduce himself when

Alyce took the opportunity to slip past the two men and lead Meg away, but the little girl stopped and asked, 'Are you really a giant?'

Richard, seeing how perplexed the stranger was, translated. Then he explained his sister's fascination with imaginary beings, although he neglected to mention his own role in encouraging her. There was a long pause before the elder Weavers watched with interest as Luis squatted down so that he was level with the child and said very slowly and solemnly in English, 'I am not a giant. I just eat too much.' Then he smiled a smile which started in his eyes before it reached his mouth and softened the sharp angles of his face.

Meg studied him for a long time, deep blue eyes serious under straight brows, then she shyly returned his smile.

Immediately Alyce warmed towards their visitor, as did her brother who said, 'Please come back this afternoon at about five o'clock. My father will be here. I am Richard Weaver.' Then much to Alyce's astonishment he added, 'Rufus—to my family and friends.'

Luis stood up. He could see the appropriateness of such an appellation for, despite the darkness of the panelled hall, Richard Weaver's bright red hair was in stark contrast to his pale skin. He made a slight bow.

'Thank you. I will return this afternoon.'

◆   ◆   ◆

When Luis left the Weavers' house he paused for some time in order to find his bearings. In front of him he could see the church, its tall spire rising to twice the height of the tower on which it stood; the position of the sun told him he was facing north. As the morning had turned unseasonably warm, he decided to explore rather than return to the inn. After the dismal, heavy squalls of the previous days the sun now shone strongly. Small puffy white clouds hung in a spring sky of such deep azure that Luis was perplexed at the change in the weather. He turned south-east and continued until he reached a fork in the road sure that if he kept to the left, he would soon see the river.

He walked very quickly; his preference as always was to run but he did not want to attract attention, and, now a fully grown man, he felt it was unseemly to do so. Away from the centre of the town the road leading east was quiet. Most of the goodwives of Bridgwater had already visited the market and had returned to their homes. He passed few people; those he did meet stared for too long, nodded, and silently went on their way. Soon he reached the river, via a lane which ran south from the quay to the bridge by a limekiln, and flopped down on the bank.

The heat of the sun was a surprise. Luis removed both his jerkin and doublet, flexed his shoulders, and ran his fingers through his hair, which had grown considerably since he had left Caors. He felt hot, dirty, and disappointed in himself for being so nervous when he had visited the Weaver household. A wave of self-doubt fought with his determination to be successful in gaining more favourable trading rights. He stared at the River Parrett. It was low tide and the debris brought downstream by the recent rain was clearly exposed.

Homesickness washed over him. He closed his eyes and imagined the deep green Olt flowing past. He thought of Johan and how they had taught themselves to swim, the water cooling as the fierce sun burnt their necks and shoulders. He thought of his grandfather who would be in his study poring over his medical books, and of Ysabel, whose belief that he could achieve anything he wanted had led him to this point, sitting alone in a foreign land. He did not think of Marie. He opened his eyes and looked across the river at the flat meadows. He took a deep breath. The determination was starting to win.

He set off towards the wharf with renewed vigour. The easiest way to find the Swan was to retrace his steps from the previous day. The quay was busy, not with the bustle of loading and unloading, but with the actions of the gangs engaged in clearing the silt and mud from the area near the Town Bridge. As he walked Luis made three decisions. First he would return to his room to wash and say his noon prayers. Secondly, he would seek out the barber's shop he had noticed earlier that morning and have his hair and beard trimmed. Finally, he would present himself punctually at the Weavers' door as a confident, competent man.

◆   ◆   ◆

When Thomas Weaver returned home to dine at noon he was met by a flustered Agnes.

'Oh Sir, you have missed your visitor. Master Richard has asked him to come back later this afternoon.'

'Good, good, Agnes,' he replied without really registering what she had said. 'I am ready to eat. It has been a long time since breakfast.' As a burgess of Bridgwater, Weaver had spent most of the morning in the Gild Hall with the Mayor, the two bailiffs, and the other burgesses. They had spent much time discussing one of the more complicated issues concerning the rental of town lands and, as a result, Thomas was very hungry. However, his housekeeper was eager to expand on the excitement of her morning.

'Your visitor was a foreigner.'

'A foreigner?'

'Yes Sir. He was a Morian.'

Her master nodded, digested this fact and repeated, 'Please make haste Agnes. I have had a very trying morning.'

'Very well, Sir,' Agnes replied, disappointed that so little interest was shown in her news. 'I have already set dinner in the winter parlour,' she added as she took his hat and cloak.

Alyce, Rufus, and Meg were in the parlour waiting for Thomas to return. His elder daughter looked up from the embroidery she was stitching, 'You are back late, Father.'

'Yes, the meeting took far longer than I expected. There was a great deal of disagreement.' He sat down wearily. 'I hear we have had a visitor this morning. He seems to have unsettled Agnes.'

Rufus laughed, 'She was very agitated when she came to tell me that a Morian was at our door, asking for you.'

'Who was it, Rufus?'

'Luis Gharsia.'

'Ah yes, is he a black man?'

'No, Father. I think he is a Spanish Moor. He is an Arab.'

'That makes sense; hence the Spanish name.'

Meg, who was sitting on the floor playing with her doll volunteered, 'He is a giant.'

'A giant!' exclaimed her father, his eyes sweeping over the faces of all three of his offspring.

Alyce smiled, 'He is a very tall, broad-shouldered young man, and Meg and I first looked down on him from the landing. He certainly did appear very big when viewed from above. Meg thought he was a giant. Unfortunately he heard us chuckling. I did try to explain her reaction to him but his English seems poor.'

Her brother interrupted, 'I think he was nervous. He probably understood more than we think, although he did appear mightily relieved when I addressed him in French. Did you notice his hands, Alyce? He had them clenched. I think you frightened him, Sister!'

Alyce, who was well used to her younger brother's teasing, retorted, 'I think for most people it would be the other way round. He is so big and his face so scarred.'

'Alyce,' her father reprimanded softly. 'It is not like you to judge on appearance.'

His daughter reddened, the pink glow giving warmth to her pale, creamy skin.

'I am not judging. I only offered an opinion. I feel many people might find him intimidating initially.' She tilted her chin upward. 'I did not. In fact I found the way he spoke to Meg endearing.'

Rufus was not going to let that comment pass.

'Is this the first time I have heard my sister admit a man to be endearing?'

'Shut up Rufus. I said his manner was endearing. There is a difference.'

'Perhaps he was frightened of you because of your beauty. A vision of loveliness, descending the stairs before his eyes!'

Alyce knew he was only joking but she could not suppress her regret that there could be no truth in his words. She was twenty-three years old with not a suitor in sight. Whether it was her fearsome intellect, encouraged by her father and honed on both Thomas and Rufus, or her habit of speaking her mind with brutal honesty that kept potential husbands away was uncertain. Although she did not see herself as comely, Alyce knew she was an excellent housewife, yet, as the years had passed since the death of her father's second wife, she had come to accept that her future lay in the role of the spinster daughter who would care for her ageing father and raise her half-sister. She hid her hurt by deflecting the attention back to her brother.

'You took to him too. You even implied he could call you Rufus.'

'Really?' asked their father.

'Yes, I did. I felt sorry for him because he was so uncomfortable. I agree he looked rather fierce—he reminded me of a hawk—but when he smiled at Meg his face changed completely. I think he would be an interesting fellow to get to know. I asked him to come back at five o'clock. If you thought it appropriate, we could ask him to sup with us, Father. I believe the conversation could well be stimulating. He could tell us all about where he has come from.'

Thomas smiled wryly.

'In French?'

'Yes, in French.'

His father shook his head, surprised that one visitor seemed to have made such an impression on all three of his children.

'We will see. We will see. We do not know why he is paying us a visit. Anyway, it is time for us to eat our dinner.'

◆   ◆   ◆

At five o'clock sharp Luis Gharsia lifted the ornate iron knocker on Thomas Weaver's door and announced his arrival with a resounding thud. This time Agnes led him through to the winter parlour where the master of the house was reading at a table. The light from the window behind the table made it difficult for the young man to see Weaver's features. Luis stood silently as the older man rose to come round the table to greet him; a man of about fifty, tall and wiry with sparse coppery hair. It grew back from a high forehead, faded from its original shade, the colour of hair that did not turn grey but gradually became paler as the years passed. His light blue eyes were friendly as he openly assessed his visitor. When he spoke it was slowly and clearly.

'Welcome, Mister Gharsia. Welcome. I trust you had a good journey?'

'Yes Sir. Thank you.'

'Is it fine for me to continue in English or would you prefer me to speak French?'

'Please speak English. I must improve.'

'Good, good. We can always change to French if need be. Please sit down.'

Luis took the stool nearest to him whilst Thomas walked to the table where a jug of wine and two cups rested.

'Will you take some wine, Mister Gharsia?'

'Thank you.' Luis sipped the liquid; it was a quality Bordèu. 'It is good.' His host nodded in agreement.

'Your patron writes that you are an excellent wine producer yourself.' Thomas saw a small frown gather between his visitor's brows and was about to rephrase his comment when Luis replied, 'I try to be.' What had caused him to pause was the term 'patron'. It seemed such a cold word to describe Ysabel and all she meant to him.

'What brings you to England, Mister Gharsia?'

The young vintner of the Olt was ready. He had rehearsed his explanation many times. He started to speak with a strong accent and laboured pronunciation.

'The wine produced in the Olt valley is of the highest quality but it is difficult to export it. England used to be a major importer of our wine but the authorities in Bordèu have the power to block our supplies and prefer to mix our Caors wine with their own to achieve a good quality wine which will travel well. I want to negotiate fairer trading rights and my first step is to establish the possibility of an English market. I do not act for myself but for all the producers of my region.'

Thomas Weaver looked at the earnest young man before him, aware of his tense shoulders and eyes shining with the challenge of a quest.

'That is no small feat, young man.'

Luis did not understand exactly what Weaver had said but he realised the gist of his host's reaction.

'I know, but if I can show an English market exists then it will be easier to put pressure on the administrators at Bordèu.'

Thomas found himself taking to the young man. There had been none of the usual machinations associated with negotiations. Luis Gharsia had been in his house for less than a quarter of an hour before he declared his purpose. Perhaps it was his unfamiliarity with the English language but somehow Thomas doubted this. His instinct told him that Gharsia was a man with whom he could do business. He made up his mind.

'Your plan will need careful consideration, Mister Gharsia. Would you care to stay and sup with us this evening?' He was heartened to see the look of pleasure cross his visitor's face and he realised that the latter's eyes were no longer focused on him but on something of interest over his shoulder. Thomas turned his head so he could view the window behind him. In the garden Rufus was throwing Meg in the air, the little girl shrieked with laughter before her brother caught her and his precious Alyce was kneeling amongst her herbs, gently weeding.

'Thank you, Sir. I am delighted to accept your invitation.'

'Come then, let us join my family in the garden. I believe you have already met them all.'

The garden was long and narrow, enclosed by a high stone wall. Fruit trees grew against it at the far end, the buds of blossom just visible, and nearer the house there were three flower beds, edged with thyme, rosemary, marjoram, and lavender, surrounding the bare stems of rose bushes. A yew hedge separated the two sections of the garden and, at intervals, stone benches were carefully placed to make the most of the sun and shade. Rufus stopped throwing Meg in the air and came over towards them, the small girl clinging round his neck. Luis, who had no experience of small children, guessed she was about three or four years old.

'Hello,' he said but the child turned her head against her brother's shoulder.

Rufus smiled in greeting.

'I think she has become a little shy.' In the April sun his hair seemed to glow more brightly, a vibrant dark red. Alyce rose from her knees to join them.

'Good afternoon Mister Gharsia.' She brushed her hands together to remove the soil and Luis noticed that they were beautiful hands, long slender palms ending in elegant tapered fingers. She was as tall as her brother with thick hair of a colour Luis found difficult to place. It was fair but deep, neither copper nor honey but somewhere in between. Her eyebrows and lashes were the same shade giving her face a nakedness that could have meant a lack of definition except for her extraordinary eyes. They were a light almost translucent green; a long buried memory of clear Pyrenean water sprang into Luis's mind as he replied.

'Good afternoon, Mistress Weaver.' He searched for one of the practise sentences he had learnt with Martin Ebrart. 'You have a beautiful garden.'

'Yes, it gives me great joy.' Alyce included Thomas in her answer and gave them both a beaming smile. 'Have you finished talking already, Father?'

'For the time being, but I have asked Mister Gharsia if he will sup with us tonight and he has kindly agreed.'

'Good.' Alyce looked directly at Luis who found himself very glad that he was staying with this family for the evening. 'I will go and tell Agnes that an extra place needs to be set.'

SIXTEEN

~

Luis had stopped listening. Instead he was watching the Weaver family, especially Alyce. Words were flying around the table with a speed that rendered them incomprehensible to his inexperienced ear. Alyce, her hands gesturing to make herself understood, appeared to be arguing with her father, who was clearly relishing the exchange. Occasionally Rufus spoke, but for the most part sat back and toyed with the chunk of wheaten bread on his plate. Luis's eyes rested momentarily on the coarse, grey bread torn to pieces on the shiny pewter. Everything he could see in the room indicated prosperity, from the new oak panelling to the excellent food he had just enjoyed. Rufus looked up from his reverie and noticed how quickly their guest had eaten the last course.

'It was good?' he asked.

'Yes. It was very good.' Luis did not recognise the fish but another distant memory had surfaced as he had tasted the first mouthful, a familiarity buried deep from his early years in Valencia.

Rufus smiled, 'Agnes told me it was caught fresh this morning in the estuary.'

Luis acknowledged the information with his customary slight movement of head but remained silent.

'Can you understand what they are saying?' Rufus waved his bread in the direction of his father and sister.

'No,' admitted his companion.

'Father, Alyce, stop talking. Our guest cannot follow what you are saying.'

Silence fell. Thomas and his daughter looked shamefaced. Alyce was the first to speak, this time in French.

'I apologise Mister Gharsia. We forget ourselves.' She glanced down at her plate where most of her uneaten fish rested and laughed. 'In my excitement I have forgotten to eat my fish.'

'As usual,' remarked her brother. 'I think we should keep to French from now on.'

'I think Mister Gharsia was coping very well with English,' retorted Alyce determined not to be criticised. 'He answered all your questions,' she added pointedly.

It was true Rufus realised. He had asked many questions in his enthusiasm to learn more about their guest. Yet he still knew very little, which was unlike him. Usually his open friendly face and easy manner prised interesting facts out of most people. He could not decide whether Gharsia's taciturn manner and succinct answers were due to a lack of vocabulary or to reserve. Luis, on the other hand, had understood but been relieved when the attention had turned from him to what appeared to be a heated but amiable discussion. No sooner had Thomas Weaver said grace and the cups of soup had been brought by Mary, the girl who helped Agnes, than Luis had been bombarded with questions about his journey and his home. No mention of the purpose of his visit had yet arisen, but that was to change. All attention was back on Luis yet he was surprised when it was Alyce who asked him directly, 'Why have you come to Bridgwater, Mister Gharsia?'

'Yes,' added Rufus, his eyes alight with interest, 'What brings you to our shores?'

Luis tried to order his thoughts. It was apparent that Thomas Weaver had not shared what they had spoken of earlier. However it was also apparent to the young man that he was experiencing a strange lightness of head. Perhaps he was ill? He must concentrate. He must show the Weavers he was the competent man he wished to be. Speaking slowly in English so that they could see his knowledge of their language, Luis repeated his explanation word for word.

'The wine produced in the Olt valley is of the highest quality but it is difficult to export it. England used to be a major importer of our wine but the authorities in Bordèu have the power to block our supplies and prefer to mix our Caors wine with their own to achieve a good quality wine which will travel well. I want to negotiate fairer trading rights and my first step is to establish the possibility of an English market. I do not act for myself but for all the producers of my region.'

Alyce smiled appreciatively, slight creases fanning out from her eyes. Rufus whistled long and low, gaining a frown from his father, before he said, 'You have certainly set yourself a challenging task, Mister Gharsia!'

No emotion showed on the face of their visitor who now decided he felt decidedly strange. Luis looked at the three adults seated at the table (the small child had been taken to bed by the housekeeper after the soup) and was filled with the warmth of bonhomie. He took another sip of the pale golden liquid which he understood to be apple juice and invited, 'Please call me Luis,' before he took another generous gulp.

If the Weavers were surprised by this familiarity, they did not show it. After all, earlier that day Richard Weaver had shared a confidence about his own appellation. Alyce watched their guest empty the vessel and place it back on the dark oak with a hefty thud. The expression of solicitous hostess sat firmly on her face, though a bubble of laughter threatened to escape from her lips. She quickly reached for the pitcher of water at the end of the table and filled Luis's goblet.

'I find it is unseasonably hot for early April this evening, Mister Gharsia.'

He nodded, drank the water and waited for someone to say something. Any snippet would do which could begin a conversation and help him to focus. Concentration was what he needed. That would allow him to fight the feeling of otherworldliness. He studied the polished wood thoughtfully. When he lifted his eyes Alyce Weaver was still watching him. Her face showed polite concern, but the set of her mouth told a different story. The memory of that morning came back with a jolt: the sound of laughter tinkling at the top of the stairwell and his belief that he was the cause of the amusement. The bonhomie was gone; Luis wanted to shrink back into himself until he became invisible, as he had frequently wished to do as a child. He spoke very formally and coldly in English, 'Excuse me, I feel unwell.'

Alyce's eyes flicked to the flagon in the centre of the table before giving her brother a meaningful stare. His attention caught, she silently indicated the significance of the drink. A great guffaw escaped Rufus's lips, followed quickly by an apology.

'Pardon me, Mister Gharsia—Luis. I fear you have drunk too much of our Somerset cyder.'

The colour leached from Luis's face.

'Is it not apple juice?'

Alyce spoke softly responding to the confusion and horror she could see in the black eyes, mortified that she had found his predicament amusing.

'It is made from apples but it is not juice.'

Realisation dawned on Rufus as their guest stuttered, 'I am intoxicated?'

'No, no, Mister Gharsia,' soothed Thomas Weaver, his embarrassment obvious. 'It is just a little strong if you are not used to it. It is our fault. We should have watered it down for you. You cannot be intoxicated, you have not drunk enough.'

Alyce turned to look out of the window. Darkness had fallen as it was early in the year but the walled garden would still be pleasant after such a sunny day. With an inviting smile she asked, 'Perhaps we could take a turn around the garden?'

◆　　◆　　◆

The freshness of the evening air hit Luis as he followed the bobbing lantern, taking careful steps so as not to stumble. Alyce held her arm high and a warm pool of light illuminated the path. Rufus was close behind, a firm hand on his guest's shoulder to steady him. Luis took a deep breath, tasting the sharp tang of the sea on the breeze as it blew up the estuary. Rufus's voice drifted past his ear.

'The tide has turned.'

Alyce stopped unexpectedly as if she had had a sudden change of mind. Luis would have bumped into her except for her brother's restraining tug backwards.

'Let us sit here.' A stone bench was almost hidden at the back of an arbour, the latter's construction difficult to distinguish in the gloom. She placed the lantern on the path a little distance away. Immediately, insects lured by the unseasonal warmth of the day danced and died in its flame. Luis watched them as a stifled groan escaped his lips. He bent forward and held his head in his hands. A sharp clap on his back made him start.

'The first thing we must do to see if your plan is feasible is to taste your wine,' announced Rufus cheerfully.

'Yes,' added Alyce, 'and then Father would need to introduce his fellow burgesses to it.'

Luis, sandwiched between brother and sister on the bench, looked up from one to the other and forced himself to concentrate.

'I do not have any wine with me.'

Rufus chuckled, 'We are not expecting a barrel but surely you have a skin for your own consumption?'

'I do not drink wine.'

'You do not drink your own wine?'

'I do not.'

Rufus was aghast.

'Do I understand you correctly? You do not drink your own wine?'

'I do not drink my own wine.'

'Why?'

Luis remained silent, his elbows still on his thighs, his spinning head cradled in his hands. Rufus continued, 'How strange! How can you assess its quality?'

'I taste it but do not swallow.'

'You will have a difficult task persuading people to buy your wine if they have not tasted it.' Rufus pointed out logically. 'Does Father know you have not brought any wine with you?'

'No, we had not begun to discuss my proposal,' replied Luis, his voice low and muffled.

His companion thought about this, torn between disbelief that Gharsia had not thought to bring any wine with him and his own increasing desire to help. He looked across their visitor's back to Alyce who was staring intently at the back of the stranger's head.

'Alyce, how do you think we should proceed?' Startled, his sister did not answer at first. Instead she moved her hands from where they rested in her lap and firmly sat on them.

'Mister Gharsia must speak to Father, but I believe a good place to start would be to clarify the customs regulations so he can assess the cost of importing enough wine for potential buyers to taste.'

'Yes, he needs to talk to the Customer of Bridgwater,' agreed Rufus. He patted Luis on the back, 'Do you feel any better?'

Luis shook his head and at once regretted the movement.

Alyce met her brother's eyes. He smiled ruefully and then addressed Luis.

'I think the best thing is for me to take you back to the Swan. Alyce will give your apologies to our father.' Rufus levered his companion off the bench and then turned to check he had his sister's approval. She appeared preoccupied.

'Alyce?' He waited but she still seemed far away. 'Alyce,' he repeated loudly, 'I will take Luis back to the inn.'

'Yes, yes,' she replied, 'that is best. I will go and speak to Father.'

Long after she had watched the two young men retrace their steps, Alyce sat in the dark with her thoughts. She became aware of discomfort: the cold of the stone bench beneath her, the pressure of her weight on her hands, and the inadequacy of the light shawl as the incoming tide brought a dampness to the air. However, what made her most uncomfortable of all was her reaction to their visitor. She was horrified at herself. As he had leaned forward, his head in his hands, the light from the lantern had lit up his hair. Glossy and black as a raven's wing, she had felt an overwhelming urge to reach out and touch it.

◆   ◆   ◆

It was Thomas Weaver's favourite time of the day, the time when the household settled down to sleep. Agnes, who retired early once her duties had been performed, had left him alone in the winter parlour. Wax candles of the highest quality flickered in their brackets, a good light by which to read. Now he was more advanced in age he found it difficult to read in dim light, especially at night. The shutters were closed against the night and a warm fire shifted and sighed in the grate. Thomas unlocked the sturdy chest resting against the back wall and carefully lifted out his copy of the Great Bible.

Back in his chair by the fire, he studied the front page first, as he always did. The page showed King Henry sitting on his throne between Cranmer, the Archbishop of Canterbury, and the chief minister, Cromwell. The monarch was presenting each of them with a copy of the new Bible. Weaver shuddered as he reflected on the fate of Henry's powerful minister. Since Cromwell's downfall and execution, the king seemed to have changed his mind about reformist ideas. Although he knew he was safe in his own home, Thomas could not resist looking over his shoulder towards the shuttered window. It was two years since Parliament had passed an act restricting access to the Bible. It was only upper-class men and noble women who were allowed to read the new translation in the privacy of their homes.

Thomas felt the accustomed thrill as he turned the pages and saw the Word of God in English rather than Latin. Ever since he was a young man, exposed to the ideas of Luther, Zwingli, and Calvin through merchants from the continent, Thomas had embraced the new religious thinking. After twenty years of reading and reflecting, he was still uncertain of exactly what to believe but on one thing he was certain: the traditional teaching and practices of the Catholic Church needed to be questioned. He had welcomed Henry's break with Rome and the reforms of the 1530s, but, in the five years since Cromwell's death, the king had legislated and written against reformist thinking. There were terrible punishments for those who did not comply. The denial of the Catholic belief in transubstantiation led to the stake, the marriage of priests was banned, as was the taking of both the bread and the wine in the Eucharist by lay people.

A log creaked and broke in the hearth. All was quiet except for the occasional hoot of an owl. Thomas finished the chapter of St Luke's Gospel he was studying and thought about what he had read. He wished Alyce was with him so they could discuss its meaning. She often sat with him but tonight she had appeared distracted and, after announcing that Rufus had taken their guest back to the inn, she had excused herself and retired to bed. He must remember to speak to her tomorrow before he forgot his thoughts. His mind wandered, now focused on his daughter. His Alyce, with her incisive mind, who debated so well, had been his companion for so long that he dreaded the time when she might not be there. However, as each year passed and no suitors appeared, he became more confident that she might always be by his side.

From an early age, his elder daughter had soaked up learning and he had encouraged her, firmly in unison with Erasmus in the belief that women should be educated. Her logical mind was at odds with the prevalent thinking about the weaker sex while Richard, though equally quick-minded, was all emotion. He had embraced Protestant thinking most enthusiastically but to his father this seemed more by instinct than by detailed study. Thomas was thinking about this when the parlour door was pushed open. He jumped.

'Rufus, you startled me!'

'Sorry, Father, I thought you would be expecting me to come to you once I had returned.'

'Yes, yes. Have you delivered Gharsia safely to the Swan?'

'Yes.'

'How is he?'

Rufus smiled.

'Feeling very sorry for himself.'

His father looked worried, a small frown between his eyes.

'I had no idea the cyder would affect him so.'

'It is because he does not drink alcohol.'

Thomas thought about this.

'He drank a glass of wine with me when he arrived.'

'Well, I think he is unused to alcohol.'

'How does he manage at the inn?'

'He would have to drink gallons of their stuff. It's like gnat's piss.'

'That is your opinion, Richard. Many find it to their liking.'

His son grimaced and changed the subject.

'Father, did Alyce tell you Gharsia has none of his wine with him?'

'No, she just explained that you had taken him back to his lodgings.'

'Do you not think it strange that he has no wine?' asked Rufus. 'Potential buyers will need to taste it if he is to have any chance of doing business.'

'I agree, but perhaps he is not ready to bring a tun with him. If the journey has been long the wine will not be at its best in a skin.'

'True.'

'What arrangements have you made with Gharsia, Richard?'

Rufus had long noticed that his father would often use his Christian name when discussing business.

'I plan to collect him from the inn tomorrow morning and take him to see John Persone, the customer, if he is home, to talk about import duties. It will do no harm to introduce him to some people of influence. Then I thought I would bring him back here for dinner. I find him an intriguing fellow.'

Thomas looked at his son with affection and knew what was coming next. Rufus continued, 'I also thought, that with your permission, I would invite him to lodge with us. At the moment he is unable to acquire a private chamber at the Swan.'

'Let us not rush. We will see how tomorrow goes.'

'I agree. I wish you a good night, Father.' Rufus grinned, already sure Thomas would acquiesce and allow their visitor to reside with them. He pushed himself up in one energetic movement from where he had been squatting in front of the fire and left the room with a spring in his step.

S E V E N T E E N

~

Everything was grey. It was raining fine rain which fell gently but still soaked him. When Luis had woken and miserably studied the low brooding cloud, he had wondered where the sunshine of the previous day had gone. Now he was perched on the corner of the mounting stone opposite the Swan's carriage entrance, watching the water run off the lead roof of the church. Already thoroughly damp, it seemed pointless to return indoors and wait there for the merchant's son who was late; very late by Luis's estimation. He was feeling increasingly grumpy as each minute passed, yet he did not remind himself that it was his choice to be outside in the fresh air rather than wait in the public room of the inn.

'Good day, Mister Gharsia,' a lively voice greeted him. Richard Weaver approached, his usual benign expression bringing cheerfulness to the dull day. 'Why are you waiting in the rain?' The glowering look he received as a reply made the Englishman momentarily stop in his tracks, but just for an instant. Weaver was not one to be discouraged by such a reception.

'I hope I have not caused you to be here long. I am hopeless. I set out in good time but have stopped to greet so many people on my way.' Richard was before Luis now, a look of such genuine concern on his face that Luis felt it was he who was discourteous and at fault for feeling out of sorts. He rose slowly from the mounting block and took Weaver's offered hand. The innkeeper, overseeing a meat delivery at the other end of the yard, watched with interest as the dark stranger was greeted by the son of one of the leading burgesses of the town and then accompanied him towards the church.

Luis was pleased that his companion walked quickly and felt his mood lighten with each step. They took a shortcut through the churchyard, crossed over St Mary's Street in order to join Friarn Street which would lead them to their destination beyond Bridgwater's old defences. As soon as they started to walk, Richard again bombarded Luis with questions, enquiring about how he had been since they had separated the previous evening. When his inquisitor ran out of things to ask Luis, he changed to a running commentary about the route.

'We cross now,' he indicated as a plank bridge came into view, straddling the town ditch. 'It is fed here by springs as the tide does not reach this far,' Richard explained.

Once across the bridge they were in the grounds of the Friary. Far ahead, Luis could see a handsome stone house and next to it what had once been a fine church, but was now in a state of disintegration. The roof was gone, as were large sections of the walls.

'What happened here, Master Weaver?' he asked turning to Richard who had noticed the lightening of his companion's mood and judged the time to be appropriate to say, 'Please call me Rufus, it is shorter!' After all they were of an age and Richard Weaver was not a young man who always followed the conventions of his elders. He waited as he realised Gharsia was not a man to be rushed and watched the closed face as the Spaniard surveyed the view. A recollection of his own intoxicated request surfaced in Luis's mind and if he had been a man to show emotion he would have winced, but all Richard saw was a nod of acceptance before his companion asked again, 'What did happen here?'

'The Friary was closed about seven years ago and the friars sent on their way.'

Luis looked puzzled so Rufus explained.

'After King Henry broke away from the Church of Rome and made himself Head of the Church in England he decided to shut down the monasteries. The smaller ones like this one were the first to go and then all the larger ones went a couple of years later.'

'Why?'

Rufus shrugged, 'The monasteries had become rich, and the monks lazy. They no longer took their vows seriously.'

'All of the monks in the country?'

'Yes. And all of the nuns and friars.'

'Do you not find that difficult to believe?'

Rufus who supported the action of the King wholeheartedly did not expect to be questioned so and replied somewhat brusquely.

'That is what was found. Cromwell, the King's minister, sent out his men to tour the religious houses and they found they were corrupt. Parliament passed two acts of dissolution.'

'What happened to the brothers from this friary?'

'There were only eight here in 1538. They were evicted.'

'Were they given any money to live?'

'No, I believe not, although some monks from other monasteries were.'

Luis, brought up within the culture of Islam with a strong emphasis on charity as well as being exposed to Roman Catholicism, was troubled by this.

'In my experience the monasteries help the sick and the poor, provide shelter for travellers, and offer prayers for the souls of the dead. They are very important.'

'No, they were rotten here.'

Luis would not accept this answer.

'Do all English people think this to be true?'

Rufus was not so quick to reply this time. He thought for a moment before he stated, 'There was a rebellion in the North but it was suppressed.' He lowered his voice, 'It is not wise to go against the King.'

This Luis could understand. They walked through the grounds towards the house. To his left, across the brook which formed part of the town's defences, he could see extensive gardens.

'This is a very big area of land.'

'Yes, it is about six acres.'

'Who took all the buildings and the land?'

'The King did.'

Luis mulled this over.

'I understand better now.'

Rufus was defensive.

'You will find it difficult perhaps to fully understand as the Church in France answers to the Pope. You will see matters as a Roman Catholic.' He stared penetratingly at his companion as he delivered the last sentence which could have been taken as a question. He was quick to notice that the Spaniard immediately became very interested in the orchards where the blossom made a delightful display.

'If the rain continues the blossom will rot and the harvest will fail,' observed Luis.

Rufus had forgotten the young man was a farmer.

'Do not worry, Luis. You are in England. The sun will shine again soon. It will be fine by this afternoon. In fact, it has virtually stopped raining now.'

Luis continued to distract Weaver.

'Rufus, you said we are going to see the chief of the customs officers.'

'Yes, he lives in that grand dwelling. It is said he rents it for two shillings a year.'

'Will he see us without an appointment?'

'We will see. I want this to be an informal visit.'

Rufus, with a confidence which came from being the son of one of the most influential merchants of the region, knocked loudly on John Persone's door. The diminutive housekeeper who answered explained that her master had just that moment left to visit his garden. It had stopped raining but was still very overcast with low cloud. Luis doubted Rufus was correct about the sun.

'Come on, Luis,' ordered Rufus as he led the way round the house to an entrance to the orchard and gardens. 'It is excellent that he is at leisure. It will be to our benefit.' He looked at Luis and put himself in the customer's shoes of seeing the Morian for the first time. He grinned a wide mischievous grin. 'Luis, you must be as charming as you possibly can.'

◆   ◆   ◆

The crunch of footsteps on the gravel path alerted John Persone to the fact that his peace was soon be shattered. He had escaped to his garden once the rain had stopped and now, as the clouds started to lift, he was looking forward to some solitary time. The wet weather, interspersed with bouts of sunshine, had made his plants grow apace and weeds were emerging everywhere. While the hard work was the domain of the gardener, the Customer of Bridgwater enjoyed the relaxing activity of wandering among his newly grassed and gravelled paths, removing those weeds that had the temerity to spoil the meticulously neat planting. He straightened, placing a hand in the small of his back to ease the action and watched the gangly figure of Richard Weaver approach with a stranger by his side.

Thomas Weaver's son always reminded Persone of a favourite puppy he had once owned as a younger man. Everything about Richard indicated energy and enthusiasm, from his over large hands and feet to the bounce of his gait. As usual, there was a wide smile on his face as he came towards the customs official.

'Good morning, Mister Persone.' The customer returned the greeting and waited for Weaver to state his business, while studying his companion with interest.

Dressed soberly, the cut of his clothes hinted at his continental origins, and the darker colouring and features of an Arab led Persone to correctly assume the man came from Spain. In contrast to Weaver, there was an air of stillness about him, an aloofness which the chief customs officer found disconcerting, accustomed as he was to sycophancy.

'Allow me to introduce my friend, Luis Gharsia.'

Luis moved forward, slightly thrown off balance by Richard's use of the term "friend" after such a short acquaintance. Rufus continued to talk, enquiring about Persone's health. The latter was keen to accelerate the conversation so he could return to his solitude.

'What brings you out to the Friary this morning?'

Rufus replied, 'We were hoping you would answer a couple of queries we have.'

Persone had enough experience in his official capacity to realise that what appeared to be a few questions invariably led to a lengthier conversation.

'Follow me,' he said as he led the young men through a gap in the hedge to another section of the garden. While they walked he was heartened to see Gharsia studying the area.

'You are pleased by what you see, Mister Gharsia?'

'Yes, it is very. . .' the Spaniard paused to think, 'ordered.'

Persone nodded in satisfaction.

'You should see it later in the year when the roses, lavender, and honeysuckle are out. Then there are the marigolds and the gillyflowers. It is full of colour.' They had reached a bench in an alcove created by the trimming of a thick yew hedge, so well established that it had obviously existed in the time of the friars. 'Please sit,' he invited, 'what do you want to know?'

Rufus had already decided what he was going to say.

'My friend Gharsia is a producer in the Pays d'Oc and has a mind to export his wine. What does he need to know?' He was aware that much of what Persone would say he already knew, but he felt it would be better for Luis to hear it from the customer. The official settled comfortably on the bench and began.

'First of all, any wine exported from Bordèu must be in an English ship.'

'Why?' Gharsia looked at him intently. Now he was closer, Persone could see that his visitor had very dark eyes set deeply in a badly scarred face.

'It is the law. The King's father passed the Navigation Act way back in the very first year of his reign. It was renewed five years ago. All goods transported to England must be in English ships.'

Rufus shot Luis a sideways glance to see his reaction but his face gave nothing away as he went on to ask, 'What duties would I need to pay?' Luis included both men in the question and saw a similar reaction which would have been imperceptible to most observers, but Hernando Gharsia had trained his grandson to read people carefully. Their survival had depended upon it. Now he noticed an unwillingness to meet his gaze. Persone answered.

'You will need to pay above three shillings on each tun of wine.'

Luis, whose grasp of English coinage was not as good as he wished, focused on the word "above" rather than the amount.

'Why do you say "above"?'

Persone studied the recently raked gravel beneath his feet.

'Because three shillings is what an English merchant would pay. As an alien you would pay more.'

Luis stared at the customs official.

'This makes it harder for a stranger to make a profit.'

'Yes,' agreed Persone. 'Also, just this year, the Government reissued the *Book of Rates*.'

'What is that?'

'It fixes the prices of goods for assessing duties. You cannot choose the price at which to sell your wine.'

'This is not good.'

Persone shrugged.

'It is how it is. Our merchants control the importation of wine.'

There was silence as Luis digested what he had been told. He watched the clouds scud past, a small patch of perfect blue sky appeared, heralding the fine day Rufus had promised.

'This is not good,' he repeated as he turned to the latter who responded with a small sympathetic smile.

The customer had not finished.

'You must not break the rules,' he insisted. 'There are harsh penalties for those who smuggle. I have a strong team with a controller, searchers, and surveyors as well as the tide-waiters down at Combwich.'

'Combwich?' queried Luis.

'A small harbour on the river, just a short distance downstream. Goods being brought up the Parrett can be off loaded there before ships reach us,' explained Rufus.

'I would never break the law,' Luis retorted. He was offended by the warning and decided it was time to leave. There was no purpose in staying longer. However, the customs official, now that his peaceful morning had been interrupted, seemed happy to chat and turned the conversation back to the subject of his garden.

It was some time later when Persone asked, 'Master Weaver, how does your father? He did not wish to accompany you today?'

'No Sir, he is otherwise engaged. Did you not know he is taking delivery of some millstones this morning?'

The customer shook his head. In practice, as with most officials in his position, he drew his salary and employed a deputy to do much of the day to day administration of the port. Rufus continued for Luis's benefit.

'There is much profit in importing grinding stones. The best come from Swansea and it is but a short journey to transport them from Bristol.'

This time Persone nodded in agreement.

'The trade is increasing at the moment and should continue to do well. We all need to eat bread.' He rose from the bench followed immediately by his two visitors; 'Can I offer you some refreshment?' Rufus was tempted to return to the house to take some ale but one glance at Luis made him change his mind.

'Thank you kindly, but we are expected to return home in time for dinner. You have been most helpful,' he said as he and Luis took their leave.

The silence was heavy between them as they walked. Luis, preoccupied as he was by the obstacles Persone had placed before him, felt disheartened whilst Rufus was thinking about his dinner with anticipation. They had reached the town ditch when Luis stated: 'Between the administrators of Bordèu and the merchants of England, there is little room for the vintners of Caors.'

'It appears so, but there may be a way.'

'How?'

'You need to find a partner in England,' Rufus suggested as he stopped in the centre of the plank bridge and turned towards Luis. 'Ideally someone here in Bridgwater.'

'Do you think your father might be interested?'

'I do not know.'

'He would know many merchants.' It was not so much a question as a statement but Rufus replied, 'Of course he could introduce you to them if he was unable to back you.'

'Do you think I will be successful?'

'I hope so.'

'If not, I will travel to Bristol. It is a bigger port, is it not?'

'Yes, but let us see what comes of your plans here.'

They started walking. The clouds had further dispersed; there was more blue sky and sunlight streamed through the remnants of the morning's gloom.

'Good,' said Luis almost to himself as they increased their pace. He looked around once they had made their way down Friarn Street as, instead of continuing to the inn, Rufus turned in the opposite direction.

'We are going home for dinner.'

'I am invited for dinner?'

'Yes.'

'That is most kind, but you are too hospitable. I ate with you yesterday.'

'You must come as Meg demanded that you be invited,' grinned Rufus, 'and my little sister will be very disappointed if she does not see the giant again!'

Luis's face broke into a smile.

'In that case, I cannot refuse.'

E I G H T E E N

~

Dinner was over. Luis sat awkwardly on the chest he was sharing with Rufus and wondered how soon was polite to take his leave. It was past noon and he had not yet prayed. The Weaver family showed no sign of urgency to continue with the business of the day but relaxed in the presence of a guest. Rufus had reported on the visit to Persone and Thomas had listened without any indication that he was interested in supporting Luis's venture. Now conversation had flagged and attention turned to the small child sitting cross-legged on the rushes, a horn-book in her hand. Luis could clearly see the alphabet printed in black beneath the sheet of transparent horn, and the little girl had been quietly mouthing the sounds whilst the adults had talked.

'Luis,' Rufus joked. 'You should listen carefully.'

A faint colour washed over Luis's face as he had been doing just that. Regretting his customary lack of witty repartee he nodded and smiled at Meg. Emboldened, she rose, her cumbersome skirts preventing any quick movement, and came towards him. She stopped a short distance away and stretched out her arm to give him the book.

'Thank you.' He studied the letters; Rufus leaned over from his side of the chest.

'A, B, C,' he made the sounds slowly, a chuckle in his voice while his sister studied Luis with her serious blue eyes.

'A, B, C,' their visitor repeated back dutifully, concentrating to achieve correct annunciation. The child continued to stand perfectly still, her feet planted firmly apart, and watch him. Rufus had reached the middle of the alphabet when Meg spoke in little more than a whisper.

'Why is your face like that?'

Her brother stopped, the pronunciation of the fourteenth letter on his lips. Thomas studied his feet whilst Alyce, very aware of the silence which followed her sister's question, held her breath until their guest replied, his eyes fixed on the small person before him.

'When I was about your age a bad man did this,' Luis pointed to the old long scar that disfigured the right hand side of his face, 'and this one is quite new.' Alyce looked at the smaller scar on his left cheek, just under his eye. Sensing her gaze, the young man lifted his eyes from Meg and Alyce felt he was speaking to her alone.

'One night, last year, I was attacked as I walked home late from the university. Three itinerants who had come up with traders from Toulon caused trouble because of who I am.' He paused. There was such sadness in his black eyes that Alyce wanted to reach across the room and touch him. He shrugged and continued, 'The King had allowed his allies to use the port over the winter. The people of the town had to pack up their belongings and hand their homes over to pirates from North Africa for a few months. You can imagine it caused great resentment. We were told they even set up a slave market in the town square.' She watched him shrug his shoulders again, all the while holding her gaze.

'Why did your king do that?' she asked.

'So the Muslim fleet could prepare to attack the Spanish and Italian coasts. Conflict between France and the Spanish Habsburgs never ends.'

'It has nothing to do with you,' she commented quietly, masking how incensed she was on his behalf.

'True, but they were drunk. The sight of me inflamed their hostility.'

She shook her head in exasperation.

'You were seriously hurt?'

Another shrug; he lifted his hand to his left cheek and replied, 'One well aimed punch did this, and I was very sore and bruised.' He did not add that his three assailants had suffered considerably as he had fought furiously, fuelled by anger of such strength that he had surprised himself. 'My grandfather sorted me out. He is a very good physician. He has great pride in his stitches.'

Rufus, aware that his sister and Gharsia seemed to be in their own private world of communication, decided to intervene at this point. He was about to speak when his friend did it for him. Luis dragged himself away from the sympathy obvious on Alyce's pale face and addressed Meg.

'My grandfather does very tiny, neat stitches, although now he needs to wear his spectacles.' An unexpected wave of affection for his grandfather caused Luis's face to soften as he remembered Hernando, his eyes enlarged behind the lenses encased in leather, his expression a cross between irritation and concern as he expertly drew the catgut through his grandson's open cheek. Luis smiled and mimicked the action of sewing for Meg.

Questions buzzed as usual in Rufus's head; he had learnt more personal information about their visitor in the last few minutes than in all his other questioning.

'You were at the university?'

'Yes.'

Rufus took an educated guess.

'You were a student?'

'Yes.'

'Which discipline?'

'Law.'

This was good. Rufus felt he was making progress although Gharsia seemed to have reverted to his taciturn self.

'You said your grandfather is a surgeon.'

'Yes.'

'Does he teach at the university?'

'Yes, but not so much now as he is advanced in years.'

'May I ask how you came to live in the Pays d'Oc?'

'Is it so obvious I do not belong there?' Luis asked sharply, annoyed by too many questions. Thomas interceded. 'Please excuse my son. He does not mean to pry but has a great interest in all our visitors.'

Their guest acknowledged the words and studied each member of the Weaver family in turn. Thomas Weaver managed to look both apologetic and authoritarian. His son rose from the chest and stood in front of the fire, one hand resting on the mantel, eager to hear more. Luis found himself drawn again to Alyce, sitting to the side of the fireplace, her cool green eyes watching him. The child, now bored with the conversation, had abandoned her horn-book to Luis and returned to her place on the floor to play with her doll. He held the book by its handle and slowly rotated it as he spoke.

'I was born in Valencia but left with my grandfather when I was very small. We travelled to Caors so that he could take up a position at the university.' That was all he was planning to say but Alyce asked, 'Was it not hard for you in Caors as the King of France was your country's enemy?'

Luis thought carefully before he answered, 'I do not remember it being hard.' If he had known Alyce better or if he had been a different person he might have added, 'because Ysabel protected us' but he did not. Instead he said, 'The Pays d'Oc is very different from northern France. We do not even speak the same language.'

Alyce did not believe him. She noted his closed expression and chewed her lip, a habit indicating she was troubled, but she was unable to proceed further as Thomas had a question.

'How have you used your studies, Mister Gharsia?'

'I assist one of my teachers, Martin Ebrart, in his law practice.'

'And you have time to make wine?'

'I do not have any land yet,' said the young vintner solemnly with decided emphasis on the last word. 'At the moment I work with Madame Bernade's brother, as I have done since I was fifteen, but I plan to have my own vineyard.' Luis leaned forward on the chest as he spoke more earnestly. 'It was through my studies that I discovered that the restrictions on our wine export are enshrined in tradition not law.'

'So that is why you were the one to come,' suggested Rufus.

'Yes.'

Rufus removed his arm from its resting place on the mantel and turned to face Thomas. 'Father, I feel Luis needs more time to establish connections here. He cannot be successful without an English partner.'

Luis looked from father to son, curious to hear what was to come next. Thomas ran his hand through his thin coppery hair and explained, 'I am not sure how much of a contribution I can make. Most of my activity centres on the export of our Somerset cloth. Tauntons, serges, and kerseys are highly prized. I have an interest in a ship which takes them to Bordèu so there is a chance that I can help you with transport, but you will need other backers.'

'I would be appreciative of any assistance, Sir.'

Thomas looked long and hard at his visitor whose face clearly showed his pleasure at the possibility of the Englishman's help. Alyce and Rufus saw it too and were struck by how enigmatic their guest was, veering from a reserve which left his expression inscrutable to obvious joy at their father's words. Rufus cautioned, 'Do not get too excited yet, Luis. You only have the possibility of transport. You need to establish a market first. Do not put the cart before the horse!'

Pleased that he could respond, Luis retorted immediately, 'I know, one swallow does not make a summer.'

Alyce's serene face lit up as she exclaimed, 'The *Adagia*!'

'Yes,' Luis smiled back.

Father and son spoke together. 'You read Erasmus?'

'Yes.'

'What else have you read of his?' demanded Rufus.

'*In Praise of Folly*, *Julius Exclusus*, and, obviously, the *Adagia*.'

'You have not read his *Paraphrases*?' asked Thomas.

Luis, confused by the construction of the sentence and unsure whether he should answer yes or no, just shook his head.

'You must, you must, Mister Gharsia.' Thomas made a decision. The prospect of a future of many evenings of discussion stretched before him and provided the impetus Rufus wanted. 'My son tells me that your accommodation at the Swan is not ideal. We would be very happy for you to reside with us while you are in Bridgwater. It may take some time to find men interested in your scheme, and I know that I speak for my children as well as myself when I say we will enjoy the stimulation of your company.'

◆   ◆   ◆

Rufus had accompanied Luis back to the Swan to collect his belongings, and fortunately, once they had reached the inn, the Englishman had opted to stay in the public room to drink ale with the landlord. Relieved, Luis hurried to his sleeping chamber which, in the still of the early afternoon, was empty. At his request, the landlord's wife, her stout figure bulging in her stained work gown, brought him water for washing. He cleared his mind of the excitement bubbling within him and prayed fervently. Then he grabbed his bag, with Ysabel's gift safely inside, and joined Rufus, who was just finishing his jug of ale.

They ambled back to the house enjoying the spring sunshine. Luis acknowledged that his companion had been correct: the wet dismal morning had been replaced by a fine afternoon. Fluffy white clouds sailed sedately across a pale blue sky, driven by a light breeze. Luis breathed deeply, the tang of the sea touched his tongue and he experienced a moment of pure contentment. The future was full of potential. He had been welcomed into the home of Ysabel's contact and there was already the hint that Weaver would help him.

'Luis, are you listening to me?'

He had not realised he had lost concentration.

'Yes,' he replied automatically.

Rufus did not look too sure.

'I was saying that I much prefer to drink at the George rather than the Swan.'

'Why?'

'Because I much prefer the ale at the George. I will take you there soon.' Rufus noted the lack of enthusiasm on Luis's part. 'Of course, you do not drink alcohol.'

Luis stopped in his tracks.

'I do, but I do not wish to make a fool of myself by becoming intoxicated.' Even to his own ears he sounded priggish, so he took a chance, hoping he was a good judge of character; 'I have promised my grandfather that I will never be drunk.'

Rufus fitted another piece of the puzzle together in his mind. He was keen to ask more but realised it was not the time for further questioning. Knowing Gharsia would soon become uncommunicative, he changed the subject.

'Luis?'

'Yes.'

'I think you need more practice at negotiation.'

'Why?'

'When my father suggested that he may be able to help you with transport, your face gave you away.'

'How?'

'Your expression—it showed how pleased you were. It was so obvious. You must not let your face reveal what you feel when you are discussing business.'

'I was not aware I did this.'

'You did,' Rufus answered, 'but it should not be too difficult to work at it. After all, you are very good at presenting a closed face when I ask you questions.' He wondered whether he had gone too far such that Luis would be offended, but his new friend only said, 'Do I?'

Rufus clapped him on the back and replied with a grin.

'Yes, you do!' The sun highlighted his hair, showing a vibrant mix of copper, auburn, and deep russet, while his smile was wide and his eyes twinkled. For a moment Luis envied him the easy familiarity and his absolute confidence in his place in his world and replied, 'You speak very plainly, Sir!'

The Englishman, taken aback at the change of tone, admitted with his usual openness, 'Yes, I do,' and looked at Luis intently, noting the crease of a frown between his brows.

'What gives you the right?'

Nonplussed, the smile faded from Rufus's face but he continued to meet Luis's eyes. 'Because last night when you were a sorry excuse of a man I saw you back to the inn.' Rufus's voice rose as he asserted himself, 'And left to your own devices, you could have fallen foul of any vagabond.'

There was a pause before Luis threw back his head and laughed, a deep throaty laugh followed by one word.

'True.'

◆   ◆   ◆

The upper floor of the Weavers' house was silent in the late afternoon. Luis followed Alyce's tall, slender figure as she led him to the guest chamber, her soft leather slippers making no sound on the uneven boards which were smooth and shiny from generations of Weaver feet. This part of the merchant's house had not been modernised, and the family sleeping quarters consisted of a series of passage rooms where curtained beds provided privacy. The ceiling was so low by the windows that he needed to walk down the centre behind his hostess. They passed three beds before she stopped at a fourth, hidden behind a screen.

'This is where our visitors may sleep, Mister Gharsia.' Her voice was low and melodious with the intonation Luis now realised was of the area. He looked at the bed, similar to the others he had passed, and could see the richly embroidered curtains, bedspread, and valance. The mattress appeared deep and promised a good night's sleep. Alyce rested a hand on one of the carved posts and smiled up at him.

'The beds are quite new,' she moved her hand to the bedspread and added, 'Father always insists on the best feathers.'

'It looks very comfortable, especially after the straw at the inn.'

She nodded and pointed to the press where he could store his possessions.

'I hope there is enough space here.'

'Thank you.' Luis removed his bag from his shoulder and placed it beside the press. He was so close to her that Alyce felt herself gabbling, 'I think the bed might be a little short but it is wide enough for you to stretch out.'

'Do not worry. It is perfect, Mistress Weaver.'

She could not think of what to say next. There was an uneasy pause before she said, 'Please may I ask how you come to speak such perfect French? You said that the language in the Pays d'Oc is different?'

'I needed it for my law degree. A few years ago King François issued an ordinance which ruled that French rather than Latin had to be used in all legal documents. My tutors were still very cross about it when I started my studies. We all have to be very proficient in French.'

'I see.'

'Mistress Weaver, your family speaks excellent French. Why is that so?'

An air of melancholy settled on her.

'My mother was French. My father took the opportunity of better relations with France after the Field of the Cloth of Gold. He travelled to Calais and then into Picardy to trade. By the time war broke out two years later, my mother had become an English housewife and I was on the way.'

'Your mother has quite recently died?' Luis said quietly, thinking of Meg's age.

'No,' replied Alyce, realising his assumption, 'Meg is the child of my father's second wife, Margaret Mercer. She died when Meg was born. My mother died when I was fifteen and Rufus, fourteen. We had two younger brothers but they died young.' She looked at him, unshed tears glistened in her eyes and she brushed them away brusquely. 'I try not to think on it. It was a long time ago.' She gave a little shake and Luis found himself saying, 'My mother is dead.' Words which he had never had to utter as there had never been the need, until now. 'She died when I was a little boy.'

'When you left Valencia?'

'Yes.'

'Do you have a memory of her?'

'Sometimes I think I do. Other times I do not know. I cannot recall her face but there is something . . . her essence perhaps?' He was going to say more but experienced the rising panic that he had tried so hard to bury since that terrible day. Alyce saw the pain in his eyes. She did not speak but rested her hand on his sleeve, a gesture of such warmth that it reminded him of Ysabel and his grandfather. Without thinking, Luis spoke in Occitan.

'I am very pleased to accept your father's hospitality.'

~

Luis lay on his back, star-shaped, enjoying the first moments of waking. He stretched his arms and wriggled his toes, luxuriating in the bed's comfort. His head rested on a plump feather pillow, linen sheets were soft against his skin, protecting him from the scratchy woollen blankets, and the deep feather mattress beneath him rested on firm new ropes. Life was good. He had been with the Weavers for over two weeks, and with each passing day his happiness had increased. Thomas had introduced him to several men of influence who had listened attentively to his proposed enterprise, and Luis felt that he had had enough indication that a return visit next year, with some wine, would be worthwhile. His relationship with Rufus had settled into one of genial sparring over the asking and answering of questions, underneath which a true affection was developing, and little Meg followed him around at every opportunity. Then there was Alyce. He found himself looking for her whenever he entered a room. With a sigh, Luis threw back the covers and parted the curtains. He did not want to go home yet. There was no sign that he had outstayed his welcome and, by his calculations, he had at least another month before he needed to look for a passage to Bordèu.

There was a basin of water still warm on the chest. Mary must have left it before she helped Agnes to organise the family breakfast. He washed, said his prayers, and afterwards made ready to go downstairs. The final action, which was so unlike him, was to check his reflection in the burnished metal mirror propped up behind the basin. A serious young man with dark, deep-set eyes looked back at him. Luis turned his head, first inspecting one side of his face and then the other. It was dim in the room and, although visible, his scars did not seem so obvious. He laughed at himself; he would never be a pretty man even without the scars. There was his beaked nose as well as his gaunt cheeks and thin mouth. He smiled ruefully and spoke to the mirror, 'At least you do not have black teeth, Gharsia,' and then added, 'thank you, Grandfather,' acknowledging the result of Hernando's insistence on personal hygiene.

There was an air of expectation in the parlour. It was May Day, a day for celebration when the cares of winter could be finally thrown off and the promise of summer welcomed. Thomas and Rufus had already broken their fast; the aroma of freshly baked bread greeted Luis as he wished them a good morning. He pulled up a stool and helped himself to a chunk. Rufus looked at his friend over the rim of his tankard and, after he had swallowed the ale, said, 'Are you ready for today's festivities?'

'I am.'

'Excellent.'

At that moment Alyce entered the room with an excited Meg in tow. She was dressed in the finest wool, for the weather was still chilly despite the bursts of sunshine. The soft green fabric hung elegantly as she crossed the floor; the gown's low square neckline was filled with a sheer linen partlet in the same hue, which emphasised the colour of her eyes. Luis could smell the perfume she used; the delicious scent of roses wafted on the air as she took the stool next to him. Meg, who had wanted to sit beside their guest, stamped her feet and threatened to misbehave so Luis swept her up and passed her across the table to her brother.

'That child is too indulged,' commented Thomas who knew it to be true, yet grief had made him soften when it came to the upbringing of his fifth child.

'Do not worry, Father. We will keep her in line,' replied Rufus as he tickled the little girl on his knee. Meg chortled, pleasure at her unorthodox arrival at the table shining in her eyes. Her brother turned his attention to Alyce.

'You look particularly fetching this morning, dear Sister.'

She shot him a warning glance, 'It is May Day!'

'Of course. Did you creep out to the garden at dawn and wash your face in the magic May dew?'

'Don't be stupid. I am not a young girl.'

'I agree,' Rufus said. 'But you might want to rid yourself of those freckles.'

'I am quite happy with my freckles, thank you. I only have a few,' she retorted. 'Which is more than I can say for you.'

'Touché.' Her brother laughed. She was right. Alyce had a smattering of the small light-brown spots across her nose whilst Rufus's face was covered with them.

'Come children, it is too early for banter and we must finish our breakfast so we are not late for church.' Thomas had chosen his words carefully with inflection on the word children and, despite being a more relaxed parent with Meg, his word was final. The family did what he said.

The church, decorated with fresh greenery, was packed. The Weavers felt uplifted by the use of the English litany instead of the Latin, although several of the congregation muttered their disquiet once they were safely returned to their homes. To Luis the interior was sterile. It had been stripped of the images of the saints and even the newly cut boughs could not mask its nakedness. At home he understood the Latin although, following Hernando's teaching, he only paid lip-service to most of the service, but over the years he had found that he enjoyed the familiarity of the prayers. Now the English words jarred. This was a different Christianity to the one he knew and he found it alien. He watched the dust particles dance in the beams of light streaming through the windows and wished that, like Meg, he had been allowed to stay in the house with Agnes.

Once the service was over, people spilled out into the churchyard. There was a noisy buzz as greetings were exchanged and everyone made their way to the Church House on the High Street. It was time for the occasion of the church ale and all its jollity. The parishioners of Bridgwater had acquired their own building for fund-raising activities five years previously and it was still a novelty to enjoy themselves away from the disapproving eyes of the church authorities. Luis saw a solid house; the door to the downstairs kitchen was open and he could hear music from the upper storey. He turned to Alyce.

'What happens now?'

'Fresh ale has been brewed and cakes have been made especially for today. We pay for them and the money goes to the poor. We have always had a church ale to celebrate festivals. They are very popular, even more so since the king has abolished saints' days.' Rufus came up, flinging an arm around both of them.

'What do you want to do? There is bull baiting in the field outside the East Gate.'

Alyce shuddered. 'No thank you. Has Father been to collect Meg yet?'

'No, he is over there, talking still with John Hammond.'

'I think we should go and get her.'

Luis was only too happy to accompany Alyce as he did not want to drink until he became riotous, nor did he want to dance. Rufus shrugged, gave the ale barrels a last lingering glance, and followed them.

◆   ◆   ◆

They visited every attraction except the baiting, although the sound of that activity could be heard from across the field. Meg was surprisingly heavy and awkward on Luis's shoulders as she insisted on squirming round for a better view from her vantage point. He walked slowly, her fat little ankles firmly in his hands. They watched the maypole dancers plait the colourful ribbons and avoided the hobby-horses bounding through the crowds; they strolled amongst the stalls in the marketplace where Luis was thrilled to see dates, figs, and the exotic spices he recognised from home. They moved aside as a pie man pushed his way through the throng, his tray full of flavoursome wares. Rufus, indecisive for once, chose both gilt gingerbread and peppermint drops from the sweet-seller and shared them out. Buoyed with enthusiasm, he bought Meg a toy lamb made of white wool with tin horns and legs and then treated Alyce to a woven girdle, finished with a silky tassel. A stall selling leather attracted his attention and he was deep in conversation with the trader when he thought he heard his name called.

'Richard Weaver, is that you? Hello, Richard Weaver.'

He turned, peering into the crowd, and his heart sank as he saw a familiar figure coming towards him.

'Cousin, it is you!'

'Good day, Cousin Matthew,' Rufus began, but before he could get another word out, the man before him rushed on, speaking very quickly.

'Richard, Richard, I am glad I have found you. I have been to the house but there was no answer. All must be at the fair.' Matthew Blake's face was flushed with exertion; his straw-coloured thatch of hair rose up from a high forehead giving him a permanently startled look. His large grey eyes darted from side to side as he spoke. 'Who is that man with your sisters?'

'Luis Gharsia.'

'I do not know him.'

'He is a recent acquaintance. He is residing with us.'

'He is in the guest chamber?' Blake looked put out. 'I had planned to stay.'

'We were not expecting you.'

'I did not know I could come until the last minute. Bishop Bush did not need me and understood my wish to visit my family.' Matthew's eyes darted back to where Luis and Alyce had stopped by a stall selling brightly painted ceramic jugs. He watched as the young man, in response to Meg's request, carefully lifted the child from his shoulders so she could see the jugs more clearly. The little girl slipped her hand in his, pointing to the jugs. Alyce picked one up for closer inspection and all three of them seemed to study the jug with great interest.

'He is an Arab,' Matthew said, pointing out the obvious.

'Yes.'

'Is he Christian?'

Rufus's eyes held a challenge in them.

'He is as Catholic as you and me, Cousin.'

Matthew's eyes swivelled back to him, but the ambiguity of Rufus's words had been missed as Matthew's attention had already wandered elsewhere.

'Are you hungry, Richard?'

'I am always hungry,' laughed Rufus.

'I am in great need of sustenance after my journey.'

'Let us go to the Church House. We can find my father. He will be surprised to see you.'

Meg pulled at Luis's hand, her attention caught by a stray dog, and, as he turned, he saw a glimpse of Rufus weaving his way out of the marketplace accompanied by a stocky man dressed in clerical garb.

◆   ◆   ◆

'You are a long way from home, Mister Gharsia.' The large grey eyes assessed him openly after Thomas had introduced his cousin to his guest.

'I am, Canon Matthew,' agreed Luis, determined as ever not to reveal too much. He need not have been so wary. Matthew Blake's eyes soon dismissed him as of little interest and continued to skim around the room. It was a small gathering of about thirty in the Weavers' hall: fellow burgesses and their wives, local clergy, and, Luis noticed, John Persone. He had been introduced to those he had not yet met and had responded politely. Now he was tired of the effort of small talk in English and leaned against the panelling, a drink in his hand which he was making last all evening. He twirled the goblet slowly. Rufus had advised him that it was an informal gathering to celebrate the end of May Day and not the occasion to discuss business ventures, but his friend had added, with a wicked grin, that it did no harm to be seen.

A sense of disquiet seeped into Luis as he watched Canon Matthew Blake. Whenever the clergyman was talking his eyes continued to sweep the room as if he was searching for someone of greater importance whom he had missed. At first Luis found it amusing, but it did not take very long for him to realise that after each restless circuit, the large grey eyes returned to Alyce.

'How goes it?' Rufus was suddenly beside him.

'Who is that man?' Quite used to Luis not answering his questions, Rufus followed his friend's line of vision.

'He is the grandson of my grandmother's sister—our cousin.'

'He is a churchman?'

'Yes. Until the dissolution he was an Augustinian canon at the abbey in Bristol. Now he is attached to the new cathedral. Three years ago, Bristol was made a city and one of the canons, Paul Bush, was made bishop. Matthew has come to visit. He came by boat from Bristol and arrived this afternoon.'

Luis studied Blake as he effortlessly moved from group to group, greeting and being greeted with a smile.

'He appears an affable fellow.' It was a testament to their friendship that he could make such a comment to Rufus.

His companion agreed, 'Yes, very affable, but he talks too much for me. The man never draws breath.'

A small smile appeared on Luis's lips and he took a sip of wine as he watched Blake start a conversation with Burgess Wallys. He talked animatedly, his mobile face adding emphasis to his words while the set of his stocky body blocked anyone from joining them. Luis could not see Wallys's expression but he appeared not to be speaking. Eventually Alyce, the practised hostess, gently touched her cousin's arm and gave her father's friend the opportunity to rejoin his wife. With her unobtrusive presence, Alyce had been circulating amongst the guests, replenishing their goblets and handing around the plates of sweetmeats which Agnes had prepared earlier, before she too had been allowed to enjoy her own May Day celebrations.

'Rufus,' Luis leaned towards his friend, 'is it true that some clergymen in England have taken wives?'

'Some did. They followed the example of Martin Luther in Saxony, but it is illegal here since the Act of the Six Articles.'

'When did that become law?'

'Six years ago. They were read out in church. Anyone who had taken the vow of chastity was banned from marriage.'

Luis felt his disquiet lessen, although he still did not like the way Matthew Blake stood so close to Alyce when he spoke to her. Rufus continued, 'Even Cranmer was forced to put away his young wife. The Act was a setback for the reformists.'

'Cranmer?'

'The Archbishop of Canterbury. Surely you know that, Luis?'

'I did not.'

They stood side by side in silence; two young men bored in a room filled with the middle-aged. Rufus whispered, 'I hope they go home soon.'

Luis continued to watch Blake.

'Your cousin is standing very close to Alyce.'

'He stands very close to everyone.' Rufus looked to see for himself, 'Alyce is being very patient. Perhaps she enjoys his attentions—forbidden fruit!' And then he laughed at his own joke. He flicked Luis on the arm, 'By the way, if Cousin Matthew refuses to use a pallet by the hall fire, you are to give him your bed and come in with me. I am not having him share my bed!'

◆   ◆   ◆

It was very late. The guests had gone, but the Weaver family had not yet retired for the night. The logs in the cavernous fireplace still glowed and Matthew was talking to Thomas about Sir John Cheke's role as tutor to the young prince, Edward. As a Protestant humanist, his influence on the King's heir augured well for the reformists. Rufus and Alyce were listening as well, so Luis excused himself and returned to his chamber for some privacy. After he had prayed, he sat for some time on the bed revelling in his solitude. His eyes fell on his pack next to the press and the germ of an idea grew into the certainty that this was the right time. He rummaged through what was left in his satchel and removed Ysabel's gift.

When he returned to the hall, the younger Weavers were about to depart but waited when they saw Luis enter. The fire had crumbled into dull red embers and the only light came from the candles in their sconces on the walls and in high sticks on the mantel. He walked towards Thomas, tall and imposing, yet with some of the awkwardness he had shown on arrival. Conversation stopped and for once Luis relished being the focus in the room. When he reached his host he spoke formally as was required.

'Sir, please may I present you with this gift from Madame Bernade?'

Thomas Weaver took the carved wooden box and the key from his guest and thanked him. All eyes were on Thomas as he slid the key into the lock and carefully lifted back the hinged lid. Alyce caught her breath, Rufus whistled, the irritating habit which so annoyed his father, and Matthew's eyes, if possible, grew larger. Finally, Thomas broke the negotiator's rule; his face lit up as he looked down and saw the spice. He was speechless.

All attention turned to Luis, but the value of the saffron did not surprise him, he had known the contents of the box since he had left Ysabel. The look of wonder on his face came from another realisation. As they had looked into the box, Rufus had lifted one of the candlesticks from the mantel high over their heads. The flame had illuminated the siblings' hair, turning Rufus's a deep bronze whilst Alyce's was paler but no less bright.

Her hair, thought Luis, *her hair in this light is the colour of spice.*

TWENTY

~

Canon Matthew Blake stayed for one week, ingratiating himself with each member of the Weaver family. Thomas was congratulated on his excellent wine, Rufus on his oratory, Alyce on her embroidery (although she would have much preferred recognition of her debating skills), and Meg on her speed in learning the contents of her horn-books. Luis watched the Weavers' cousin turn affability into a fine art; Matthew even managed to please him. The clergyman had valiantly declined a comfortable bed stating that, as a man of God, he was used to humbling himself; a pallet by the fire in the hall would suffice. Happily, Luis still had his privacy, albeit as a result of Blake's wish to impress Alyce.

The Weavers were also happy. They appreciated another academic mind in their evening discussions and although Luis could not follow the detail of what was said, for the exchanges were always in English, he realised that Matthew made a welcome contribution, often initiating ideas. From what he could understand, Luis believed the four were dissecting the minutiae of Christian doctrine, which had puzzled him. Over the week he had reverted to his taciturn self, mainly ignored by Blake who saw no advantage in befriending a trader from the Pays d'Oc. They were polite to each other on the rare occasions they spoke, but Luis soon realised he was of little interest to the Weavers' cousin. It suited him to be left alone, yet he often wondered whether the family had observed, as he had, the miasma of obsequiousness which Blake wore like a cloak.

The day after the canon's departure, Thomas called Rufus into to the parlour.

'You wished to speak to me, Father?'

'Yes, Richard.' Weaver was standing next to the table, the carved spice box before him.

'Ah, the saffron,' murmured Rufus.

Thomas nodded, 'What do you think about taking this to Edward Mercer?'

'All of it?'

His father laughed, 'You know better than that, Richard!'

'Yes, I do,' agreed Rufus, 'but why involve Edward?'

'I believe the saffron to be of superior quality and my brother-in-law has better contacts in the spice trade than us. It is not as it was when my father first had dealings with Michel Bernade. If Mister Gharsia can provide us with such a commodity there is no need for him to think about exporting wine. After all, we are quite happy with the wine of Bordèu.'

Rufus frowned.

'I think Luis's heart is in his wine production and gaining fairness for the producers of his area, not in making money the easiest way.'

'It could well be so. Mister Gharsia appears to be a man with whom I can do business; he is an honest man, but he is very inexperienced and a little naive.'

'That is a bit harsh, Father.'

'Nevertheless, I have come to see that it is true.'

Rufus thought for a moment.

'I cannot go soon as I am due in Bristol next week. We must finalise our negotiations with Henry Cooper.'

'I know, and my bones feel too old for such a journey. My enthusiasm for sailing has gone.'

'What are you thinking of then?'

'I promised Edward that when Meg was old enough to travel, she could reside in his house for the summer. She cannot go alone, Alyce must go with her. I had already decided that it should be this year and sent word to Edward last month.' Thomas paused and placed both hands on the edge of the table. 'What do you think about moving the visit forward and asking Gharsia to accompany the girls?'

Rufus tried to suppress his disappointment.

'I had hoped to take Luis to Bristol with me. He has mentioned more than once that he wishes to go there.'

'But you do not need his assistance in Bristol. If he escorted Alyce and Meg to Lewes, he would be helping us and he can forge links with Edward.'

'I can see that, but will he have time to make the journey and return in time to go home?'

'He should. If the winds are kind, they can be in Lewes in five days or fewer. Let us say, two weeks to get there and back at the most. He would still be ready to sail to Bordèu by early June.'

'You have it all worked out, Father.'

Thomas had, but there was a fleeting doubt.

'You do believe Gharsia to be an honourable man too, Richard?'

'Yes, Father. He will keep Alyce and Meg safe. Anyway they will sail in one of our cogs so they will not be alone,' stated Rufus. He chuckled. 'I doubt Luis will rob Alyce of her virtue!'

Thomas glared at his son.

'That is not what I meant.'

'I know, Father, I know. You had better ask him if he will go.'

◆   ◆   ◆

After supper that evening, Thomas proposed his idea to Luis with Alyce listening carefully, already aware that a visit to Lewes was planned for the summer.

'Mister Gharsia, or, in the light of my request, may I call you Luis as my son has since the earliest days of your acquaintance?'

Luis nodded, interested to hear what was to come next. Thomas continued, 'May I ask a kindness of you? My daughter Meg is to spend the summer with her uncle, Edward Mercer, brother of my dear late wife Margaret. Alyce is to go with her. May I prevail upon you to accompany them on their journey?'

Luis tried hard to control the surprise he was sure showed on his face. He needed time to think so he did not reply. Thomas elaborated, 'It will require a coastal voyage of a few days in one of my cogs which will take you to Lewes. Once there you can return to Bridgwater as soon as you are refreshed. Rufus will collect the girls at the end of the summer.'

Alyce stole a glance at Luis but, as was his habit, he was sitting stiffly, a guarded expression on his face.

If I do not hope for it, perhaps he will agree, she thought, unable to bear the suspense, but still he did not speak. As she sat, eyes cast down and hands with fingers entwined resting in her lap, Alyce heard her father continue, 'I feel it would be beneficial to show my brother-in-law the quality of the saffron Madame Bernade gifted.' Thomas did not want to say too much as he was well aware of the pitfalls of moving too fast when negotiating, but he asked, 'Did you know that our family's first association with her husband was because of the saffron trade?'

Luis found his voice.

'Yes, Madame Bernade told me of this but she thought you no longer traded in spices. The saffron was a gift, in no way was it to rekindle a business arrangement.' He looked at Weaver keenly, watching the older man's reaction, determined not to be distracted from his own original purpose of meeting the English merchant. Alyce kept her eyes down, trying hard to stifle the regret that he did not speak of accompanying them.

'Yes, yes,' replied Thomas, 'but it will do you no harm to show it to such an influential merchant as Edward Mercer.' Then because he realised the conversation was not proceeding as he wished, Thomas changed tack. 'Luis, saffron aside, you would be doing me a great service if you could escort my daughters.'

Alyce, uncertain whether their guest objected to the role of escort or to the proposal of taking the saffron when in fact it was neither, pressed her fingers more tightly together. Luis felt thwarted; he had wanted to go to Bristol with Rufus to explore possible partners for importing wine and now that opportunity would be closed. Yet, at the same time, the possibility of enjoying Alyce's company exclusively, except for Meg, filled him with anticipation. Also, he was not as naive as the English merchant believed him to be: he had seen the light in Thomas's eyes as he espied the orange threads, more valuable than gold itself.

Alyce thought, *if only he would show some emotion, give a sign that Father's request pleases him.* It seemed like an eternity to her before Luis spoke again, his dark direct gaze fixed on Thomas.

'Sir, I will be honoured to travel with your daughters and, if you feel it is appropriate, I will take what you wish to Edward Mercer.'

'Thank you Luis, I am reassured my girls are in safe hands.'

Only then did Alyce raise her eyes to see Luis watching her, his face inscrutable.

◆   ◆   ◆

Even though it was still daylight, a full pearlescent moon hung low in the pale greying sky, partly obscured by dark scudding clouds. The south coast of England was clearly visible as the small cog worked her way eastwards to her destination. Luis, leaning against the side, wondered where the rain still came from as a brisk wind had started to blow the showers away but, as he looked directly above the bobbing boat, a pot-bellied cloud was releasing its last droplets. Rain stippled the surface of a puddle where the uneven deck allowed the water to gather; the planks were slick and slippery, dangerous for those who had not yet found their sea-legs, though the nimble crew moved without faltering.

The cog was a small coastal vessel with most of its capacity dedicated to cargo. Luis could see it tied securely and stored under canvas on the area between the stern castle and the bow. There was limited accommodation: a large area at the stern provided very cramped cabins, each with a hanging bed, a pole for clothes, and a night bucket. They had been at sea for three days and Meg was becoming increasingly fretful and grizzly despite the occasions when they could disembark. That morning, after a sedate journey up the Exe, they had spent a welcome few hours on dry land.

Luis turned at the sound of his name to see the small solid figure of Meg hurtling towards him.

'Be careful!' he called, just as she lost her footing on the wet deck, sliding forward on hands and knees. Initially shocked into silence, the little girl was soon wailing in pain. Alyce, who was just behind her, was first to reach Meg and saw the bright red stain spreading on her petticoat.

'She has hurt herself,' shouted Alyce, raising her voice above the flapping of the sail. Luis was there an instant later. He scooped the child up and turned towards the stern.

Dark and claustrophobic, the cabin felt like a tomb. Meg sat on the narrow bed whimpering while her sister held her hand. The candle once lit, flickering and dim, was totally inadequate for seeing clearly. Alyce turned to Luis, her eyes wide with concern.

'She must have cut herself on one of the raised treenails. I have some chamomile salve in my bag to clean the wound.'

'Wait,' said Luis, 'I have something which is much better. I will get it from my berth.'

He returned quickly with a phial, wads of cotton, and bandages.

'What is that?' demanded Alyce.

'Distilled alcohol.'

'Why do you use it?'

'It will clean the wound and prevent infection.'

'Why are you so sure?' asked Alyce, her voice full of doubt.

'My people have known this for centuries.'

She watched him dampen a wad and gently clean Meg's knee. The little girl flinched but stopped whimpering, too interested in watching Luis. Alyce held the candle high so he could see more easily. All was quiet in the cabin except for the creak of timbers, a closed world so restrictive that it was impossible to move without touching each other; a safe place for confidences to be shared.

Her beautiful, melodious voice was barely a whisper.

'What do you mean when you say your people?'

'The people of Islam,' he replied, continuing to wipe the injured knee.

Many unanswered questions hung in the air. Alyce started with, 'You learnt this from your grandfather?'

'Yes.'

Another whisper, 'Is he a follower of Islam?'

'He was.' The bleakness in his voice startled her.

'But he is Christian now,' she stated. 'Is he not happy?'

Luis did not answer, he continued to clean Meg's other knee, which was less seriously scraped. He knew what he should say but he had an overwhelming need to tell Alyce the truth. When he did speak it was to ask a question and still he did not look at her.

'How would you react if you were forced to reject your religion and accept another?'

It was too difficult a question for her to answer, but she realised what he was saying, so Alyce chose to ask her own question instead.

'Were you born a Christian?'

She watched as he continued to attend to Meg. He started to bandage the child's knees.

'I was a baby when we were baptised.'

'So your grandfather would have been a man of some years.'

'Yes.'

The enormity of what he was telling settled into her mind.

'It must have been hard for him.'

'Yes.'

She was quiet while he pulled Meg's dress down and checked the child's palms for abrasions. Then she repeated, 'It must have been hard for him to turn away from all that was dear to him.'

'Yes.'

'I am so confused,' Alyce admitted. 'I am glad that your grandfather was baptised, yet I feel unsettled.'

Whatever Luis was about to say was lost as a little voice piped up, 'Will I need a stitch?'

'No.'

'Not even a tiny, tiny one like your grandfather does?'

'No,' replied an amused Luis, 'fortunately your knees are just grazed. Grazed badly, but no stitches needed.'

Meg looked up at him, her blue eyes luminous in the candlelight.

'Are you a great surgeon like your grandfather?'

'No, I am no surgeon at all. You would not want to be stitched by me!'
'Oh,' was all she said as she held out her arms to be hugged.

◆   ◆   ◆

Moonlight crept through the gaps around the door dispelling the utter darkness of the cabin. Alyce lay on her side listening to Meg's steady breathing and imagined, rather than saw, the little girl's chest rising and falling. Cramped together on the bed, sleep had come quickly for the child, but Alyce's mind was too busy for slumber. Recollections jostled and thoughts tumbled in rapid succession as she picked over her conversation with Luis like a crow with a carcass. Every word that he had used, every inflection of his voice, each movement of his head was dissected, analysed, and committed to memory.

She tried to make sense of what was happening to her. She questioned herself.

Why was she so interested in him? Was it because he was so different from the other men she had met through her father and brother? Why had she reached twenty-three and never experienced feelings like this? Was it infatuation? Alyce mulled over the questions without finding any answers until her busy mind hovered over what she was afraid to ask. *Was he interested in her? Did he enjoy her company? Why did he seem more relaxed with Rufus? Was it because he returned her feelings?*

She turned over onto her back; Meg stirred but settled again, her warm little body snuggled up closer. The timbers creaked and groaned as she stared upwards into the inky blackness; the child muttered softly and still sleep eluded Alyce. She admonished herself for being fanciful, told herself she was foolish, and gave herself a warning. *He is not of your world, Alyce Weaver. Soon he will be gone. Enjoy the days you have but do not hope for more.*

T W E N T Y - O N E

~

As the early afternoon sun was warm for the second day in a row, a thin
wiry man in servants' garb perched contentedly on one of the wooden
capstans. His master had sent him down to the jetty at the same time as
the previous day to see if a boat had arrived. It was such an enjoyable task
compared to his other duties that he was disappointed to see the small
cog make its way up the river on the final stage of its journey. He rose to
allow the mariners to catch the ropes to secure the vessel and watched,
with a hint of regret, the speed and efficiency of the berthing. Soon three
passengers began their descent down the gangplank and Mark Baker
narrowed his eyes to decide if they were the ones he sought.

A woman, still young but well past girlhood, was the first to disembark
behind a sailor shouldering a large travelling trunk. Her unbound hair
declared her unmarried and, as she turned to speak to the man behind
her, its beauty was revealed. Thick and straight, it cascaded down her back
almost to her waist. She was tall and slender with a face neither comely
nor plain. She could be Mistress Weaver, but Mark decided she was not
because of the young man behind her.

Broad-shouldered with closely cropped black hair and beard, the
colour of his skin and his continental clothing proclaimed him a foreigner.
But then Mark looked closely at the child in the man's arms. She looked
about four years of age, a plump bundle still in baby clothes. She scanned
the scene before her with great interest. Her eyes met Mark's and, in that

moment, he saw more than a passing resemblance to his master's son, John. He moved forward.

'Mistress Weaver?'

The woman nodded.

'My master, Edward Mercer, has sent me to collect you. I am Mark Baker.'

'Thank you. That is most welcome,' she replied as she looked over his shoulder and saw the cart behind him. 'Is it far to Uncle Mercer's house?'

Baker swivelled round pointing away from the river.

'It is towards the Priory of St Pancras. My master's house is the large house just off the High Street, before you reach the priory grounds.'

'I think I would prefer to walk. What do you think, Luis?' Her green eyes were studying him expectantly. She had started to call him by his given name once her father had done so, and it was still such a novelty that it did not flow easily in her Somerset burr. She tended to shorten the 'i' as she forgot the pronunciation, which confused Luis. It sometimes took a moment for him to realise it was his name; it also surprised him as her French was excellent and she did not seem a woman who was content with inaccuracy. He replied, the English coming more easily after a month in the country.

'That would be very pleasant after being on board for so long. I think Meg will enjoy it too.'

'Very well,' the servant answered, 'I will take your trunk with me.' He looked at the satchel slung across Luis's chest. 'Shall I take your bag, Sir?'

'No, thank you. It is not heavy.' Out of habit, he preferred to keep his belongings with him, yet he knew the box of saffron would have been perfectly safe.

They set off behind the cart which, as it made such slow progress, remained in sight. Several beggars were in the vicinity, one of whom was obviously lame. Luis took a coin from his money pouch for an old man, who blessed him and thanked him profusely. The young man walked away feeling uncomfortable. Meg skipping beside him, her hand in his.

'Alyce,' he said loudly, as she was slightly in front of them, having increased her pace past the beggar. She half-turned for him to catch her up. 'Alyce, I have noticed many beggars since I came to England, and not just the old and infirm.'

A puzzled expression on her face, she asked, 'Do you not have beggars in the Pays d'Oc?'

'Yes, but not like this. I have seen so many here. We have hospitals for the poor and in many towns there are relief organisations. These help the poor in their homes. People who can afford it pay taxes to support them.'

'We help the poor. Think of the church ale, Luis. Yet it is true there appears to be more beggars. The end of the religious houses seems to have made it worse, although there have always been beggars and vagabonds.' She looked back to the ragged figures. 'That old man,' pointing to the beggar Luis had given alms to, 'will have a license from the justice of the peace to beg by the dock. If he begs outside of his area he will be placed in the stocks. Those men over there,' continued Alyce as she inclined her head towards three unsavoury looking characters loitering by the unloaded cargo, 'they appear to be able-bodied. If they are caught begging more than once, they are whipped and could also lose part of an ear.'

Luis raised his eyebrows. 'It is to discourage vagabondage,' Alyce explained, 'although Father has told me that that there have been complaints that such measures are not implemented.' She glanced down as Meg reached for her hand so she could be swung by both adults. They started to trot, the little girl running between them.

'One, two, three, jump!' shouted Alyce as they swung Meg off the ground on every fourth step.

'One, two, three, wheeeeeeeee!' echoed the child, gurgling with glee.

They had progressed some way to their destination in this fashion when Alyce decided it was time to calm Meg down, ready for their arrival at the house. Also, she wanted to continue her conversation with Luis, so they walked the remainder of the distance at a sedate pace, Meg straining forward on their arms.

'I read recently a book by a man called Henry Brinklow. He believes that society should be changed. He suggests the wealth from the Church and the monasteries should be used to help the poor. There should be free schools where Greek and Latin can be taught so there is more learning. He also believes there should be a physician and surgeon in each town.'

'He is a man who speaks sense,' agreed Luis. 'I would be interested to read his writings.'

'It is my father's book. I am sure you could read it.' Alyce looked up at him with a smile which faded quickly as she realised that soon he would be gone. There would be no time for reading books.

'Do you know the works of Juan Luis Vives?' Luis asked.

'I have heard Father speak of him but I have not read any of his writings. I know he was a friend of Erasmus.'

'Yes he was and he spent some time here in England until he lost favour with King Henry. My grandfather was very interested in his ideas. Vives came from Valencia and his family suffered greatly under the Inquisition. They were persecuted for still practising Judaism. He left the country just as we have. He wrote about the problem of the poor and suggested schemes to help them. I expect Henry Brinklow knew of him. Vives believed schools should be established in every town, paid for by the municipal authorities. I enjoyed reading about his ideas on how children should be taught. He said each child's inclinations and abilities should be considered.'

Alyce's face glowed as a wide smile made her beautiful.

'What is it?' he asked.

She continued to smile up at him, her eyes dancing.

'When you speak about wine and learning you say a lot more than usual. I have a feeling you have not finished on the subject of Juan Luis Vives.' She pronounced "Luis" correctly, as he had just done.

He grinned back at her.

'I suppose I do.'

◆   ◆   ◆

As a symbol of mercantile success, Edward Mercer's house outshone that of his brother-in-law. Older than Thomas Weaver's, the building had been remodelled and appointed in the very latest style. A new ceiling had been added to the hall to create an extra floor, yet the entrance hall, with its new staircase, was still impressive, despite an area of it having been taken for a solar and a dining room, both snug with elaborate wainscoting. Luis, sitting forward on the settle in the solar, Meg wedged firmly between himself and Alyce, started to relax a little as Edward Mercer made his guests welcome. He sipped the sweet spiced wine slowly to make it last and ate as many of the almond cakes as politeness allowed. While Alyce and their host caught up with family news, Luis silently studied the room and its occupants.

There was a fresh scent in the air from the newly strewn herbs scattered across the floor whilst plaited rushes, obviously recently laid, covered the stone flags in the centre of the room. There were signs of a readiness to impress, perhaps for their arrival as Thomas had sent word ahead by boat as soon as it was decided that the girls were to arrive earlier than originally planned. Everywhere there were signs of Mistress Mercer's skill, loudly applauded by her husband. A tapestry carpet hung over the oak panelling opposite the fireplace; another, worked in petit-point, covered a side table.

Luis had not expected Catherine Mercer to be so young; he doubted she had reached thirty. Her husband looked no more than mid-thirties, a good decade younger than his brother-in-law. Yet Luis told himself he should not be surprised as Margaret Mercer had been Weaver's second wife; the mother of Meg, not of Alyce and Rufus. Sitting side by side in new chairs, complete with arms, the Mercers were as physically different as a husband and wife could be. Edward Mercer was a rotund man, full of life, but Catherine was thin, almost to emaciation, with an ethereal, fey quality about her. Luis noticed that, as her husband and Alyce talked animatedly, Catherine sat quietly, as if her thoughts were far away, her hand continually stroking the lapdog nestled on her knees. The animal, though, was attentive, eyeing the strangers with an air of superiority.

As they had not yet been shown to their chambers, Luis had his satchel on the floor next to the settle. Realising there was an opportune break in the conversation he leaned over and opened the bag. Meg slid off the seat and helped him retrieve the spice box. Considerably smaller than the one he had brought from home it nevertheless contained a substantial quantity of the precious saffron. He placed the box securely in the child's chubby hands and asked her to present it to her uncle. Her face alive with the pleasure of being given such an important task, Meg stepped carefully across the room, crushing the herbs as she went. She reached her uncle and aunt; the dog yelped, a loud noise for such a small animal, and startled Meg. She thrust the box at Edward Mercer, retreating quickly to the security of the settle, unshed tears brimming in her eyes. She snuggled up to Alyce as Luis spoke.

'Please accept this gift of saffron. It has been grown on the land of my patron, Ysabel Bernade.'

Edward opened the box slowly, his expression giving nothing away. He nodded approvingly before he commented.

'It is most generous.' He looked sideways at his wife who still appeared to take no interest in her guests or her son, who was watching the newcomers, especially Meg, with the same intensity as the dog.

John Mercer was six years old; a sturdy child, a smaller version of his father. Luis wondered how Catherine Mercer could have given birth to such a boy, but perhaps he had been born early, before the full term. His grandfather had told him of such births and some babies did survive, with the children growing strong and healthy, aided by a good wet nurse. There was a noticeable likeness to Meg; the same large blue eyes and light brown hair. As yet the boy had not spoken other than the greeting prompted by his father.

'My dear,' Edward now addressed his wife, 'I think it is time to show our guests to their chambers.' He smiled broadly, a man very content in his achievements. 'When we had the ceiling added to the hall it enabled us to make separate bed chambers. We have plenty of room. We have plenty of room.'

◆　　　◆　　　◆

There was half an hour before supper. After seeing their chambers and washing away the dust of the journey, Luis, Alyce, and Meg were again on the settle, their only companion John. The new chairs appeared very comfortable but were obviously reserved for the master and lady of the house. Early evening sun shone through the small mullioned window of the solar, and Luis had seen the large garden beyond, the view distorted by the thick, uneven glass. It had looked so inviting but Alyce had felt they should not explore without permission, and the adult Mercers had absented themselves until it was time for the meal.

Luis was amusing Meg, letting her play with some coins from his money pouch. She chose one and he had to identify it before it joined a small pile growing on the seat. After an unsuccessful attempt to engage John in the activity, Alyce was totally content watching them. The boy sat on the floor on the other side of the room, eyes focused on the coins. Meg held up a silver coin, discoloured where the base metal showed. 'What is this?' she asked.

'A groat,' replied Luis, 'look, you can see it is heavily alloyed,' pointing to where the silver had worn away. The child reached into the pouch and took another coin.

'What is this?'

'A penny.'

Meg turned the coin over in her hand. It was discoloured too. In fact all the coins in the pile on the settle's seat showed areas where the base metal could be seen. Alyce contemplated the pile sadly.

'All the old good silver coins are being hoarded. The only ones we see now are these base metal ones. It is the same with the gold coins. The king has reduced the weight of the sovereign. People hoard the old ones or take them overseas when they travel, and all the while prices are rising sharply.'

Luis replied ruefully, 'It is the same in my country. The coins are worth less and the prices increase year on year.' He picked up a groat from the pile and asked Meg a question which was too difficult for her. 'If you wanted to buy some ribbon which costs a penny and you give the tinker this groat, how many pennies would he give you back?'

'Three,' piped up John.

'Well done!' Alyce congratulated him, pleased the boy wanted to participate. 'However, Luis, that is very expensive ribbon.'

'I know, but prices are rising!'

Alyce laughed, despite herself.

'That is not amusing,' she said, affection in her voice.

Meg was not pleased. Her mouth formed a perfect pout as she swept the coins off the settle. John rushed to the floor and collected the scattered money.

'Meg,' reprimanded her elder sister.

'It was my game.'

'You must learn to share.'

'Why?'

'It is polite to share. Also, it will be fun to have a cousin to play with.'

Meg was not convinced and glared at John as he handed the silver discs to Luis, who thanked him and met Alyce's eyes over the boy's head. He studied her for, what Alyce felt was, a very long time.

'I do not like it here!' The pout was gone, replaced by defiance. 'I want to go home! I want to go home!' Alyce sighed. It could well be a long summer.

'Come, Meg,' said Luis. 'Shall we play seesaw?' The child looked from her sister back to Luis, deliberately ignoring John, and then back again to Alyce. She loved the game she often played with Rufus and lately with Luis, but she was tired and grumpy.

'There is no point playing if you are bad-tempered,' commented her sister.

'I want to play.'

'Come on, then,' invited Luis.

He stretched out his right leg so Meg could sit over his calf. Holding her hands in his, he lifted and lowered his leg as he pulled her backwards and forwards. All traces of ill-humour disappeared and peace reigned until the patter of tiny paws on the stone flags at the edge of the room announced the arrival of the dog. He took one look at Luis's moving leg and dived, nipping the ankle viciously. Alyce could not believe the speed of what she saw. Luis pulled Meg off his leg and into his arms, before kicking his leg with force. The dog lost purchase, flew across the room with ears flying until he thudded against the wainscoting and fell to the floor with a whimper.

There was a heavy silence. Horrified, Luis was speechless until he used a coarse expletive, one he must have learnt from Rufus.

'Luis Gharsia!' exclaimed Alyce, 'I did not know you knew such words.'

'Sorry! Do you think I have killed him?'

John was shouting, 'I will tell my mother. I will tell my mother.' His face contorted with self-righteousness, he pointed at a frightened Meg, still clinging around Luis's neck. 'She did it! She did it!'

'Be quiet, John,' ordered Alyce, 'It is nobody's fault. It was an accident. The dog attacked Luis.' Meg's tears, threatened all afternoon, finally came. She started to weep, quietly at first, then working up to great, shuddering guips. Alyce, usually so serene, taking in the scene before her, felt a bubble of hysteria begin to surface. She suppressed it firmly and walked over to the dog. He was breathing; stunned but alive, eyes open and fixed on Alyce. 'Look, the dog is fine.' She gently picked up the animal, feeling for injuries; he did not cry out as she stroked methodically, as Catherine had done. Luis's relief was tangible.

'He obviously prefers you to me.'

'Yes, he is a lady's lapdog. He seems to have an aversion to you.'

John moved closer to Alyce to inspect the dog but, she noticed, he did not pet it. Then he turned and walked out of the room.

'Do you think he will tell his mother, Alyce?'

'I do not know, but all is well now. And,' she added impishly, 'I think with a gift of such saffron, you will be forgiven your magnificent act of self-defence.'

A moment passed; Meg made a last hiccup and, thumb in mouth, nestled down to sleep against Luis's neck. He looked so solemn, so worried about what he had done that Alyce thought he had not understood what she had said.

'It was such a magnificent act of self-defence,' she teased, before adding sincerely, 'The dog could have bitten Meg.'

'Yes.'

'I have never seen such fast reactions.'

'Yes.'

'Did it hurt?'

'Yes.'

'Really?'

'Yes.'

They both looked down and watched the blood oozing through Luis's hose, above his shoes. Alyce commented, 'You should have kept your boots on.'

'Yes.'

'You will need some distilled alcohol.'

'Yes,' he agreed with a twinkle in his eye.

'Luis, say more than "yes"!'

'Yes!' he laughed then, a deep throaty sound which she had not heard before.

She laughed too, but with a touch of hysteria. A laugh born from the stress of the journey, a laugh nurtured by the strain of their arrival, and, finally, a laugh precipitated by the sharp teeth of a tiny dog. The tears started to flow, and what comeliness she possessed was soon forfeit to red eyes, blotchy skin, and acute embarrassment. Moved, Luis delved into his pocket for his handkerchief and pressed it into her hand.

'Put the dog down,' he commanded.

She obeyed him and the small animal gave them one slow accusatory glance before it scampered for the door. She wiped her eyes and blew her nose.

'Thank you.' She closed her hand around the cloth and looking directly at him, she smiled weakly. 'I am glad you are here.'

'So am I,' he replied, with such intensity that Alyce, uncharacteristically shy, could no longer meet his eyes.

TWENTY-TWO

∼

Caors, February 1546

Luis moved methodically along the row of vines, pruning with accuracy that seemed at odds with the speed at which he worked. His breath condensed as it met the winter air and he had to continually stamp his feet to keep them warm. It was February, one of the most desolate months of the year and, despite the straw packing his sabots, Luis could feel the cold creeping up from the ground. The weak, wintry sun was already sinking in a grey, metallic sky, a sign that this would be the last row before he hurried back to the farm, saddled Solomon, and returned to Caors.

It was Sunday, the day of rest, but Luis never rested. Over the winter, his busy life had taken on a rhythm which had enabled him to fulfil all of his obligations. During the week he worked for Martin Ebrart as they wrangled with the legal issues which flooded Martin's office, and very early each Saturday morning he rode out to the Gaulberts' farm. Ebrart, realising the benefit of such an able assistant, had continued to prove remarkably flexible, allowing the young man to adjust his commitments by the season. In return, the lawyer had the advantage of Luis's legal astuteness and a cellar always amply supplied with the highest quality, deep black wine. Thus Luis, on his return from his travels, was able to take a full and active part in the vineyard's summer preparations and the following excellent harvest.

It was eight months since he had left Lewes after four days in the Mercer household and a few final days in Bridgwater while he waited for favourable winds. As he had bade farewell to Rufus at the dock, he had reason to deem his visit a success. Thomas Weaver had summoned enough support for the importation of three tuns of wine the following year, while his brother-in-law had guaranteed a market for as much saffron as Luis could bring. Nevertheless, as he had boarded the ship, Luis had recalled another leaving and felt a sense of loss rather than gain. He had been accompanied to the jetty at Lewes by Alyce and Meg. The little girl had cried, her chubby arms tight around his neck, once it was obvious he was leaving without them. Alyce's pale face had remained impassive as she brushed her windblown hair back with beautiful, slender fingers. She had smiled as she wished him a safe journey, the polite smile of an acquaintance. All he had planned to say was strangled by the cords of his reserve. The most he had managed to utter was, 'I will return next year.'

Her eyes steady, Alyce had replied. 'God, go with you.'

'I will return,' he had repeated before he turned towards the gangplank. He had walked stiffly, an aloof figure once more. He did not look back; he did not see Alyce's face crumple as she no longer fought her own tears; he did not see her pick up Meg so the child would shield her from view. When finally he did look back and raise his hand in farewell, they were already making their way back to where Mark Baker waited with the cart.

He reached the end of the row. If his calculations were correct, he would finish the winter pruning within another couple of days and then he could start planning for his next visit to England. It would follow the same pattern as the previous year, setting sail towards the end of March, although this time he could not justify being away so long; just long enough to deliver the wine and see the Weaver family. He was gathering the last of the day's prunings, ready to be burnt, when he heard Guilhem hail him from across the field. Luis watched as the vintner made his way through the vines until he joined him and looked approvingly at his mentee's skill.

'Good work, Luis. I have taught you well.'

For some time, both men stood silently, as cultivators sometimes do, studying the vista. Row upon row of skeletal vines, twisted, gnarled, and newly cut, climbed the slopes before them ready to burst forth once spring arrived. Satisfied, Guilhem gave Luis an affectionate slap on the back, 'How long have you been with us now?'

'It is my sixth year.'

The older man nodded and began to speak, his eyes still firmly fixed on the land.

'You have proved your worth, time and time again.'

'Thank you.'

They watched as the sun dipped lower, changing the light across the hill-side. Guilhem cleared his throat.

'One day, I will no longer be here.' There was a long silence; for Guilhem it seemed impossible that someday he would no longer be with his beloved vines. He scuffed the earth with his sabot. 'Henri must have his inheritance and I need to provide a dowry for Marie. It is time she was married.' Small pieces of white limestone continued to be dislodged as Guilhem dug away with his clog. 'If the right suitor comes along, I will divide my land equally in two,' he added, almost to himself as he glanced up at Luis.

Luis continued to contemplate the vines he had just pruned while he wondered whether Piere del Mas was the right suitor. There had been no sign of a betrothal with Marie when Luis had returned from England, although since then Piere had been a frequent visitor to the farm and had helped with the harvest.

Perhaps there was an understanding and an announcement was imminent? What was Gaulbert trying to say to him? Was it a warning that Luis could no longer rely on working this area of land? Was his mentor giving him permission to court his daughter? Surely that could not be? He dismissed the last thoughts immediately and became aware of the cold dampness on his back where Guilhem's hand had pressed his clothes against his skin, for, despite the chill in the air, he had sweated profusely. Only then did he look at his companion who continued to survey the land before him.

'Come, Monsieur Gaulbert, let us finish now. I must return home.'

Loise was spinning wool by the fire when they entered the farmhouse. She looked up, immediately peeved by the easy companionship between the two men. Luis had changed since he had returned from England. She was pleased to see he was still wary of her, but his confidence had grown; she felt the balance of their relationship had shifted another notch. It was a long time since he had been the watchful, puny boy who had avoided her sharp tongue with an adroitness she welcomed. Even when he had come to live with them, he had continued to limit his contact with her to only what was necessary; contact always conducted on his part with unfailing politeness. Now, when she had found him asleep in front of the fire that morning instead of using the icy attic, her barbed comment had dried on her lips in the face of his composure. In one swift movement, he had thrown off the sheepskins and had risen, fully clothed, to his feet. After a curt greeting and scarcely a glance, he had turned his back on her and walked slowly from the room.

The spinning wheel whirred.

'I thought you would have finished the pruning before now. Henri has been back some time,' Loise said sourly. At the sound of his name, Henri looked up from where he was dozing on the settle, a flagon of wine on the floor beside him.

'Shut the door,' he grumbled, 'you are letting the cold air in.' He saluted his father and friend with the wine goblet.

Guilhem suppressed the treacherous feeling of sadness, which arose when he saw Henri alongside Luis, and said brightly, 'We have just been talking.' His benign gaze settled on Marie, who was helping her mother by winding wool. She smiled at her father and Luis, giving her most engaging smile.

'You must be very cold, come by the fire.' Tilting her head on one side coquettishly, she addressed Luis, 'You must stay and eat with us.' She kept her eyes firmly on him to avoid seeing her mother's pursed lips, but Marie was destined to be disappointed. Luis shook his head.

'Thank you, but no. I must set off at once if I want to be home before dark.'

◆　　◆　　◆

Badly swollen with damp, the ancient door scraped across the floor. Johan woke with a start, exasperated by the sound, for however much he had tried he could not banish the winter cold that rose from the river. It was the same every year despite the fires he laboured continuously to feed. He spoke towards the dim candle.

'You are very late.' He heard Luis, too tired to comment, flop down on the bed opposite and pull off his boots.

'Have you eaten, Luis?'

'Yes, I have just grabbed something from the kitchen.'

'You did not eat with the Gaulberts?'

'No, I needed to get back before dark.'

'You didn't succeed then.'

There was no response. Johan, snug under the covers sat up carefully to avoid any heat escaping, and verified what he already knew. Luis had fallen asleep, almost instantly, without undressing. Following what had now become a routine, Johan left the warmth of his bed, quickly pulled a blanket from the press, and threw it over Luis before he retired back to his side of the room, candle in hand. It was an action he performed most nights and he had perfected it so skilfully that he was back in bed before the icy chill of the room could penetrate his nightshirt. Johan regretted that since Luis had returned from England he worked very late at Ebrart's office or arrived well after supper from the farm. There seemed little time for talking, and even Luis's reading was being neglected.

They rose at dawn; Luis to wash and pray while Johan stoked the fires and ran to the baker's to purchase a fresh loaf. When he returned, a welcome sight with bread still warm from the oven, Hernando was at the table in the kitchen, watching Luis fetch cheese, figs, and walnuts from the cupboard. An unconventional family, it had been decided long ago that it was easier to break their fast where the servants normally ate rather than dine in the parlour. After all, there were still no servants in the house.

They ate in silence, as was their custom, especially so early in the day. Three men busy with their own thoughts. Hernando was rehearsing the key points he wanted to explain to his students that morning. As he had become older, he had the uncomfortable feeling that his memory was not what it was. He had not yet experienced the ignominy of forgetting to teach a vital operating technique, but the spectre of a mistake made him prepare more thoroughly than he had ever done. Johan was organising the demands on his own time, trying to work out whether he could fit in a companionable drink in the town, while Luis was thinking about the Weavers. He recalled the easy talk that accompanied each of their meals, whatever time of day; conversation which had ranged from local issues to the latest ideas Thomas was studying. He thought about his host nostalgically, remembering Thomas's enthusiasm for philosophy and theological debate, shared with his elder children. Luis even missed Rufus's endless probing and Meg's entertaining ways, but most of all he missed Alyce. He could not define what it was that he missed, he just knew that as each day passed and March approached, he felt a lightness of spirit, an excitement that had nothing to do with the export of wine.

Hernando's voice broke his reverie. 'I presume you will not be as late as last night, Luis?'

His grandson looked up from his plate, his expression revealing his preoccupation. Hernando repeated his question with a nuance of displeasure.

'I presume you will not be so late tonight.'

'I do not know. It depends on what needs to be done.' Luis's mind quickly ranged over the case he was working on; a particularly tricky issue of disputed property ownership, the origins of which were proving difficult to trace.

'You are working too hard. Even Ebrart agrees with me, although he says you are indispensable.'

Luis, torn between pride at the compliment and his pique that his grandfather and employer had been discussing him, answered somewhat tersely, 'I am the person to decide whether I am doing too much.'

Hernando acknowledged the statement with a raised eyebrow, which Luis knew was a sign his grandfather did not agree. The younger man was about to say more when Hernando started to rise from the bench and quickly spoke, 'It does not matter to me tonight anyway, as I am dining with Ysabel. You two can eat when you want.' With that final word he turned from the table, wished them a good day, and left the room.

◆   ◆   ◆

Hernando was worried; he was worried about Ysabel. She had lost weight. Just when he could not say, but, as he studied her across the table, it was clear that something was not right. The shimmering candlelight could not hide the obvious. Her rich chestnut hair, now liberally peppered with grey, lacked its usual lustre, her eyes no longer sparkled, and her pretty face, normally round with pleasing plumpness, appeared sunken and lined. Unsure of how to proceed, Hernando for once did not eat with enthusiasm, for in the relationship Ysabel had always been the open, enquiring one, the perfect foil to his own reserve. She noticed him picking at his food. 'The meat is not to your liking, Hernando?'

'No, the meat is good. I am not hungry tonight.'

She smiled and met his eyes warmly, 'That is not like you.'

He responded with a smile.

'I know!'

'Are you ill, my dear?'

He kept his eyes on her.

'No, I am fine, but, Ysabel, I feel something ails you?'

He watched her give a little start and place her knife on the side of the plate.

'What makes you think that, Hernando?'

He took a sip of water, still cold from the well, and slowly returned the goblet to its position on the table. He twisted the base, deciding where to begin. Ysabel followed suit, but her drink was the inky black wine of Caors. She drank deeply. Hernando coughed a nervous cough before he said, 'You do not look well. You have lost weight. I am worried about you.'

Joy filled Ysabel's heart, as it always did, when he revealed his concern for her.

'You are right,' she said softly. She knew him too well to expect him to reach across the table and caress her hand, which she noticed was shaking, so she leaned forward and took his firmly in both of hers. The moment was pregnant with emotion.

'You are right,' she said again.

'Of course I am right. I am a physician,' he almost barked, unable to bear what he could see in her eyes. He made himself angry to mask his fear, pulling away his hand as if he was scorched. 'Tell me,' he ordered, 'tell me!'

'Stop shouting, Hernando, please.' Her voice was very small to his ears.

'I am not shouting!'

'Yes, you are, my love,' she whispered.

He inhaled slowly, forcing himself to calm down.

'What is wrong, Ysabel? Please tell me what is wrong.'

Her clear hazel eyes were full of love.

'If I do, you must make me a promise.'

'What promise?'

She took his hand again.

'You must promise not to tell Luis.'

TWENTY-THREE

~

It was March at last. In the hour before midnight the streets were deserted, but rather than stay within the narrow confines of the city centre, Luis made for the river. He walked as quickly as possible without breaking into a run, buoyed up by the possibilities ahead of him. A perfect half-moon rode high in the sky and all was quiet except for the soft sigh of the Olt as it flowed westwards, its rhythm occasionally broken by the distinctive plop of a water rat as it slid from the bank. Luis was tired, so very tired, yet he had done it. He had finished all he needed to do for Martin Ebrart and was free to finalise the details of his trip to England.

At the vineyard, three tuns of the finest Caors wine were ready to load onto the barge at Douelle for the first stage of the journey. As a result of a hefty incentive paid to a port official, Luis had secured some storage at Bordèu, and all that he needed to do was to rendezvous with Weaver's ship and accompany the wine to Bridgwater. In readiness, he had already packed a substantial quantity of saffron which he would carry himself. He passed Ysabel's impressive house, dark and shuttered against the night, and felt a twinge of remorse that he had been too busy of late to spend much time with her. He told himself that he would visit the following day and he increased his speed until the small house in the Place St Urcisse came into view.

On reaching home and entering the dim hall, the first thing Luis noticed was a line of light filtering under the parlour door. His grandfather had not yet retired. Tired as he was, Luis had initially intended to creep into the kitchen for a bite to eat before going straight to bed, but the change in Hernando's routine drew him to the parlour. His words of greeting died on his lips when he saw his grandfather's face. Instead of a brief acknowledgment he asked, 'What is it? Are you ill?' Hernando did indeed look distressed; he was very pale with a reddening about his eyes while an unsteady hand was raking through his thick silver hair in an agitated fashion. He sighed by way of an answer to Luis's question and the younger man retorted firmly, 'You should be in bed if you are not well. It is nearly midnight.'

Hernando looked at him sharply.

'Is it that late? Why are you so late?'

Luis forced himself to be patient.

'I needed to finish writing the notes for Martin Ebrart. You know I will not see him again until I return from England.'

'I do not see why you have to go away again,' Hernando grumbled.

'We have been through this, Grandfather. I want to accompany the wine and assess how well it is received. Also, the saffron is too valuable to be trusted to anyone else. I will not stay in England as long as I did last year.'

The older man made a sound which could have meant anything, a sound that riled Luis, hungry and tired as he was.

'I am going to bed now,' he said curtly and turned to leave. As he did so, he saw his grandfather's eyes become misty with tears. Exasperated he snapped, 'Stop that! You are not going to die while I am away.'

Hernando's hand stopped raking through his hair. He lifted his head proudly and gave his grandson a defiant stare.

'It is not what you think.'

'No?'

'No.'

'What is it then?'

'I cannot tell you.'

'Cannot tell me?'

'Yes.'

'Why?'

'I made a promise.'

'A promise?'

'Yes.'

'To whom?'

Hernando continued to hold Luis's eyes; there was a long pause then he rose stiffly and stood by the fire. He took the poker, stabbing and breaking the glowing embers ready to add some new wood. Sparks crackled and danced. He reached into the basket beside the hearth and selected two large logs; they could be in the parlour for some time. A defeated air hung about Hernando, something his grandson had not noticed when he had first entered the room. Luis made his way towards the fire. There was only one person close enough to his grandfather to demand a promise.

'It is Ysabel,' Luis looked sideways at Hernando, waiting for affirmation. His grandfather continued to stare into the fire, arranging the new logs with the poker. 'What was the promise?' Luis asked quietly. To his horror, he saw two fat teardrops fall onto the flags as Hernando blinked and echoed his own words, 'It is Ysabel.'

'What is the promise? Tell me. It must be serious if it distresses you so.'

Hernando shook his head, as if pushing away the memory, and then he turned to look at Luis, unable to keep the burden of the secret any longer, 'She has a tumour.'

Luis felt as if icy fingers touched the back of his neck, 'She is ill?'

'Yes.'

'Very ill?'

'I think so. She has become so thin.'

The icy fingers took a firmer hold of Luis. The question came out as a whisper.

'When did she tell you?'

'About a month ago.'

'A month ago and neither of you told me!' he shouted.

'She made me promise.'

The icy fingers were replaced by anger.

'What am I? A child that has to have such things kept from me?' He could feel the anger rising, 'Can you not remove the tumour?'

'I believe so but she won't let me.'

'Why?'

'Ysabel says that if it is God's will for her to die, so be it.' Unable to bear the thought, Hernando found the tears welling up again.

Enraged that he had been left out, Luis demanded, 'Can't you make her have the operation?'

A smile stole across Hernando's face, at odds with his red, watery eyes.

'Since when can Ysabel be made to do anything she doesn't want to? I certainly cannot force her.'

White, hot rage flared in Luis, fuelled by the sight of his helpless grandfather coupled with a dawning realisation.

'You would have had the authority if you had been her husband! It is your fault!'

Stung, Hernando shouted back.

'How could I be her husband? How could I marry her? She is a Christian!' He almost spat out the last words.

'But you love her. I can see it in your face and she is going to die,' he flung the words in his grandfather's face.

'How naive can you be? What has love got to do with marriage?'

Luis felt he was about to explode, he knew he was losing control and fury made him cruel. 'All these years; all these wasted years. The two of us stuck in this miserable house with Johan, separate from everyone. We could have lived with Ysabel, in a home filled with light and laughter.'

'Luis!' Hernando's voice came out in a screech as he raised it to interrupt the tirade. 'Luis, calm down!' But Luis was beyond listening to his grandfather. He stormed out of the room, thundered across the hall, and shut himself in the kitchen.

◆   ◆   ◆

He did not know how long he had sat at the old scrubbed bench, his fingers idly tracing the outlines of the knots. At one point he had rested his head on his folded arms and closed his eyes. Guilt consumed him. Guilt about the way he had neglected Ysabel. Guilt that he had missed the signs of failing health, and guilt about the way he had spoken to his grandfather. He must have slept for when he stirred someone was stroking his hair gently, with great tenderness. Luis looked up to see Hernando, still dressed, next to him. He appeared strained but composed. He moved his hand from Luis's head and rested it on the young man's shoulder. Luis spoke first, his voice unnaturally flat, 'Is Ysabel really going to die?'

'That I cannot predict but, without surgery, I would suggest yes.'

'How long?'

'Again, I cannot say. It could be a year or two, or as short as a few months.'

'She must have surgery!'

Hernando squeezed his shoulder.

'Speak to her, Luis.' He saw a spark of hope in his grandson's dark eyes. Maryam's eyes, his beloved daughter Maryam's fathomless black eyes. 'Speak to her in the morning,' he suggested, 'if anyone can make her change her mind it is you. Surely she will do it for you.'

With those words Hernando left and made his way slowly to his bed chamber. Luis sat alone for some time. Neither of them had mentioned his furious outburst, as was their custom. Like other less ferocious exchanges it would be left to fester, creating another wedge between them. Exhausted, he eventually pushed the stool away from the old bench and left the kitchen, but he did not climb the narrow uneven stairs to the upper storey. Instead he went back to the parlour and sat at Hernando's desk. The room was cold, the fire having died down, but he did not notice. He penned a brief letter, his hand unsteady from tiredness and emotion. On completion, he folded it carefully and sealed it with a blob of wax. He took his time writing the address to ensure it reached its destination. When he was finished he still did not go to bed but remained completely still, his eyes on the address. It read:

Thomas Weaver Esq.,

St Mary Street,

Bridgwater, Somerset,

England.

◆   ◆   ◆

Her face lit up when she saw him, as it always did; soft hazel eyes studied him carefully and, for a moment, he basked in the warmth of unconditional love.

'You look as if you have not slept, Luis,' she said, as she pulled him towards her for a hug. He hugged her back, swift and closely, and she knew.

'Your grandfather has told you.'

'Yes.'

'And you are angry because we kept it from you.'

Luis did not answer. There was no need; he had accepted the accuracy of Ysabel's perception long ago. He glanced around the garden, struggling with what he planned to say while she continued her pottering, enjoying the early spring sunshine.

'What are you doing, Ysabel?'

'I am checking what is growing, and seeing which plants, if any, I have lost over the winter.'

'I need to talk to you.' He had stopped with the sun behind him, his face in the shade, and she could not read his expression.

She smiled up at him, squinting in the sun.

'Is it going to be a long conversation?'

'That depends on you.'

'Then we had better sit down.'

They sat on the nearest bench with their backs against the wall where latent heat emanated from the rough stone. Luis leaned forward, his elbows on his thighs and looked at his feet. He was unsure of where to start so he stated the obvious.

'You have become much thinner.' The prominence of Ysabel's bones had shocked him when he had embraced her.

'Yes, but I was getting too fat,' Ysabel answered cheerfully. 'Lisette had to take out my best silk dress. It was becoming far too tight and uncomfortable.'

'And now she will have to take it in again, even more.' He commented morosely.

'Yes,' laughed Ysabel, determined to keep the mood light.

'I do not think that is amusing.'

'You are right,' she conceded.

'Are you in pain?'

'No.'

'Then why are you so thin?'

She touched his hand.

'I think I am worrying about myself. It has stopped me eating.'

'Ysabel, you must have surgery. It can make you well again.'

'Your grandfather told you that?'

'He is right.'

'You and Hernando agree. That is cause for celebration!' Ysabel squeezed Luis's hand affectionately.

'It won't last long,' he said dully, keeping his eyes on his feet so he did not have to look at her. 'I was very disrespectful last night.'

'Oh Luis,' her hand still rested on his and he noticed the veins, blue and prominent. 'What did you say?'

He told her, keeping nothing back and only faltering briefly when he recounted how he had blamed Hernando for not taking a husband's role. Ysabel sat quite still, aware that she must pitch her response perfectly.

'Oh Luis, Luis, Luis,' she said, 'You must listen to me carefully.' She took a deep breath. 'I have a growth in my breast which I expect will kill me, as it did my mother. I will die when it is time for me to die, when God wills it. It is how it should be. Your grandfather wants to cut it out; he assures me that it can be done but he cannot promise, nor should he, that it will prolong my life.'

Luis started to speak but Ysabel held up her hand to silence him and continued, 'I know what you are about to say. You will tell me that Islamic medicine has practised such procedures for centuries. You will tell me that I will not feel the cut as I will have a narcotic-soaked sponge over my nose. You will tell me my wound should heal cleanly because of the liberal application of distilled alcohol, and finally you will tell me there is a risk but it is better than dying.'

The expression in his eyes told her she was correct. She smiled ruefully.

'I have heard all this from your grandfather but I say in reply: why avoid death when I have had such a blessed life? I am ready to meet my Lord.'

Luis tried to speak; she held up her hand once more.

'Listen to me, Luis, and remember what I have said always.' He leaned back against the wall, felt the uneven stone through his shirt, and did as he was told. Ysabel spoke quietly in the voice she had used when he was a child, yet he was not offended. It was the voice reserved for explanations and comfort, and as such he did not feel patronised.

'When I was widowed for the second time, I was thirty-seven years old and childless. That year I fulfilled a promise to my husband, Michel, and went on a pilgrimage to the shrine of St Jacques. On my return I stayed in Auch, longer than planned, as my maid was ill. One idle afternoon I looked out of my chamber window and saw a man with a small boy. Over the next few days something happened which I can only explain as a gift from God. I felt a surge of protectiveness for that little boy, which grew into a fierce love beyond anything I had ever experienced. You, Luis, are my gift from God. My child, the son of my heart. How can I be afraid to die when I have been so blessed?'

Her calm, hazel eyes surveyed him.

'Do not be embarrassed, Luis. You must hear what I say.' For a moment Ysabel tilted her head back and closed her eyes, the better to receive the sun's rays, before she started again. 'I found your grandfather difficult to understand at first; he came from a different world. Yet we became bound by love for you, and then by love for each other.' He raised his eyebrows quizzically at her words, a gesture so reminiscent of Hernando that it made her smile. 'Come,' she said, 'I want to show you something.'

Luis followed Ysabel back into the large rambling house, its jumble of rooms comfortingly familiar. Her bedchamber, a room he had not been in for several years, had not changed. The old-fashioned box bed, the presses where she stored her many clothes, and the rough oak table where she displayed her treasures were all as he remembered. Out of habit, long dormant, he immediately went to the table and fiddled with the objects, as he had done as a child. He picked up the beautiful Venetian mirror, a wedding gift from Bernade, and could not resist pulling a face; he cradled the scallop shell from the shrine of St Jacques in the palm of his hand, running his fingers over its ridges; and he pulled the stopper out of the exquisite perfume bottle and inhaled the fresh, flowery scent.

'Have you quite finished?' inquired Ysabel, mock annoyance in her voice. Luis shot her a sheepish glance. He looked incongruous as he stood next to the treasures, yet she could still see the small child in the man before her. He had grown into his features but he was recognisable still as the thin scrap of a boy who had stolen her heart. His deep-set black eyes, although always arresting, did not dominate his face quite as much as they had done; his angular bone structure suited his more mature face and she could not pinpoint the time when she had stopped noticing his disfigurement.

'Sorry', he said as he sat down on the end of the bed.

'I want to show you this.' Ysabel went to one of the presses against the far wall and carefully removed a length of green silk, protected by a wrapping of muslin. 'Do you recognise this, Luis?'

'No.'

'Your grandfather gave this to me, the day after I told him about the tumour.' She walked over to the bed and stood in front of him. She spoke so quietly, he just heard her say, 'That is when I knew he truly loves me.'

'Because of a piece of cloth?' Luis reached out to touch the luxurious material, snagging it on his rough farmer's hands.

'It is the cloth your mother was embroidering on the night she died. She had not started on this length yet.' He pulled away, catching his breath as he felt the old panic rise up. The atmosphere in the room felt heavy, as if they were not alone. Ysabel saw the fear in his eyes and regretted showing him the silk, but she steeled herself as he needed to understand. 'Your grandfather has given this to me to have a new dress made. He wants me to have a future.' She skimmed her fingers across the silk before she ran them over his hair. 'Of course I am not going to use it. I am saving it for you, for the woman you choose as your bride.' After placing the silk on the coverlet, she cupped his face in both of her hands. 'You know where it is if I am not here.'

He pushed her hands away as he stood up, declaring angrily, 'You are not going to die! You must have the surgery. Why did you not marry Grandfather?'

'Luis, you know why. My position in this city rests on the fact that I am Michel Bernade's widow. In turn, your safety and Hernando's rested on that in the beginning. How could I have married your grandfather—an Arab, a foreigner—and allow all I had inherited become his. Such a thing is beyond imagination. You think that, as my husband, Hernando would have the authority to order me to have surgery, but you know that it is not so. It is true that a husband controls everything legally in a marriage and has authority over his wife, but could a husband make me, Ysabel, act against my will? Of course not!'

'That is what he said,' Luis informed her with an air of resignation, which told Ysabel that she was succeeding in making him understand.

'Luis, you know that you are both tolerated because of me. Hernando pays lip service to the Christian Church and Johan is very discreet, but there have always been questions and mutterings. I know your grandfather is respected at the university, but toleration only goes so far.'

'And what of me?' he said suddenly. 'Sometimes I do not know who I am. Sometimes I think I am a great disappointment to him.'

She knew what he meant.

'Your grandfather is very proud of you, as you should be of him. He gave you a life. At forty-nine years of age, he embarked on that perilous journey across the Pyrenees and his one concern was to keep you safe. Think what an ordeal it must have been. The day-to-day activity Hernando did was as now. He walks from his home to the university and back. He wanted to preserve your faith, your heritage, and your way of life. It has not been easy for you both; you must feel isolated, but your grandfather has done his best. He has taught you well.'

Luis sat back down on the bed and looked at her miserably.

'But I drank alcohol when I was travelling. I even got drunk on cyder and I did not always pray five times a day. I have asked Allah for forgiveness, yet at times I find I want to ask the Virgin Mary for help as I did as a small child.'

Ysabel replied honestly.

'I cannot give you an answer, Luis. I do not know what to say. You are a good man, an honourable man, and you must find your own way.'

He thought for a moment.

'There is so much confusion in my mind. Did you know that in England they are continually changing their minds about doctrine and argue about tiny differences in the wording of the Bible?' Ysabel shook her head. She remained standing for the bed was so high that, if she sat next to him, her legs would have hung inelegantly in the air. She touched his hand. 'It is all so mysterious to me, but I do know that you must keep attending church. When you go to the farm at weekends, do you worship in Douelle?'

'No,' he answered truthfully. 'I hope that the citizens of Caors will think that I do and that the good people of Douelle will believe I attended Mass before I travelled there.'

'I thought as much. You must be careful, Luis.'

'I will.'

Ysabel folded the silk almost reverently, wrapped it in the muslin, and returned it to the press.

'What are you doing today?' she asked.

'I thought I might spend it with you,' he replied nonchalantly.

'No, you are not.' She felt she needed to rest, to recover from the emotion of the morning, but, more importantly, she did not want him to shadow her, his forehead creased with worry. 'You must have many things to do for your journey.'

He did not tell her what he had done. There would be time for that later.

'I will go then.' He stood up and gave her a quick, tight hug. He crossed the room to leave but turned to speak to her, his hand on the door latch.

'Ysabel.'

'Yes?'

'If I am a gift from God, I think it very ungrateful of you to leave me alone and unprotected. I do not think that is what God would wish.'

'Luis Gharsia!' retorted Ysabel, 'it is not for you to presume what God wishes.'

'But you think you know what He wills.'

'Go,' she said good-naturedly, 'I am too busy to argue with you. Go!'

'Think about it?'

'Go,' she repeated before she added what he wanted to hear. 'I will give it some thought.'

TWENTY-FOUR

≈

Bridgwater, June 1546

Alyce waited until she knew the rest of the household was occupied before she left the house, Meg dancing excitedly by her side. Her father had already departed, anxious not to be late for his meeting with the mayor. Agnes was busy in the kitchen, assisted by Mary, while Rufus was deep in discussion with their cousin Matthew Blake, who had become a regular visitor since the previous summer. The reason for her subterfuge was not apparent as Alyce pushed the heavy oak door shut and set off for the Market Place at a brisk pace. However, if anybody had accompanied her, other than Meg, they would have been surprised to see her bypass the stalls and continue down Forstret in the direction of the jetty.

'Are we going to see if any ships have arrived?' asked Meg, who enjoyed this new activity, which was beginning to become routine.

'Yes,' replied her elder sister. 'We might be lucky and be on the jetty at the precise moment a ship docks.'

As they skirted the castle wall, Alyce held her breath in anticipation. *Perhaps today would be the day he would arrive?* During April and May she had visited the docks occasionally, but once June had arrived it had become almost a daily occurrence. At first, when Luis had not come, she had blamed the hostilities with France which had broken out shortly after he had left. However, now there was no danger. News that an advantageous peace had been signed with the old enemy had been read out in church earlier in the month and Alyce had become certain he would come at last. Sadly, as with all the other occasions when she had made that detour, she was to be disappointed for there was no ship in view.

Deflated, Alyce stood for some time staring at the empty dock. Normally the quay was busy; there had even been a vessel from Bordèu a few days earlier but it had not brought the person she longed to see. *He said he would come. He said he would come. He should be here by now.* She chided herself for her thoughts, for her expectations, for her foolishness in willing the winter months to pass quickly so that spring would return and, with it, Luis Gharsia. Now it was summer and with each passing day her hope had begun to dwindle. Soon it would be too late for him to come and return home in time for the grape harvest. The tug of Meg's hand broke her reverie. Alyce smiled wanly at the little girl and said, 'Come let us go to the market and see what the morning catch has brought. Then we will go to the baker by the West Gate and buy a fresh loaf.'

As they approached the church, the old bell started to peal and a crowd gathered around the church gate. A newly-wed couple, arm in arm, paused at the door. Alyce wanted to carry on but Meg pulled her back.

'I want to see the bride! I want to see the bride!' Reluctantly, Alyce agreed. She watched the bride and groom squint as their eyes became accustomed to the bright sunlight after the dim interior of the church. Dressed in blue, the colour of love and fidelity, the girl was young and pretty; markedly younger than the man. She radiated happiness as her new husband led her proudly down the path. Alyce suppressed a flash of envy as he bent his head, to catch what his young bride had said, a look of adoration on his face. She could see it was a fortunate match, a love match, which was not always the case with other couples who left the confines of the parish church to begin their life together.

'Come on,' she encouraged, keen to leave the environs of the church.

'I want to stay,' demanded Meg, assertion dominating her sturdy little body as she crossed her arms and refused to budge.

'We will come back another day, Meg.'

'No.'

'There will be other weddings soon.'

Meg put her head on one side and eyed her sister knowingly.

'How do you know?'

'June is a popular month for weddings.'

'Why?'

'It is summer. The weather is warm and June is a popular month, coming immediately after May which is considered an unlucky month for marriage.'

'Why?'

Alyce was about to fabricate a reason when her characteristic honesty triumphed.

'I am not really sure, Meg. I feel I should know but I don't. We will ask Agnes when we get home. Please come, we have much to do before dinner.'

'No! I want to watch the bride.'

Thwarted, Alyce tried to think of a distraction, 'Shall we see if the button man is at the market?'

'Yes, yes please!' Meg clapped her hands with glee, executing a complete volte-face as she turned her back on the happy couple and made for the stalls.

The button man was there with his wonderful range of wares. There were wooden buttons, glass buttons, buttons of bone and horn, and, if you caught him on a good day and you were a special favourite, as was Meg, he would reach into the box he sat on and show you delicate buttons of mother of pearl, shiny buttons of copper, and precious buttons of silver and gold. Meg was lucky; it was a good day and her face shone with pleasure as she was allowed to handle the iridescent mother of pearl. She turned her wide blue eyes expectantly on Alyce but to no avail. Her elder sister took the opportunity to purchase six horn buttons for their father's jacket before bidding the stallholder farewell and continuing on to the fish stall.

It was almost dinner-time when they returned to St Mary Street to find Thomas home from his meeting and waiting in the parlour with Rufus and Matthew Blake. When Alyce entered the room she was flushed from the exertion of walking vigorously from the West Gate, fearful that she would delay the serving of the meal.

Matthew Blake watched her covertly as Thomas broke the news of the letter. With his connections in the Diocese of Bristol, the canon had heard the gossip from court and he could feel a new wind blowing. The old king's health was deteriorating. Surely he could not live much longer? It was hoped that Henry's heir would promote a more reformist Church of England. Edward's uncle, Edward Seymour, was known to embrace Protestant ideas. Two of the young prince's influential teachers, Richard Coxe and John Cheke, were known humanists, and the former was a Protestant while the prince's French tutor, Jean Belmain, was a follower of Calvin. Matthew Blake could be patient. If the time came when clergy could safely take a wife, Alyce Weaver would be an ideal choice. As he continued to watch her, it became clear to Matthew that the high colour which made her glow when she entered the room had drained away at her father's words.

'He is not coming?' her voice sounded strange.

Thomas looked puzzled.

'That is what I said, Alyce.'

She fought to compose herself, sitting down carefully and arranging her skirts.

'Tell me the content of the letter, Father.'

'It is very short. Gharsia apologises for being unable to come to England this year as his patron is very ill.'

'That is not much of a reason,' grumbled Rufus, making no secret of his disappointment. 'Why does he have to stay?'

Matthew, eager to contribute to the conversation, intervened with, 'Sometimes it is very prudent to put one's patron first.'

Rufus was not convinced.

'I could understand it if it was a member of his family, but a patron? Surely she has others to support her?'

Matthew was quick to respond, disliking his views being disregarded. He felt he should clarify.

'Perhaps the lady is near death and Gharsia wants to be available to receive any possible benefits.' His chest expanded noticeably on delivery of his wise words but, as he looked directly at Alyce to add emphasis, Matthew was surprised at her words of dismissal.

'Luis would never be so mercenary. He must have genuine affection for his patron—he would need a valid reason for not coming.'

Frustration coloured Rufus's reply.

'I cannot agree. I feel it is poor repayment for all the efforts we have put into making this enterprise possible.'

'So it is. So it is,' murmured Blake.

Alyce looked from her father to her brother, ignoring her cousin. The letter hung limply in Thomas's hand. She wanted to reach out for it, to take it in her hand and run her fingers over his words, and to read them, for he must have said more than her father had summarised. But now was not the time. The room seemed stifling; afraid that they might witness her real distress, as the very action of pretence was making her ill, she excused herself.

'I feel a little unwell. I will go and lie down. Please eat without me.' She did not hear Matthew, his voice most solicitous, say, 'Of course, Cousin Alyce, you look so pale.'

The tears she expected did not come as she left the room, nor had they arrived by the time she reached her bedchamber. She sat motionless and dry-eyed on the stool next to the chest as she chided herself again for being a fool. Although she had defended Luis, she felt betrayed. *He said he would return. He promised to return. You are stupid, Alyce Weaver. Why would he want to see you? You imagined an intimacy which did not exist. You are ridiculous to have hoped.* She climbed onto the bed. Turning on her side, she drew her legs up until she was in a tight ball and wrapped her arms around her wounded heart. She remembered the dark, claustrophobic cabin where, for a time, she had felt closer to him than any other man as he had gently bathed Meg's leg. She remembered his magnetism, the way she wanted to touch him, and again she chided herself for acting like a fanciful girl. She would not make that mistake again.

◆   ◆   ◆

Meg sat quietly, as she was listening. It was a new habit she had recently acquired and she found it very rewarding. Now, just past her fifth birthday, the youngest Weaver had made a discovery or, as she sometimes thought, two discoveries. The first was that adults talked when she was in the room as if she was not present, unaware that her understanding had developed considerably. The second discovery, which was even better, was that the knowledge gained could be stored, ready to be used to her advantage at a later date.

At first, the conversation around the table had bored her. It was the usual talk of prices, taxes, and, because Matthew Blake was present, religious matters pertaining to his role in the neighbouring diocese. His bishop, Paul Bush, was mentioned frequently, always with the hint of obsequiousness which characterised the canon. Meg watched the clergyman, his face animated, converse with her brother and father. She did not care for Cousin Matthew as he paid her no attention; experience had shown her she was invisible to him. The little girl was about to excuse herself when the conversation took a turn for the better. There had been a lull while the three men finished their cyder when Rufus announced, 'Why don't I go to the Pays d'Oc?'

His father was startled.

'You go?'

'Yes, it makes sense. It is only late June now. If I sail with our next consignment of cloth, I can be in Bordèu within the month and with Luis by early August. I could bring the wine, and, more importantly, the saffron, back with me.' Rufus studied his father, suddenly conscious that he very much wanted an answer in the affirmative.

Thomas pushed his hands through his fading gingery hair. He was unsure.

'It is a big undertaking at such short notice and I am not convinced it is necessary. Gharsia will come next year.'

'How do we know?' questioned Rufus with a skill practised through many negotiations.

His father smiled, recognising what Rufus was doing.

'I thought we both agreed Gharsia was an honourable man who would keep his word. It is only unfortunate circumstances which prevent him from coming.'

Rufus had to agree but added, 'If I don't go we will lose a year and will need to re-establish our buyers. If I go I can really check the feasibility of the enterprise and return with the goods.'

It made good business sense but Thomas was still reluctant to give his consent. 'You would be travelling in a foreign country with a very substantial amount of money on you, Richard.'

'Yes, I agree, but my French is fluent and my purpose unknown.'

'You must not go alone, Richard.'

Rufus could feel his father's capitulation coming.

'I won't. What if I take Ralph Brewer with me? He is a big, stout lad.'

Thomas nodded. Their maid, Mary, had a brother who worked on the family's small holding out on the Taunton road.

'We will see if James Brewer can spare his son for a couple of months. If we pay him enough, I am sure he will.'

Rufus beamed at his father and Blake; the germ of an idea was becoming reality. He sat back from the table and became aware of Meg, sitting very still. He gave her an exaggerated wink.

◆　　◆　　◆

Alyce heard the patter of small feet but kept her eyes tightly shut.

'Alyce?' whispered Meg as she reached the bed, 'Alyce, are you asleep?'

'Yes.'

The little girl giggled.

'No, you are not. If you were asleep you wouldn't answer.' The mattress sank as she clambered up and snuggled down on her side in the soft feathers.

Alyce opened her eyes, her sister's face was so close it was out of focus. She inched back slightly. Meg's small plump face was full of the importance of the information she was about to impart.

'Rufus is going to see Luis Gharsia.'

Alyce took a moment to digest this information, continuing to stare at Meg. Her brain registered the irrelevant; the blue of the child's eyes and the thickness of the brown lashes framing them, the faint dusting of freckles sprinkled across the neat retroussé nose, and the mischievous curvy mouth. She felt a rush of love for her younger sister.

'Where?'

'The Pays d'Oc.'

'How do you know?'

'Father and Rufus were talking about it just now.'

'Is he really going?'

'I think so.'

'When?'

'Soon.'

Alyce propped herself up on one elbow, the better to see Meg.

'Is he going alone?'

'No. Father is going to ask if Mary's brother can go with him.'

Alyce turned and lay on her back. Meg copied her and said, 'I want to see Luis.' Bright June sunshine streamed through the small casement window, dust motes danced in the light. Suddenly there seemed no air. Alyce rose in a quick jerky movement and pushed the window open.

'Can you remember Luis from last year?'

'Yes. He was a giant and he used to play with me.'

Alyce laughed, a sad brittle laugh.

'He is not coming to see us.'

◆   ◆   ◆

On the same morning when Alyce's hopes were crushed, Ysabel woke early. She heard Lisette stir in her sleep, saw the sunlight edge around the shutters, and again pondered on the miracle that she was still alive. It was now eight weeks since she had arrived at the surgery, terrified that she would never see another sunrise. Her hand had gripped Luis's so tightly that he had been forced to peel her fingers away when they reached the room where the operation was to take place. Hernando had been there but she had been unable to look at him. Instead her eyes had met those of Lorenzo Zametti, the surgeon who was to perform the procedure. His calm, steady gaze had been intended to reassure his patient but it had not. She had remained in a state of almost paralytic fright until the sweet-smelling sponge, administered by Hernando, had rendered her unconscious.

Ysabel moved so she was more comfortable. It had been a long, slow recovery, and although the wound had healed, it was still very tender. Hernando had devised a schedule for her to decrease, and then stop, her dependence on the poppy juice that had deadened the pain and she felt he had been rather too eager with his timing. Nevertheless, as she stretched and winced with discomfort, Ysabel was glad with every fibre of her being that she had been brave enough to agree to the operation. It had taken some time for her to make up her mind, sure as she was that she must accept God's will. In the end it was not Luis, however strongly he argued, who changed her mind. It was Hernando. After weeks of indecision, she had asked him a question, one she had wanted to ask for years.

They had been sitting in her garden, enjoying the freshness of a spring morning when she had looked at his beloved face and said, 'When you first arrived in Caors, did you intend to settle here permanently?'

'No.'

'What made you change your plans?'

He had studied her with his dark intense eyes, so serious under stern brows and had simply said, 'You, Ysabel. I could not bear to leave you.'

He had affirmed what she had always hoped but could never quite believe. As a cloud obscured the sun momentarily, the temperature dipped and she remembered that morning, many years ago, when she had found him distraught, slouched on the floor and weeping for all that he had lost. She had known then that she could not let him suffer again. She knew she would not let him suffer again and so very quietly, in almost a whisper, Ysabel had spoken, with some of her old teasing spark.

'Are you really a great surgeon?'

He had moved his head so it touched hers, uncertain he had heard correctly.

'What did you say?'

'Are you really a great surgeon?'

Puzzled, he had nodded and then he had smiled as he heard her say, 'Then I will allow you to cut out my tumour on one condition.'

'What is that?'

'What do you think?'

'That I wear my spectacles?'

'Yes.' She had watched his smile spread until it illuminated his whole face and she had known that, whatever the future brought, she had made the right decision.

TWENTY-FIVE

Caors, July 1546

The imperious knocking increased in volume as Johan rushed towards the door of the small house on the corner of the Place St Urcisse. The unusual occurrence of unexpected visitors, combined with the resounding thuds, made his heart race as he approached the sturdy oak and released the heavy metal lock. Astonished, Johan viewed the caller with trepidation for before him stood a great bear of a man whose height was increased by the turban framing his fleshy face. A face with a wide forehead and a neat mouth, half obscured by a bushy beard. Small eyes, dark and hooded, studied Johan aggressively.

'Does Hernando Gharsia live here?'

'My master is not at home,' Johan stuttered.

'Is his grandson here?'

'No, Luis Gharsia is not here either.'

The small dark eyes narrowed into slits.

'Luis *Gharsia*?'

Johan's discomfort was growing. He repeated, 'My master is not here.' The visitor pushed past him. Johan was helpless against the momentum of the big man's weight and, as the words were uttered in Catalan, he understood there was no point arguing.

'It does not matter. I will wait.'

Instinct told Johan that Hernando would not want such a person in the study so he invited the visitor to take a seat on the settle in the hall. Quickly dismissing the idea of offering wine, he brought a jug of fresh well water from the kitchen. The man growled his thanks and gulped the water back in one swig.

'I am uncertain when my master will return,' Johan lied as he knew Hernando was dining with Ysabel. In response the man removed his outer gown of thick fine wool to reveal a cotton caftan and baggy trousers. He threw the expensive article nonchalantly over the back of the settle and then grinned at Johan. He shook his head from side to side; the beautiful pear-shaped pearl in his right ear swung rhythmically, as did his jowls. Small eyes dancing, the man addressed Johan, 'Do not worry, lad. I mean no harm, but I have waited many years to confront your master. A little more time will not matter. Bring me some food.'

◆   ◆   ◆

Two hours later, the visitor was snoring lightly, his carefully manicured hands, festooned with ornate rings, resting on his ample belly. Johan crept quietly across the hall so he could be as near the door as possible, ready to warn his master of his unexpected visitor. But he was too late. A mighty roar echoed around the high ceiling as Hernando espied his son-in-law slumped on the settle.

'How dare you come back after all this time!' Hernando had returned from Ysabel's using the back entrance.

Yusuf awoke instantly with the skill of one who is always watchful and moved with surprising grace for such a heavy man. He chose to smile.

'Old man, old man. I greet you.'

Hernando felt the buried hatred rise within him, so strong that he could taste it in his mouth. He swung round, accusation in his eyes, and asked Johan, 'Why did you let him in?'

It was Yusuf who answered.

'He had no choice. If you need a guard dog, old man, you should hire a bigger beast.' He continued smiling. 'I have come to see my son and I think you, Hernando Gharsia, owe me an explanation.'

Hernando felt cornered. He wanted Yusuf away before Luis returned yet he knew he did indeed owe his son-in-law an explanation. He refused to look at his visitor, but told him to follow as he made his way to the study door. Just before he raised the latch, Hernando turned and addressed Johan, whose friendly face wore a stricken expression.

'It is fine. Can you bring us some sekanjabin, please?' He then paused and continued, hoping the younger man would understand his meaning, 'Make sure we are not disturbed by anyone. Anyone at all.' He was unsure when Luis would return.

Yusuf started before they were seated.

'Why does my son not bear my name?'

'I thought it was safer for him not to.'

'What gives you the right to make such a decision?'

'The right of the person who saved your son's life.' Hernando gave Yusuf a long, slow look and then waved him towards a stool. The big man shifted uncomfortably when he sat down.

'The attack had nothing to do with me.' His father-in-law raised an eyebrow, a habit which had always maddened Yusuf, and did not speak. 'I repeat, the attack had nothing to do with me. I was in Istanbul when it happened.'

Hernando worked hard to control his feelings and his voice, when he spoke, was eerily calm. 'No other Muslim household was attacked that evening. It was not like the days of the Germania. It was only your family. What did you do? Who did you cheat?'

Yusuf kept his eyes down. He sat motionless, his head bent, his elbows resting on his massive thighs.

'Was Maryam dead when you found her?'

'What do you care after seventeen years?'

'I care.' Yusuf spoke so quietly, Hernando had to strain to hear him.

'Yes, she was dead. So was the baby.'

'Little Layla,' Yusuf mused, 'I hardly knew her. I left shortly after she was born.'

'Yes,' continued Hernando in his eerily calm voice. 'Luis was as good as dead. Without me he would have joined his mother and sister.' In the past Yusuf would have challenged his father-in-law's statement but, to Hernando's surprise, he remained quiet and did not question the claim. Eventually Yusuf raised his eyes and said, 'I want to see my boy.'

Hernando's calm drained away.

'He is not a boy,' he snapped. 'He is a man. In case you have forgotten, he is twenty-two years old.'

Yusuf shrugged.

'Yes, he is a man. A man who can choose who he sees. Where is he?'

'You will not find him here.' Hernando flung the words at Yusuf. 'He is busy organising a trip to England to export wine.' It was a lie. The trip had been postponed for a year, but Hernando was determined to thwart his son-in-law.

Yusuf's eyes lit up.

'Export wine! My son, my son is a trader. He is not a dried up stick of a physician-surgeon like you. He travels and trades.'

As soon as he had spoken Hernando realised his mistake. The big man's demeanour changed, he pushed himself up off the stool and started to pace the room. He laughed, 'My son is a trader. He is a trader. My blood flows in him. Hah! He is not the next in line of a family of eminent physicians from the great centre of Granada!' He turned and his eyes glistened as he strode back to Hernando, 'Perhaps he and I can go into business together?'

Yusuf returned to the stool.

'Tell me. Tell me about my son.'

The door opened to reveal Johan with the refreshments and Hernando noted with satisfaction that, as usual, he had taken the initiative and added a plate of his master's favourite almond cakes. Without a word, Johan placed the tray on the table and withdrew. Yusuf repeated, 'Tell me about Luis.' The eagerness in his son-in-law's voice incensed Hernando.

'What right have you to know anything about your son? Where have you been all these years?' He looked Yusuf up and down, 'Getting fat—no doubt at other people's expense.'

'Legitimate trade, old man. I'm earning an honest income to support my family.' Yusuf's shrewd eyes focused on Hernando, 'I was not the one who fled in the middle of the night with another man's treasure.' His father-in-law raised an eyebrow. Yusuf continued as he surveyed the room. 'What have you done with my gold, old man? You obviously haven't spent it on this gloomy house.' He did not expect an answer. He looked at his adversary and said, 'This is a very small house. Where are the women's quarters?' He watched Hernando carefully, with dawning realisation. 'You have no women,' he stated in astonishment, his voice rising on the last word. Yusuf revelled in the opportunity to needle the old man, 'You live without wives?'

Infuriated Hernando rose to the bait.

'I have a woman.'

'And my son?'

'I do not know,' Hernando hissed in exasperation, 'no doubt Johan has introduced him to one of the accommodating widows of the town.'

Yusuf grinned and fingered his bushy beard then instantly he was serious.

'My son, he is a true follower of Islam?'

'Yes,' replied Hernando, for it was the truth.

'But you have both been baptised Christians.'

'Well, what of it?'

Yusuf shrugged.

'It must be difficult for you. I left.'

'We do as we have always done.'

There was an uneasy silence before Yusuf spoke. 'You could always come back with me to Istanbul.'

His father-in-law did not reply.

◆   ◆   ◆

Yusuf's patience was rewarded. Three days after his visit to Hernando, one of the ostler's boys, whom he had paid generously to watch the house on the Place St Urcisse, came with news. The young master was home and the physician had left early that morning for the university. Doubts that he would never see his son disappeared, for soon he was due to move on with the merchants of Marsilha, and Yusuf left the inn with a light heart.

He was surprised to see his hand trembled slightly as he lifted the knocker, but that was insignificant to the surprise he felt when he beheld the man who opened the door. Since his recent decision in Venice to travel to the Pays d'Oc, Yusuf had imagined this meeting. In his mind he had seen a younger version of himself: loud, gregarious, larger than life. A man who would shout with glee when he saw his father. They would embrace, thump each other joyfully on the back, and exclaim at their similarity. None of this happened. There was no sign of Yusuf's bulk, although the young man before him was tall and broad-shouldered. He was lean and muscled, and the expression on his thin face was inscrutable.

Yusuf felt a surge of guilt as he noted the scar which dominated the right-hand side of his son's face. It crossed the young man's temple, puckered the skin at the corner of his eye, and then traversed his cheek before it became partially obscured by his closely trimmed beard. Yusuf thought he knew the weapon which had left that mark, he had been threatened with it more than once. Maryam's eyes, black and intense, studied him and Yusuf found himself stumbling over his words.

'Luis, my son. Do you not know me?' He thought he heard a whispered 'Papa' but he could not be certain. What he did hear clearly was his son ordering him to enter the house quickly to avoid the neighbours seeing one of the Gharsias conversing with an Ottoman on the doorstep.

Once inside Yusuf tried to embrace Luis but met with a stiff, unyielding reaction. He dropped his arms, took a step back and said, 'Let me look at you, my son.' Luis looked back at his father, raised an eyebrow but remained silent, an action so reminiscent of Hernando that Yusuf felt crushing disappointment so great that his eyes welled up with tears. He regarded the hard settle in the hall without enthusiasm for it was too narrow for his comfort. He thought of the soft cushions of his home and let out a little sigh as he lowered himself onto the polished wood. Luis remained standing.

'I thought you were dead. All these years, I thought you were dead.' It was Yusuf's turn not to reply but he did not avert his eyes; instead he watched Luis warily as the young man continued, 'Why did you not come for me?'

'It was difficult.'

'Why?'

Rather than provide an answer, Yusuf posed his own question: 'Do you know how difficult it is to trade across vast distances? From Valencia to Venice, from Venice to Istanbul or Damascus, from to Istanbul to Baghdad, and then back again?'

'I can imagine.'

'I did come back but you were gone.'

Luis eyed his father keenly. 'How did you find me now?'

'The old man left a note in my strong-box after he had removed most of my treasure.' Yusuf was pleased to see a flicker of emotion cross his son's face.

'Treasure?'

'Yes, *my* treasure. The fruits of all my hard work.'

'I am sure Grandfather would never steal.'

'Are you?'

'Yes.'

'Then ask him where my Venetian gold ducats are. Ask him where my rubies and emeralds are. Ask him where the lapis lazuli I bought from the tribesmen of Afghanistan is.' Yusuf's voice rose with each sentence uttered.

'I will,' said Luis coldly. 'Where were you when Mama and Layla died?'

'That year, I spent much time in Istanbul. It is the centre of a trading empire, Luis. You should see the imaret of the great mosque of Aya Sofia. There is a huge market with over twelve thousand traders, a magnificent stone vaulted roof covers the whole area, and the trading opportunities are unsurpassed.' As Yusuf warmed to the subject of his much-loved adopted city he continued enthusiastically, '1530 was a marvellous year. The festivities celebrating the circumcision of the royal princes were spectacular. I had never seen such magnificent fireworks.' Suddenly, he registered Luis's disapproving face.

'I dislike cities, with their narrow streets and dark corners.'

'But I thought you were a trader. Your grandfather said you are preparing to ship wine to England.'

'I am, but I helped produce the wine. That is what matters to me.' The pride in his voice made Yusuf study his son more closely. He noticed Luis's hands for the first time, so unlike his own bejewelled ones. The hands in front of him were those of a peasant, scarred by cuts, calloused by manual labour. Yusuf experienced another disappointment.

'You are a peasant?'

Luis saw him staring and smiled a slow smile. Yusuf had the feeling his son was enjoying himself at his father's expense.

'No Papa, I am a lawyer.' Yusuf's pleasure at the familiar appellation was tempered by his confusion.

'Let me understand this. You are a lawyer yet you have the hands of a peasant. You produce your own wine and you are preparing to go to England to sell it?'

'That is correct. And I will take saffron too, next year.'

Sensing his son's guard had weakened, Yusuf joked, 'Perhaps I will come to England,' but one glance at Luis's face told him that he had misjudged the mood. He had no way of knowing that the idea of arriving at the Weavers accompanied by a Mudejar in the full Turkish dress of the Ottoman Empire filled his son with horror. 'Perhaps, not,' said Yusuf quickly. 'I have no interest in visiting that foggy little island.'

Luis was still standing.

'Why did you come now? What really kept you away?'

Yusuf thought carefully before he spoke. He would not mention the two wives in Istanbul who had dutifully produced children, albeit daughters rather than the much-desired sons. Nor would he mention the impressive house he had managed to acquire with its pleasing proportions, shady courtyard, and cooling fountain. But he would tell the truth, or rather part of the truth. Long ago Yusuf had discovered that if there was a germ of truth in his words, they were more easily accepted.

'I have always longed for you, my son, but, as I said, circumstances were difficult. I returned to Valencia two years after you had left. The house was intact; I found the old man's note. Ahmed had been looking after things. I knew you were safe and what life could I give you? I could not take you with me on the road. I always meant to come and see you but the years just passed. Then three months ago, when I was in Venice, I had an overwhelming desire to see you. I had met some merchants who were coming to the Pays d'Oc so I came with them.'

Yusuf stopped for he knew his tongue had a habit of running on and he did not want to admit that he had become resigned to the fact that Luis would be his only son. He had considered taking a third, younger wife but he was a man who enjoyed harmony, and now, as he planned to spend more time at home, he did not want to spoil his peaceful household. Knowing that timing was crucial in all negotiations, Yusuf rose from the settle and looked forlornly at Luis.

'My son, I must go now. I have one more day before I leave Caors. It would give me great pleasure if we could meet tomorrow. I am at the inn by the Pont Neuf.' He did not make the mistake of trying to embrace Luis but turned towards the door. Walking slowly, he was almost across the uneven stone flags when he heard, 'I will come to the inn tomorrow—after noon prayers.'

◆   ◆   ◆

Luis had spent a disturbed night haunted by images of the past. Lying tensely in the dark, he had drifted in and out of sleep, always accompanied by Johan's heavy breathing from across the room. They had come to him: Mama, Papa, and Layla, not clearly as he had been so young, but as threads of forgotten memory. He had felt the whisper of his mother's lips as she kissed him goodnight, the bristle of his papa's beard as he had been hugged tightly, and the gurgle of the baby as he had dangled her rattle above her cradle. Intertwined with these was Hernando's earnest face as he had explained to his grandson about Yusuf's treasure.

Walking quickly, Luis reached the inn without seeing anyone he knew and found his father's room with as much discretion as he could manage. Yusuf opened the door, relief on his face. His son had arrived as promised.

'I was afraid you might not come.'

'Why?' said Luis sharply. 'I said I would.'

Yusuf shrugged and invited Luis to enter. He returned to his position, leaning against the windowsill. 'I am afraid I cannot offer you any refreshment.'

Luis regarded the room. It was plain and sparsely furnished, but his father had been lucky to acquire a private chamber.

'I have already eaten.' He joined Yusuf by the window: he felt better not meeting his father's eye. There was a long silence; it seemed there was nothing to say until Yusuf spoke. His voice, when it came, tried to be relaxed and conversational.

'I saw your grandfather this morning as I was looking through the window. He was with a woman.' He felt his son's attention in the slight movement of Luis rearranging his legs as he shifted against the window ledge to be more comfortable. 'She was a small fair-skinned woman, a cheerful woman who was smiling as she spoke. She made him laugh. Who is she?'

'Ysabel Bernade.'

'His woman?'

'Yes.'

'She is younger than him?'

'Yes.'

'Is that why you stayed here, away from our people?'

'Perhaps,' replied Luis cautiously.

'These fair-skinned women can be bewitching. It has happened to our Sultan. It is over ten years since Suleiman married the slave girl given to him by the Grand Vezir Ibrahim. It is said the Hürrem, the laughing one, has great influence over him.'

Luis listened but did not comment. Yusuf continued.

'Your grandfather appeared content.'

'Yes.'

Yusuf surveyed the room as if he was searching for words.

'You have been happy, my son?'

'I have been safe.'

Yusuf nodded slowly; it was not the answer he wanted, the answer which would assuage his guilt. 'Your grandfather tells me you are a scholar. I expect you know the Qur'an better than me,' he said honestly.

'I have tried, but it is difficult without an imam.'

Yusuf pretended to think for a moment but he had already planned what he wanted to say, 'Why don't you come to Istanbul with me? You would be free to practise our faith. The old man could come too, and his concubine.'

A smile played around Luis's mouth at the thought of Ysabel being termed his grandfather's concubine.

'Madame Bernade is a very wealthy business woman in her own right. It is she who produces the saffron.' Yusuf's small eyes lit up with interest.

'Is it quality saffron?'

'The best.'

'I would be interested in saffron. I do not plan to return to Persia again. The border warfare in the north is too fierce. Relations are not good between the Sultan and the Shah.'

'There is not enough to export to the East.'

'Ah, well, she could still come. We have Jews, Armenians, and Christians in the empire. They are allowed to worship freely and keep their traditions as long as they don't interfere with the state.' He paused and then added, 'Although the Sultan doesn't like Roman Catholics, but if she was Orthodox that would be fine.'

Luis shifted against the window ledge and stretched his legs out further.

'I talked to Grandfather last night.'

'Ah!'

'He said he did take the treasure.'

'I told you so!'

'He explained that he has used some of it for me but never for himself. He is willing to return what remains of the gold minus the amount of Mama's dowry.' Luis turned his head, met his father's eyes and said coolly, 'He believes you forfeited that as you were not a good husband.'

Yusuf was about to argue but the ugly scar across his son's face made his father-in-law's words ring true. He answered quietly.

'I am very sorry I was not there for you all.' He appeared so sad that Luis felt a softening in his attitude towards him. It soon passed as his father then boasted, 'Tell the old man not to worry about my gold and jewels. I have increased my wealth four-fold since then.'

Luis pushed himself off from the window ledge and looked out onto the river below. The Olt flowed gently past, green and deep. It always calmed him.

'I must go, Papa. I wish you well.'

Yusuf pulled his son into his arms before he had a chance to resist. Luis allowed himself to rest his cheek against his father's bushy beard for one fleeting moment and inhaled the evocative scent of sandalwood. Yusuf's voice was urgent as Luis stiffly extricated himself from the embrace.

'Promise me, my son. Promise me that if you ever need sanctuary you will come to me in Istanbul.'

'I will.'

'Good,' Yusuf boomed. 'I will be easy to find. Go to the market of Aya Sofia and ask anyone for Yusuf al-Balansi!'

T W E N T Y - S I X

~

Caors, August 1546

It was the hottest August Luis could remember. The sun had parched the earth and the grass edging the vines was brown and brittle. Its heat seared his skin through his clothing even though it was not yet mid-morning. He glanced at the cloudless sky; there was no sign of the clouds which would bring relief to the land, people, and animals. He surveyed the rows of his grapes and hoped that the roots were deep enough to find water; he became aware of the song of the cigales. Except for them, the countryside was strangely quiet for the sheep, pigs, goats, and milking cow had been brought into the barn to protect them from the merciless heat and the chickens had entered of their own accord. The result was an uneasy stillness that pressed down on the valley and made Luis irritable. It exacerbated his warring emotions of relief and frustration: relief that Ysabel appeared to be on the road to recovery and frustration that he would not return to England that year.

As he stared down from his vantage point, he became aware of two figures in the distance. They moved slowly, almost gingerly, picking their way across the hot stony ground. There was a familiarity about one of the men, but Luis's brain refused to register his identity: it was impossible. Yet, as the distance between them shortened, disbelief gave way to certainty as the gangly frame of Richard Weaver approached, accompanied by an unknown younger man. Richard's face was burnt and sore from the sun and, as he removed his hat, Luis could see that his flaming red hair was plastered with sweat against his scalp.

There was a moment of awkwardness. Hot and tired as he was, Richard felt at a disadvantage. The man standing above him did not resemble the Luis he remembered. His face and height were the same, but the man Richard saw was a stranger. He was clad as a peasant, in a loose tunic and trousers, with his feet in clogs. His skin, tanned by outdoor labour in the intense sun, was much darker than it had been in England, his hair and beard were no longer neatly trimmed, and there was no sign of the friendship they had enjoyed on Luis's face. Richard's smile started to fade and, knowing that Ralph Brewer was watching with interest, he was beginning to think that it had been a mistake to come when Luis's countenance changed. He suddenly grasped Richard's hand, smiling broadly, and spoke in his heavily accented English.

'I did not expect to see a pink Englishman today, Rufus!'

All was well. Rufus clasped Luis's rough, calloused hand in both of his and replied, 'Two Englishmen, Luis. This is Ralph Brewer.'

Luis nodded at the younger man, a boy of about seventeen but tall and strongly built, whose weathered complexion had coped much better with the Quercy sun.

'You are both welcome. Let us walk back to the house.' He studied Rufus closely. 'You need to go indoors. You really are very pink.'

It was easy to slip back into their previous camaraderie.

'And you, Luis Gharsia, are looking very brown.' The slight tilt of Luis's head as he acknowledged the comment without replying was so familiar that it confirmed for Rufus that he was after all in the presence of his friend. 'I will have you know that it is quite painful.'

'I can see that. We will need to get some salve from my grandfather. I planned to return to Caors tomorrow but we can go back this evening together, if you wish.'

Marie had been collecting eggs and had just emerged from the barn when the three men entered the yard. Rufus and Ralph stopped in surprise as she bestowed her most radiant smile on them, confident of the impression she was making. She had prepared for this moment as soon as her mother had informed her that two foreigners had called asking for Luis. She had brushed her hair until it shone and tied it back with a bright red ribbon. To the Englishmen, she was an incongruous sight in that rural setting, an exquisite creature with a perfect heart-shaped face, a cloud of brown hair, and knowing tawny eyes. Rufus automatically removed his hat, unhappily conscious of his sweat-soaked hair, and executed his most elegant bow. Ralph remained rigid while Luis continued across the yard, oblivious to Marie's tactics. He stopped once he realised he was alone, and turned to see Rufus complete his gesture of greeting.

'Marie, this is my friend, Richard Weaver, and his companion, Ralph Brewer,' he said, and turned to Rufus. 'And this is Marie Gaulbert.'

Marie returned a greeting and invited the two men to follow her up the steep stone staircase which led to the upper storey. Rufus barely noticed the building with its characteristic turret, the grey sandstone shimmering in the heat, as he followed the young woman's swaying hips. Luis followed behind, finding it difficult to believe the extraordinary turn of events of the morning.

It was markedly cooler in the long, dim room and, after a meal of goats' cheese and bread, accompanied by the very wine which he had travelled to taste, Rufus felt much better. He had been introduced to Guilhem Gaulbert and the rest of his family. The vintner seemed an affable man, although his wife, Loise, appeared withdrawn and peevish. Their son, a man in his early twenties, was as handsome as his sister was lovely, but had a dissolute air about him. Rufus sat opposite Henri, who drank copious amounts of the inky black liquid. He could also study Marie, who was flanked by her brother and mother, while Guilhem occupied the head of the table. He noticed how attentive the young woman was, especially towards Luis and himself, each gesture accompanied by a flirtatious glance under thick lashes. Rufus found he was enjoying himself immensely (he had never imagined his friend would live in the same house as such a beauty) and was disappointed when Luis suggested they repair to the barn where the wine was produced and discuss business.

The early afternoon was spent thrashing out the details of exporting the three tuns, ready and waiting since Luis had prepared them for his journey in March. It was decided that Luis and his visitors would leave as soon as possible that day and call at Douelle on the way back to Caors to arrange transportation to Bordèu. Guilhem would also accompany them to Douelle, and then be responsible for the wine travelling from the vineyard to the river. Neither he nor Luis could envisage any difficulty, other than the water level might be so low that progress would be slow. After a brief stay in Caors, the Englishmen were to travel to Bordèu in readiness for the wine's arrival and then sail with it to Bridgwater.

On their return to the house, Ralph stayed with Loise and Marie to enjoy another cup of wine, but Rufus, curious as ever, refused the refreshment and followed Luis up to the attic, despite being encouraged to support the younger man in his struggle to be a good guest. When he reached the top of the ladder, Rufus surveyed his friend's sleeping arrangements with amazement. The space was spartan and stifling in the hot August afternoon. There was a small window at the gable end but it afforded no circulation of air. Unbearably hot in summer and obviously chillingly cold in winter, it was not what Rufus expected. Luis told his friend to sit on the rough wooden cot while he hastily packed a bag. Rufus's eyes were everywhere, noting the old sheepskins rolled in the corner and the paucity of clothing hanging on a makeshift pole. He watched with interest as Luis reverently took what appeared to be a book wrapped in calfskin from the only other piece of furniture in the attic, a chest made of planks crudely nailed together.

'What is that?' he asked as Luis placed it in its own bag. 'A book?'

'Yes,' Luis carefully fastened the leather satchel. 'But you cannot read it.'

'Why not?'

'It is written in Arabic.'

Luis expected Rufus to continue his questions as he always had when they were together in Bridgwater but his friend's inquisitive mind was more than happy with what he had seen that day. Another piece of the puzzle that was Luis slotted into place. There would be so much to tell his father and Alyce when he returned home.

◆   ◆   ◆

Hernando examined the Englishman's face with thorough concentration. It was one of the worst cases of sunburn he had seen: the skin was raw and peeling and the whites of his patient's eyes, with their green irises, stood out against his livid face. His overall appearance was of vulnerability, which evoked the physician's sympathy.

'It must be very painful.'

'Yes, Sir,' replied Rufus, although Luis's grandfather was speaking quietly, as if to himself.

'Some chamomile salve, I think, would be best at this stage, as the skin is broken.'

'Thank you.' Rufus was still not certain whether an answer was needed and he wished Luis had not left him alone with this stern, distant man, in whose presence Rufus's natural ebullience seemed inappropriate. There had been none of the pleasantries he was used to. His friend had introduced them and then departed with the explanation that he needed to wash.

While Rufus waited for Hernando to come back with the ointment he studied the parlour he was in. It was small, as were all the rooms he had seen so far in the house on the Place St Urcisse. The greatest surprise had been Luis's sleeping chamber where they had dumped his belongings on arrival. Rufus had seen the two beds and had asked, 'Who sleeps here?'

'Johan.'

'Who is Johan?'

His friend had thought for a moment before answering, 'Just Johan. It is difficult to explain.'

'Try.' Rufus's interest had been raised.

'There are three people in this house. Johan is the third. He looks after Grandfather and me but he is not a servant, although he is paid an allowance.'

'He is a relative?'

'No.'

'How did he come to live with you?'

Luis looked at Rufus and knew the barrage of questions would continue until the Englishman was satisfied. Rufus gave him an impish grin, 'Surely you can tell me?'

'Alright, I will give you the shortened version.'

'You always give me the shortened version,' Rufus pointed out, playfully punching Luis on the upper arm.

'When we left Valencia and crossed the Pyrenees we stayed at the inn in Gavarnie, owned by Johan's family. The following year Johan turned up at the university asking for my grandfather. He had lost his parents to the sweating sickness; his sister and his husband had taken over the inn and he had wanted to see what was beyond the mountains. He has been here ever since.'

'Just like that?'

'Yes,' Luis said. 'Just like that.'

'I look forward to meeting him and your grandfather.'

'Johan will probably be with friends in the tavern, and I am not sure where Grandfather is. It is late for him to be working so he is probably with Ysabel.'

'Ysabel?'

'Madame Bernade.'

'Ah.' Rufus fitted another piece into the puzzle.

As Hernando returned with the salve, Rufus could see how alike Luis and his grandfather were. There was the same stealth they used when entering a room, as if they did not want to be noticed, yet ironically they attracted attention by their very height, bearing, and intense gaze. He determined to be his most agreeable.

'I wish to thank you again, Monsieur Gharsia, for your ministrations.' In return he received a slight nod but no answer, so similar to Luis that Rufus felt a smile coming to his lips. He was racking his brains for something interesting to say when Luis saved him the effort by returning. Rufus directed his next remark to his friend.

'You look much improved.'

Luis did indeed. His hair was newly washed, although still too long, and he had trimmed his beard and changed his clothes. He acknowledged Rufus's honesty.

'I have been to the river. The water was so refreshing.' He grinned, 'Now I am ready to eat.'

Hernando glanced from one young man to the other but addressed Rufus.

'Madame Bernade has told me she has offered you hospitality.'

'Yes Sir, when I called on her this morning she very kindly suggested Ralph and I lodge with her rather than stay at the hostel. Ralph has gone to retrieve our bags and check on the horses. He should be back soon.'

'Excellent,' said Luis. 'If we leave now we can meet Ralph and then all go to Ysabel's.'

◆　　◆　　◆

The candle flickered in the slight draught from the open casement, a welcome relief from the blanketing heat, while moths fluttered in from the night and danced around the flame. The soft glow was kind to Ysabel; it masked the pallor of her complexion and she almost looked her old healthy self. Hernando, even though he had seen her earlier that day, searched her face for any signs of relapse. He told himself not to worry so much, it was too soon to know whether all he had done was gain her a little more time. Talking animatedly to the young Englishman with the burnt face, Ysabel paused, caught Hernando's eye, and smiled. She was enjoying the stimulation of new company, and his mood lightened as he registered the sparkle in her eyes. She was asking Richard Weaver about his family, having already covered his journey from England to Quercy. Weaver's companion was very quiet although he was eating with relish, as was Luis.

Hernando was only half listening, his attention never captive when it came to conversation about people. If the talk had been about ideas, any ideas from a range of subjects, it would have been different and probably Luis would have said more. He did not notice that his grandson seemed to be concentrating on his food even more when Ysabel asked, 'And your sisters, Monsieur Weaver, I remember something of them from Luis?'

Rufus responded enthusiastically. He had warmed to this small woman whose hazel eyes showed genuine interest.

'Yes, Madame Bernade. My elder sister, Alyce, is only one year older than me but my younger sister, Meg, has just turned five. They are inseparable.'

'Your elder sister is not yet betrothed or married?' Ysabel was sure a daughter of Thomas Weaver would be an attractive match.

'No, Madame Bernade, she is not and I believe never will be.' Ysabel's eyes opened a fraction wider. Nobody noticed Luis had stopped chewing. 'My sister is my father's companion,' Rufus continued, 'and she takes great satisfaction in her learning. Also she would never leave Meg. She is not interested in marriage.'

'A truly devoted daughter and elder sister,' commented Ysabel.

'Yes, I feel my father could not bear to lose her,' Rufus stated. 'However, I feel he need not worry as there have been no suitors.' There was a pause then he chuckled. 'Except for Cousin Matthew.' He turned to his friend, who had been very quiet throughout the meal, 'You remember him, Luis?'

'The priest?'

'Yes.'

Ysabel was confused.

'Surely a priest cannot be a suitor?'

Rufus was still chuckling.

'Not a true suitor but he pays Alyce much attention. You thought so, didn't you Luis?' He pointed his knife at Luis and said jokingly, 'I think Luis is rather partial to my sister Alyce.'

'I think Matthew Blake pays too much attention to everyone,' Luis replied frostily. He continued eating. Ysabel looked at him keenly but he kept his eyes on his food which told her everything.

Hernando was suddenly interested.

'A priest as a suitor? Is this man a follower of Luther?' He watched as Richard Weaver shifted uncomfortably. Ysabel noticed the latter's sly glance at Ralph Brewer before he retorted, 'No, no, I was just joking. My tongue runs away with me.' He held up his goblet. 'This is excellent wine,' he said, redirecting the conversation with the consummate skill of the negotiator. 'I am pleased I can take the three tuns back with me, as we were disappointed Luis could not come to England. We value the opportunities this enterprise has to offer.'

Ysabel acknowledged the change of subject.

'I am sure all will be well next year.' Luis had stopped eating. He reached for the pitcher of water and refilled his cup, his eyes meeting Ysabel's as he lowered the jug. As Rufus witnessed the silent affectionate exchange it became clearer why Luis had postponed his trip to England.

'I am sorry there is no saffron for you this year, Rufus,' said his friend. 'We have already sold it, but we can fulfil our commitment to you next year.'

'Thank you.'

'Monsieur Weaver, can I interest you in a visit to my saffron fields?' Ysabel asked. 'There is no colour at this time of year but it is a pleasant ride. Although it would mean a very early start to avoid the heat.'

'Thank you, but no,' Rufus replied politely. 'I am familiar with the production of saffron. Several years ago my father had business in the east of England and took me to the fields there. I think I would prefer to explore Caors. From what I have seen it looks an interesting city.' He smiled, the wide smile which made him so endearing, and included everybody around the table in its friendly beam. He had a mixed response. Ralph Brewer who had travelled with him for the last month continued eating his mutton, the older Gharsia studied him but did not return his smile, while Madame Bernade did smile back, her clear eyes full of good humour. Luis raised one eyebrow quizzically and said nothing, but Rufus continued to smile. He would have so much to tell everyone once he returned home.

◆   ◆   ◆

Later that night Luis was unable to sleep. His body, slick with sweat, stuck to the scratchy sheet beneath him and whichever way he tried to lie, it was uncomfortable. The small chamber was airless and Johan, although not snoring, was making strange rattling sounds which became increasingly irritating. It was impossible to relax. The more he tried to ignore Johan, the more he was aware of the noise and of his own blood pounding in his head. A good night's sleep had evaded him since his father's visit and now Rufus had arrived. Luis's quiet life of predictable routine had been disturbed by two unexpected visitors that summer and both had unsettled him. He tossed and turned until, in the end, he felt he wanted to scream.

In the small hours of the morning he pulled on his clothes and made his way stealthily through the house, across the Place St Urcisse and onto the towpath. A full moon cast her silvery light over the dark river, illuminating the shadowed banks where the water whispered between the exposed stones. The Olt was alarmingly low, another casualty of the intense heat, with the central channel just passable for the barges. It was almost as hot outside as indoors so Luis removed his shirt, rinsed it in the river and wrapped it around his shoulders. He walked idly towards the deserted Pont Neuf and climbed the steps up to the road. Crossing the bridge to the halfway point, he stopped and rested his elbows on the rough stone. From there he could see the outline of Ysabel's house etched against the moonlit sky. There was a light in one of the windows. Someone was awake. *Perhaps Rufus was unable to sleep too? Plagued by his sunburn, he might decide to come outside in search of cooler air and they would be able to talk freely.*

Luis watched the house for some time, thinking about the Englishman, but nobody came out and eventually the candle was extinguished. He recalled the glance he had witnessed between Rufus and Ralph Brewer, a reaction to his grandfather mentioning Martin Luther, and hoped that his friend would be cautious. The reformer's books were forbidden in France and, although they were far from Paris, such matters should remain secret.

His mind wandered to his father, who had returned after so many years. Mourned for so long, it seemed inconceivable to Luis that the man had been in Istanbul all that time, living, trading and laughing his great booming laugh, while his son pined for his parents and baby sister. His emotions were raw, he would never forget the pain of his yearning, yet Luis could not deny the glimmer of affection he had experienced when his father had offered him sanctuary. He hoped he would never need it but the future was uncertain. The Church was increasing its campaign against unorthodoxy and his grandfather, aware of the precariousness of their identity, was watching developments carefully, always conscious of the possible need to flee.

There was still no movement of air. Luis stretched his shoulders, feeling the wetness of his shirt on his neck taking some of the heat from his body. He tipped his head back and stared at the moon, its luminous orb dominating the star-studded sky. He thought about Alyce and wondered if she might be asleep or if she too was looking at the moon, thinking of him and dreaming of what might be?

Lightning Source UK Ltd.
Milton Keynes UK
UKOW06f1431170317
296878UK00007B/204/P